D0921538

THE NEW KID SERIES

The New Kid
The Rising
The Sword of Armageddon

THE RISING

THE NEW KID: BOOK TWO

THE RISING

Temple Mathews

BenBella
DALLAS, TEXAS

BenBella Books, Inc.
10300 N. Central Expressway
Suite #400
Dallas, TX 75231
www.benbellabooks.com
Send feedback to feedback@benbellabooks.com

Printed in the United States of America
10 9 8 7 6 5 4 3 2 1

Library of Congress Cataloging-in-Publication Data is available for this title.

ISBN 978-1936661-89-3

Copyediting by Oriana Leckert
Proofreading by Erica Lovett, Gregory Teague, and Stacia Seaman
Cover design by Laura Watkins Matura
Text design and composition by PerfecType, Nashville, TN
Printed by Bang Printing

Distributed by Perseus Distribution
perseusdistribution.com

To place orders through Perseus Distribution:
Tel: 800-343-4499
Fax: 800-351-5073
E-mail: orderentry@perseusbooks.com

Significant discounts for bulk sales are available. Please contact Glenn Yeffeth at glenn@benbellabooks.com or 214-750-3628.

For my angels:
Manon Lucy Mathews
Lucy Lydia Mathews

TABLE OF CONTENTS

Chapter One:
The Power Rod

Will was running hell-bent through the pitch-black forest, his heart hammering in his chest, the blood roaring in his ears. He wanted to stop and rest, but he couldn't. Because *they* were trying to kill him. Even though he had time-bending speed, they were gaining on him. Mainly because he had a sixty-pound body pack strapped to his back. He considered ditching it, but that would be suicide, pure and simple. He needed the pack, knew that at this point it was the only thing that gave him a rat's chance in Hell of staying alive. He kept on running, feet pounding the ground, his night-vision contacts helping him see like no other human, or rather *half-human*, could. The thought of who—or *what*—he was, haunted him.

The universe had tossed the dice and they'd come up snake eyes for Will Hunter. He'd never be a normal teenager. He would always be what he was: a half-breed. He knew tons of kids who were of mixed heritage, and lots of the combinations were pretty cool. Kids who were half Italian and half Costa Rican, half Nigerian and half Swedish. That was the beauty of America: nearly everyone was a refined mutt of some sort or another. But Will's particular brand of half-breed was totally and utterly unique. His mother was English with a little French thrown in, and his father—well, his father wasn't just from another continent, he was from another time, another place, another world.

His father was the Devil.

It was a fact Will was still processing, a fact he'd learned at a critical moment during a skirmish with a few demons. More than a few, actually; there had been 277 of them. And truth be told, it had been much more than a skirmish; it was a battle royale, a war in the bowels of Mount St. Emory only minutes before it erupted, destroying much of the quaint little town of Harrisburg, Washington. The explosion, which was captured by the United States Geological Society and a half-dozen amateur videographers, was number one on YouTube for six weeks straight. It made most 4th of July fireworks shows look safe and sane by comparison. The skies had belched smoke and leached wet ash for days. How Will had managed to survive was a glorious twist of fate. It was providence. It was his destiny. Now, exactly *what* his destiny held for him, he did not know. All he knew was he wasn't going to sit around waiting for it to come knocking on his door.

The creatures weren't far behind him now. He could hear them. He could smell them. He could sense them. He didn't know how many there were, only that there were too many for him to stop and make a stand, even with his cache of weapons. To have any chance at wiping out an entire horde of *them*, he needed his Power Rod, which was not currently in his possession. Finding his precious Power Rod was what had brought him out here in the first place.

His Power Rod was one of three potent crystal shafts that formed the mystical Triad of Power, and it had been blown out of the cone of the volcano of Mount St. Emory along with everything else. Will had returned to the site of the blast weeks later. He'd had no idea if the Triad of Power had survived the eruption, if it was intact, or if the three crystals had been blown apart. The only thing he knew was that he had to make every effort to find his Power Rod. The first thing he did was to attempt recovery of the rod by tapping on the flesh-colored retrieval-transmitter patch on the back of his neck. For years this had served him well; all he had to do was tap a code, and the sleeve he'd built for the Power Rod would activate and his blessed weapon would come soaring down out of its hidey hole in the clouds—as if thrown by mighty Thor himself—into his waiting palm. When Will activated the laser saber function on the rod, he could chop down an evergreen with two strokes. Switching into another mode, he could shoot fireballs capable of exploding boulders. And he could activate the freeze beam and turn an entire raging river into a sheet of ice. All in all, it was a pretty fine piece of weaponry. His Power Rod wasn't just an extension of his arm or his hand, but of his being, of his very soul.

But . . . the retrieval sleeve or the patch must have been damaged in the blast, because no matter how many times Will tapped in the code, no Power Rod. Logically, he concluded that the rod—possibly even the Triad itself—was therefore, if not destroyed, earthbound, maybe even buried somewhere deep in the ground. So he began programming his computers, calculating the probable trajectory of the rod from the blast, taking into account the fact that adding intense heat to an already potent power source such as the ancient Power Rod crystal would result in a considerable boost. So whatever the original numbers were, they had to be modified and graphed accordingly. The bottom line was, Will had a ton of ground to cover. Fortunately, he had equipment to assist him in the task. He'd used the Thermal Sweep Telescope and the Gamma Ray Spectrometer, but he'd only gotten trace readings that had led him to this particular forest quadrant, which happened to be crawling with demons no doubt looking for the Power Rod, too. Will took the danger in stride. What else could he do? Nobody ever said being a Demon Hunter was going to be easy. He missed his father Edward, cursed the foul beast that had taken Edward from this world. Even though Edward was not Will's biological father, he would always be Will's *real* father, the man he loved, the man he missed every minute of every day. The beast would pay for killing him. Will would make sure of that.

Cruel winds lashed the forest, whipping the pine trees into a savage dance. The sky above roiled in thunder-cracking anger. Sheets of rain began to hammer down. Will had already been on the move for over an hour, and even though he had—on account of his lineage—über-human strength and endurance, he was starting to tire. One of his boots caught a root and he went down hard. He jumped back up and was running again in a flash, but the two seconds had cost him: he saw an ugly blur to his left, another to his right. And he heard snarling. Angry, deep growling. Whatever manner of demon beasts these were, they were intent on malice. He sensed what was about to happen and whipped his wrist. A Flareblade snapped up into his palm. His instinct had been right; the creature on the left pinballed off a fir tree and sprang right at Will, knocking him sideways. His head slammed into a boulder. The creature had drawn blood and Will was down, seeing double.

As the creature swooped down, Will slashed upward with the Flareblade. The moment it made contact with the demon's chest, the Flareblade shot out a dual-directional red-hot burst of flame. The creature howled, doubled over, and jawed down, trying to take a death bite out of Will's forehead. But Will crouched out of harm's way as the demon particle-vaporized. Will retracted the Flareblade and took off running again.

Thunderbolts began to rip down out of the clouds, one striking a treetop. The ensuing howl made Will smile; one of the creatures waiting to ambush him had been hit by lightning. *Well, that'll teach you*, he thought. But there was no time to gloat. He could feel them gaining on him as he scrabbled up a rocky incline toward a plateau. He made the mistake of looking back. What he saw caused his blood to curdle. Eyes. Evil yellow eyes like molten lamps, at least two dozen pairs, maybe more. He was ridiculously outnumbered. If he stopped now and tried to fight them hand to hand without his

Power Rod, he'd be dead in under a minute. He had to reach the plateau.

Bam! He was hit from behind and rolled through a tangle of blackberry bushes, the unruly northwest variety, Mother Nature's mutants, vines thick with brutal thorns that tore into his face. The attacking demon, a teen male, wielded a rusty scabbard and he swung it at Will with all his might while howling for backup. Will rolled left—*wham!* Then right—*wham!* He was barely avoiding getting chopped in half. Not fun. Will popped a Flareblade up into each of his hands, and with a cross-swipe he beheaded the creature, taking care to step quickly away from the geyser of toxic blood that gushed out of the beast's neck. Now *that* was fun.

He knew the others would smell the kill and come swarming after him, so he hauled himself up the hill and then kicked it up a notch, running as fast as he possibly could—right toward the edge of a sheer cliff with a six-hundred-foot drop. And they were right behind him, their nostrils flaring as they smelled his blood. Will glanced back. There were even more of the monstrous demons than he'd thought—at least four dozen. No way was he going to let them catch him and tear him apart, because he knew that they wouldn't be in a big hurry. No, they'd flay him slowly to cause the maximum amount of pain possible, probably keeping him alive for days in the process. The cliff ahead seemed a much better option. He only hoped all his hard techno-design work would pay off. If it didn't, he'd be dead for sure.

With the throng of demons bearing down on him, he dove head-first off the cliff, plunging down, dropping like an anvil. And then he yanked the cord on his chute.

Up on the cliff, the gathered demons burst into a rabid frenzy, some fighting among themselves, others grunting as they sprouted their own hideous fleshy wings and took flight, swooping down after Will. But Will's body pack contained far more than an ordinary parachute. Pulling another cord transformed the chute into a hang glider. And with a short burst from a small jet pack, Will jettisoned upward and caught an updraft, sky-riding into the clouds like a human hawk. Michelangelo would have been proud.

By Will's prior reckoning, demons could only sustain flight for short distances and at a maximum altitude of five hundred feet. So he was literally able to fly up and away from them. The only problem was that he was heading straight into the roiling bowels of a lightning storm. Anvil crawlers—long, sideways, in-cloud bolts—were erupting with frightening frequency at the very spot Will was flying toward. He veered left, but the sky was lit up in every direction. He knew he should start descending, just abort and tuck into a dive and get the hell out of there. But something was drawing him into the vortex of the maelstrom. So he flew higher, climbing right into the center of the ongoing explosions. It was madness, like a fireworks show on steroids, the clouds erupting with bursts of ball lightning and heat lightning and sprites and jets. The atmosphere was breaking all the rules; the clouds were alive with pure malevolence. Will had an ugly thought that somehow he would meet the Dark Lord up here. How ironic that would be, to face the Lord of the Underworld on a celestial battlefield.

He continued to be inexorably drawn upward, deeper and deeper into the heart of the churning, explosive storm. His body was overcome with a vague yet powerful yearning, a desire to reach into the light. Maybe he hadn't escaped after all. Maybe the pursuing demons had killed him and this was his death flight and he was on his way to meet his maker. At least he was going in the right direction. He sailed higher, up toward the flashing lights. A bolt of lightning crashed past him, so dangerously close it seared his leg. *Damn,* he thought, *that hurt! Good news: I'm definitely alive. Not-so-good news: I'm alive in the middle of the whup-ass mother of all lightning storms.*

He kept flying up and up in an arc, over the blinding tumult, and found himself looking down at the pulsing mass of white-hot energy that he concluded could only be the Dark Lord. He was losing strength. He was getting dizzy. He cursed himself because he'd miscalculated again, underestimated his enemy's prowess. This was it. He'd been lured to his doom. He was going down for good this time. His brain buzzed from the proximity of the electrical energy. He felt weak and he knew he was going to black out any second. He could have used the jet thruster to boost himself sideways, but the clouds . . . they wanted him . . . they beckoned to him. *Come to me.* With the last burst of energy he had left, Will went into a tuck and dove straight into the core. *You want me? Well, here I come.*

He knew he was going to die. He took a deep breath and did his best to hold on to consciousness, but he felt it slipping away, his past mistakes racing by him in a kaleidoscopic blur. Will said goodbye to everyone and everything. *I'm sorry I wasn't able to kill off the Dark Lord, Natalie, so that we could be together.* He wished his life had been longer, wished he'd accomplished more, wished he'd been able to love Natalie the way she deserved. Instead, it was all over now. *Hasta la vista*, baby.

But then he saw something, something that sent waves of tingling relief racing up and down his spine. There it was! His Power Rod. Shimmering like Excalibur, waiting for him in the clouds like the best friend he'd ever had. There was no sign of the other two crystal rods, but for all he cared right now, they could have been blown to bits. The only thing that mattered was that his rod, his Power Rod, was intact, and waiting for him. As he dropped down, closer and closer, he reached out for it. It was agonizingly close . . . there! His fingers curled around it and he held it fast to his heart. He was home again.

His batteries suddenly recharged, and infused with a new hope, a new energy, he adjusted his glider and swooped down out of the sky to land on terra firma. He looked around and saw no demons converging on him. Up above there were a few of them circling, still looking up into the lightning storm. Hopefully they thought he'd been killed within it. That would buy him a little time. He quickly folded up his glider and ran through the woods. So far, so good—no demons. He ran another half-mile to where he'd hidden his rocket on wheels, his Mitsubishi EVO. He whipped the camo tarp off it, stowed his gear, and climbed inside. His hands were shaking as he fired up the 300-horsepower engine and gunned it. As he sped away, the forest retreating in his rearview mirror, he realized he'd made it. He'd managed to find his Power Rod, save his life, and kick some ass in the process. Not bad for a day's work.

Now all he had to do was save humanity from the greatest evil the world had ever known.

Chapter Two:
The House of Five Turrets

Rudy glared out of the Demon Trapper with blazing bloodshot angry eyes. He wanted to kill someone (*Anyone, something, anything!*) so bad he could taste blood. But of course that was only a figment of his imagination, because in his present state his molecules had been rearranged in such a manner as to make tasting anything impossible. He could, however, *see*, and as he blinked he scanned the laboratory, his eyes moving across the cache of weapons that he knew to be the brainchildren of his best friend–turned–mortal enemy, Will Hunter. Will had saved Rudy's butt in the boys' room at Harrisburg High School, and way back then Rudy had thought Will was the coolest guy on the planet: the New Kid. He enjoyed hanging with Will, being his only friend. Until he tagged along on one of Will's hunts and hooked up with his true soul mates, the demon-teens. Man, were they ever having *fun*. He'd embraced the dark side (been "infected," Will had called it, but what did he know?), and for a few precious weeks he was on a white-knuckle thrill ride, juiced up good, his blood pumping with maximum adrenaline.

But then Will had to go and ruin everything by denying his birthright and wasting the Dark Lord. Rudy couldn't believe it! The dude had actually capped the big DL himself! That brought down a hail of hatred from Rudy and the other assembled demons, and they attacked Will, the New Kid, the Power Rod–wielding S.O.B. who had just whacked their leader's head off. Rudy had gone after Will with everything he had. That was when Will—rather than toast him—sucked him into *this* contraption, the Demon Trapper, and man oh man was it some kind of tight fit. Rudy *had* to get out or he was going to go even more bug-eyed crazy than he already was, cooped up in this appalling piece of equipment. This was way worse than being crammed into a locker in high school. He moved his lips and croaked out some sounds that were vaguely amphibian, like he was gargling or something. But with continued effort he was able to form words, and as soon as he knew he could speak, he began to yell.

"Hey! Hello already! Get me out of here! Crap on a cracker! Somebody help me!"

He waited but no one came. He was all alone. But that didn't stop him from screaming.

"When I get out of this thing I'm gonna skin you alive and crush your bones! I'm gonna make you wish you were never born!"

His threats fell on emptiness, and after a while he shut his eyes and did his best to coax the good dreams to return. Last time he'd dreamed of kissing and fondling Sharon Mitchell, the awesome cheerleader from Harrisburg High. She'd been hot when she was a full-blooded human, and even hotter as a demon. But of course she was dead and gone now, hacked to pieces by Will Hunter after she'd tried to tear his head off. What a waste. Rudy tried to conjure up another dream starring Sharon, but each time he did the same thing happened: she morphed into a corpse. He was a demon, but he wasn't *that* depraved. But he kept his eyes closed just the same because he couldn't bear to face the reality that he was like some pickle stuck in a jar. He floated for what seemed like an eternity and then sensed something and opened his eyes. Two Natalies were staring at him! He screamed. Then he had an idea. Natalie liked him okay, right? They were friends, sort of.

"Natalie! It's me, Rudy! Get me out of here!"

The two Natalies continued to stare at him like he was a pig embryo in a jar of formaldehyde. Why was he seeing double? Maybe it was this contraption messing with his eyesight? But then he figured it out. It wasn't two Natalies staring at him, it was Natalie and her twin sister, Emily, who'd been missing for months and who everyone had thought was dead. Turned out she was just spending some time as a special guest of the Dark Lord.

"He looks so creepy," said Emily, peering in at Rudy's bizarre visage.

"We shouldn't even be in here," said Natalie. "Come on, let's go."

"Look at him. He's trying to say something. He recognizes us!"

"Well, he should, we went to school together in Harrisburg for years. But Em, uh, let me refresh your memory here. Rudy went to the dark side. He's a demon now."

Sensitive to her sister's history, Natalie said the word "demon" softly.

Emily winced, and the memory of being held prisoner in those caves for what seemed like an eternity hit her like a slap in the face. She used to feel kind of sorry for Rudy, back in high school. She'd ignored him just like everybody else, but it used to make her stomach turn when she'd see him getting pushed around by Todd Karson and Sharon Mitchell and the rest of the popular crowd. But now all traces of mercy were instantly gone, replaced by unbridled malice.

"Why is Will even keeping him alive? We should just smash this thing to bits, put the rat bastard out of his misery."

Natalie looked at her sister with concern. Ever since Will had rescued them, Emily had been basically bipolar. She was getting better; some days she was her old naughty adventurous self. But the rest of the time she swung back and forth between being little more than fear in a shell and so angry Natalie didn't even recognize her.

Inside the Demon Trapper, Rudy continued mouthing words.

Emily stared at him. "Look," she said, "he's actually saying 'help me'! You want me to *help* you, little guy? Well, how about this: How about I get a baseball bat and come and bash your squishy little ferret head into a pulp?"

"Emily, don't be gross," said Natalie.

Now Rudy was putting his hands together in supplication and making a sad face.

"Oh my God! He's . . . he's *praying* to us!"

"Will's going to do everything he can for him, okay? He thinks he can put him back the way he was. Now let's get out of here and back to practicing," said Natalie.

"Gladly."

As they left the laboratory, Rudy watched them go, alternating between wanting to hug them—*I love you guys!*—and thinking of ways to maim them with rusty gardening tools.

On his way home after recovering the Power Rod, Will was rocketing along in the EVO. He'd been driving for hours and his eyelids felt like lead. He pulled into a rest stop, parking under a grove of tall pines, intending to get out for a minute or two and stretch his legs. But as soon as he turned the key and the deep rumbling of the engine shut down, he just closed his eyes, exhausted. He listened to the faint sound of the engine ticking. He heard his own breath. And then sleep overcame him and he dropped into darkness and began to dream.

A catacomb. Howls of agony bouncing off the stone walls. Moving faster now, through a tunnel, into a massive cavern. Cries of pain, mournful in nature. Bats, thousands of bats, frantic in flight. Down below, demons! Floating down closer to them now. They file past a body lying on a marble altar. They weep for the body, they genuflect before it. It is the body of the Dark Lord! He is not moving. He is dead!

Will heard a noise and opened his eyes, hand already closing on his Power Rod. But it was just a brilliant white dove landing on the hood of the car. It looked around and then flew into the sky. Will smiled, relaxing again. Maybe the dove was a sign that the darkness *had* lifted, that a new dawn would soon begin. For the briefest of moments, he let himself imagine what his life might be like if things were different.

And then . . . *wham!* The dove slammed into the hood of the car. Dead. Will's fleshed crawled as he watched what happened next. Neck broken, eyes bleeding, the dove rose up, stared balefully at Will, and then flapped painfully, awkwardly, hideously away into the night.

Will shook his head. His dream had just been wishful thinking. The Prince of Darkness was not dead. Not yet. *That* would be up to Will Hunter.

Will pulled up to the massive wrought iron gates of the stone mansion he'd chosen for his new home and pressed the remote. The gates swung open. He entered and parked, looking up at the magnificent old mansion and admiring the choice he'd made. He loved the fact that the place had marble statues and animal topiaries, not to mention five turrets and an Olympian skylight. He'd found the house on eBay when he and Natalie and Emily—and Rudy in the Demon Trapper—were still on the road, fleeing from Harrisburg. They'd stayed at a succession of four-star hotels, decompressing. Thanks to the money from his ownership of the *Demon Hunter* game franchise, he'd been able to treat Natalie and Emily to days of luxury, buying them all the spa indulgences they wanted and insisting that they order anything they desired from room service. They needed time to recover, but also, Will needed them to stay calm and quiet while he thought about what his next moves would be. He'd vanquished the Dark Lord and blown his whole organization to smithereens. But demons were a hearty lot, and Will knew they would recover, reorganize, and attempt another attack on humanity. He just didn't know how or when. And because he was a Demon Hunter, like his father and his father's father before him, it was his mission to find out.

His stately, palatial new home was called the London Mansion because it had been built by Leopold Anthony London, a shipping magnate. London had commissioned it and had it built in 1902, but he only lived there for three years—thirty-six months of unbridled debauchery—before he changed his wicked ways and moved out, bequeathing it to the Seattle Society for Moral Preservation, which converted the mansion to a home for "wayward" girls. London himself became a man of God the very day he moved out. It was not known whether any of the girls who lived there were pregnant as a result of London's own seductions, but rumors abounded.

Despite its sordid past, the six-thousand-square-foot mansion had three-foot-thick walls and was the perfect place to house Will's well-equipped computer laboratory and weapons design facility. His earnings from *Demon Hunter* netted him hundreds of thousands of dollars per week, so money was never an issue, and he spent it freely on researching and developing the kinds of weapons needed to battle demons. Before he and the girls had moved in, he'd paid for the house to have extensive renovations, including the addition of a state-of-the-art system of rapidly deployable security shutters. Will had also installed remote-controlled pulse-blast laser cannons atop each of the five turrets. He hoped he would never have to use them, but it was always good to be prepared.

At the main entrance, he pressed his thumb to the print-reader lock and the huge wooden doors swung open. Then he went in search of Natalie and Emily.

He found them a few minutes later in another wing of the house, in the gaming room, stick fighting in their padding and protective headgear. Will had them using bamboo Kettukari staffs now, but once they mastered those he would switch out the sticks and give them something far more lethal. When they had first moved in, he had worked with them both, showing them the various Kendo moves and maneuvers. If they were going to stay with him, they needed to be able to defend themselves. He'd taught them that while power was good, speed was better. Speed was what counted, not the ability to clobber someone with all your might. Better a series of staccato hits than one haymaker. The twins had always been competitive growing up, it turned out, so giving them sticks and having them fight one another was a recipe for bruises. It also meant they'd been learning quickly, each of them pushed further by the other one's progress.

He'd barely entered the room when Natalie saw him, dropped her staff, and rushed up to hug him. She wanted to kiss him, but instead she settled for him hugging her gently back and forming his lips into something vaguely resembling a smile. She cocked her head to the side like an inquisitive puppy.

"So, *did* you?"

"Did I what?"

"You *know* what! Did you find it? When you left, you said you had a good fix on it but didn't know if you could find it, or if it would work."

Will was stone-faced.

"I can't read you," said Natalie. Her eyes narrowed. "You did! Didn't you?"

"I . . . might have," said Will.

"Don't tease me," she said, trying to appear angry. But the truth was, she loved it when he teased her because he so rarely did. When he did, it was a sign that he was actually relaxed, right in the moment, really *with* her, instead of worrying about the fate of the human race. He smiled and she flushed with a wave of warmth. His smiles did that to her.

"Yeah, I found it. And I've got work to do on it, so I've got to go into the lab." His smile left as quickly as it had come.

That's Will, thought Natalie, *all business, 24/7/365. Hot as fire one minute, cold as ice the next.* But it was hard to blame him. He had a lot on his shoulders.

"While you're in there, would you mind putting Rudy—or whatever vile creature he's become—out of his misery? He looks disgusting," said Emily.

The room went dead silent as Will fixed them both with a stare.

"I thought I instructed you to stay out of the lab."

"Will, we're sorry, it won't happen again," offered Natalie. Then she looked at her sister. "Isn't that *right*, Em?"

"Can you blame us for exploring?" Emily asked instead of agreeing. "What are we supposed to do, cooped up all day in this spooky castle? I mean, the swimming pool and Jacuzzi are great, and the bowling alley and theater . . . but you can only watch so many movies . . ."

Natalie gave Emily a dirty look. How on earth could she be anything but totally 100 percent grateful to even be alive, let alone hanging out in a totally pimped-out, one-of-a-kind mansion?

But Will understood. Emily was getting claustrophobic. Having been held prisoner in the guts of a volcano would do that to you.

"I get it. You need to breathe. A caged bird sings a sad song and all that. Just let me clean up and we'll all go out."

"Rudy, too?" asked Emily, kidding, but in a sarcastic way that made Will frown. He knew it couldn't be easy living in a house with one of the things that had tormented her for so long, but she'd have to figure out how to deal with it.

"Rudy's not going anywhere until I can find a way to bring him back to our side. Now, how about you two get ready? Or are you going out like that?"

They looked at each other, still in workout clothes and sweaty from stick practice. "Give us ten minutes," said Natalie, and they went upstairs, veering off to their separate bedrooms and what Emily liked to call "waltz-in" closets.

Will knew by now that with these two, ten minutes meant an hour, easy. He didn't really have time to take Natalie and Emily anywhere, but it looked like maybe they were starting to come a bit unraveled so he justified the outing as damage control. While they were upstairs getting cleaned up and changing, he took the Power Rod into the lab. He peeled the retrieval patch off his neck, opened it up, and took out his loupe and micro tools and started tweaking. He didn't mean to spend so much time on it right then, but he was so into it that an hour sped by in a blink and he had the patch synched up with the retrieval sleeve on the Power Rod with time to spare before Natalie and Emily finished getting ready. Time to test it. He went up the stairs and made his way to the roof.

Will scanned the neighborhood for buttinskis and then flung the Power Rod skyward. It shot up like a bullet into the clouds and then held and hovered at two thousand feet. He waited a full minute, breathing in the clean damp northwest air. He had chosen this place in no small part because of the amazing, nearly 360-degree view. He could see Lake Union and snowy Mount Rainier shining in the distance. He loved this part of the country, and not just because the people were smart and polite and made awesome coffee. Somehow the evergreens, the water, and the mountains all worked together to make him feel welcome. He wasn't sure he would ever be able to live a normal life, but if he could, this is where he'd want to live it. For a few brief seconds he allowed his mind to venture into the daydreams where he and Natalie hung out and snowboarded up at Whistler and went to movies and made out like normal teenagers. But he knew better. He nixed the daydream, shaking it off, then tapped the code on the retrieval patch. In a manner of seconds, his trusty Power Rod came screaming down out of the sky and slapped into his waiting palm. *That felt good*, thought Will. Then he sent the Power Rod skyward once again, for safekeeping. He thought about the other two crystal rods that had been blown out of the volcano. They could be anywhere. Will would, of course, do everything he could to find them. But he had other matters to attend to first. For one thing, he had sent his mother April away before the battle in the volcano, to keep her safe in case he didn't make it, and now he had to find her and bring her back. Satisfied the Power Rod was back in working order, he went back inside and down to the first floor where Natalie and Emily were waiting for him.

In the weeks since he'd rescued her from the hell of being a captive of the Dark Lord and his legions of demons, Emily had come a very long way. At first he was certain she'd be frightened and withdrawn for months. But she turned out to be incredibly resilient. Most days, she was able to function more or less normally. Sure, she still had brain-bending nightmares, but they were becoming less frequent, and with each healing night's sleep her frisky independent side grew stronger. She was still fragile, still carrying the pain and trauma from her experience, but she was, just like her twin sister, strong and independent. She was quite a match for Natalie, and the two of them—well, they were a pair to be reckoned with.

Just then, though, they looked like any two teenage girls ready to go out for the night. Natalie smiled when she saw him, and he couldn't help smiling back. It felt good. Maybe they weren't the only ones who needed a night off.

Chapter Three:
A Night on the Town

Instead of ripping around town in the kickass Mitsubishi EVO, Will drove the stately prowler, his BMW 750Li. With 400+ horsepower and dual nitro boosters, it had plenty of muscle if they needed it, not to mention double bulletproof glass, and front, side, and rear armor. Just because he was taking the night off didn't mean he could leave himself unprepared for an attack. So as they cruised down from the hill and around the city, Will had a unique feeling. It would no doubt pass, but for the time being he actually felt somewhat safe.

They drove past the Experience, the beautifully bizarre Frank Gehry–designed building that housed the Experience Music Project as well as the Science Fiction Museum and Hall of Fame. They ate dinner in a private dining room at El Gaucho. Though they were just teenagers, everywhere they went they were treated like royalty. Natalie and Emily were convinced that the way people treated them was due to Will's nearly immeasurable wealth. But Will knew better. It was all in how you carried yourself, what your eyes told people. And when people saw the quiet power in Will Hunter's eyes, they knew he meant business and treated him as such.

After dinner, they went over to the Seattle Center. Natalie and Emily had told him about how when they were kids their family used to drive down from Harrisburg to spend the day at the Center, riding the Wild Mouse and eating cotton candy and playing the arcade games. Will looked up at the towering Space Needle and decided to take the girls up for a spectacular view of the Emerald City.

On the observation deck of the Needle, Will, Natalie, and Emily gazed out at the vast sea of city lights sparkling in the crystal clear night air. A vigorous gust of wind buffeted them, and Natalie leaned against Will for support and warmth. He ached for her when she got this close. He put his arm around her as she moved in tight, tucking her head into his neck.

Seeing the way Natalie and Will were standing, Emily smiled to herself, happy that her sister had finally found someone she really cared about. There had been a lot of time to talk the last few weeks, and Natalie had told her all about Will's arrival in Harrisburg and the way they'd gotten together. And she knew they hadn't had much time alone since they'd escaped the volcano. Deciding to give them some space, she circled around the deck, enjoying the feel of the breezy night wind on her face and neck. For the first few moments she loved being up there, outside. But then the fear began to gnaw. For all she knew, demons could come swooping down on her at any second. She shuddered and held herself against the wind. The memories of being held captive by *them* still dogged her. She knew she had to train her mind to forget, but it was hard. How do you forget weeks of unrelenting torment?

Natalie wanted to get lost in Will's embrace. She felt so amazingly *safe* when she was with him. Not only was he a genius, he was unbelievably strong; his muscles were like steel. And she'd seen him move faster than any human. She wondered what it would be like to have such powers—to feel like she was really a worthy match for Will. For a moment she wondered what it would be like to be a demon. If Will was half demon, then how bad could it be?

Will breathed in the scent of Natalie's hair. Having her in his arms sent waves of pleasure rolling down through his chest and into his stomach. She turned her head to look up at him, and her ear brushed across his face. They were, in that moment, so incredibly attuned to their senses that they could feel each other's heartbeats.

"Will?" she said.

"Yeah?"

"It feels so good to be with you. To be together."

"I know."

She looked into his eyes and found heaven. Neither of them blinked. Instead of speaking further, they held their breath and lingered in the moment, tasting it, feeling it, being with it totally. Natalie felt like they were somehow melding together, all the unspoken words between them dissolving, their souls merging, dancing slow and close. Their cheeks touched, but they didn't kiss. Natalie couldn't help herself and asked: "How long . . . ?" *How long can we stay like this?*

"Shhh . . ."

Will brushed his lips against her cheek as he made the sound and a tingling sensation spread from her face to her scalp and then trickled down into her body like a thousand raindrops. She held Will and breathed him in. In truth, she didn't want to hear the real answer to her question. She only wanted to hear, "Forever, forever, *forever.*" The thought of any other words spilling from Will's lips— anything, no matter how innocent, that might contradict her core desire—would kill her right there on the spot. So when it looked like he might speak, *she* made the sound.

"Shhhh. You're right. Let's not say a word."

He understood. They wouldn't have this conversation now. Not when they were on top of the world, the handsome prince and his beautiful princess gazing out over their kingdom, their bodies close together, the heat between them fierce, overpowering, relentless and growing. Will knew that Natalie wanted him to kiss her. Right here. Right now. He hadn't since they'd escaped Mount St. Emory back in Harrisburg. And a dull ache to do so lived inside him every minute of every day. But he was afraid. For her. For him. For what it would mean for humanity if he let his guard down so much. He told himself he must remain strong and vigilant, and above all he must stay in control. Natalie sucked in some jagged breaths through her nose—she'd forgotten to breathe again, something she often did when touching Will—and her body shuddered as she felt a lightness lifting her head into the sky.

Will's lips found her forehead and he rested them there, kissing her, *kissing her*, for a long time. Her eyes fluttered closed. She felt like someone had poured warm liquid into her skull and it was slowly flowing down through her body. She tightened her arms around him and her mind was singing, *Come in, come in, come in! I want you so bad!* She was going to kiss him on the lips, and this time, he was going to let her. She could feel it. She tilted her head up. Her lips parted. And then:

"Hey, you two," said Emily as she completed her circular journey around the deck. She'd really wanted to give them more time, but she was starting to stress out, the dark dreams coming at her from the shadows. Still, she felt guilty for it now, seeing the way they were looking at each other.

"Um . . . I can take off if you want, get a cab back home. It's no problem."

Natalie squeezed Will's hand. They all knew that they would never let Emily go traipsing off by herself.

"No," said Will. "We should stick together. We'll all go."

As they were leaving the observation deck, Will thought he saw a flash of lightning and heard thunder. But when he scanned the sky, it was clear: The sounds and images seemed to be coming from inside his head, and they were faint, distant, and otherworldly. Maybe it was a memory. Or maybe it was his seventh sense, his ability to read tiny meta-communications all around him, the unspoken, nonverbal cues that passed between people and animals, even plants. He could even sense minute chemicals emitted and exchanged, as well as atmospheric alterations. Now he was struck with a strong feeling of foreboding. It was definitely time to leave. They climbed into the elevator and stood silently as the car descended, making its five-hundred-foot journey to the ground in just under a minute. As the doors hissed open, Will stepped forward protectively, moving out of the elevator and quickly scoping out the lobby. All was quiet.

They got in the BMW and when Natalie reached to turn the radio on, he shook his head. Picking up on Will's anxiety, she and Emily were silent. He drove with the windows down so he wouldn't miss anything happening around them, the night air rushing in and swirling around them like cool caressing fingers.

Suddenly Emily's head jerked to the right. "What was that?"

"What was what?" asked Natalie.

"I thought I saw something."

"We'll be home soon," said Will. He didn't think Emily had really seen anything, but his bad feeling still hadn't gone away.

But Emily *had* seen something. Or rather, some*one*. It was a tall older man in a tattered coat, and he was stalking them. As they drove, he moved like a ghost, floating, his long coattails flapping in the wind. When they stopped at a light he dropped down onto the BMW from an overpass—*WHAM!*—his boot heels denting the hood, his horrible eyes glaring.

Emily screamed as her blood ran cold. Barely flinching, Will sped up and then braked hard, and the man was thrown backward like a slingshot and disappeared as though swallowed up by the asphalt. Will knew better, knew the creep wasn't dead—he'd seen the man's ugly hooded black eyes—and so he goosed the throttle while keeping his left foot on the brake. When the tall man rose up like some apparition, Will released the brake and the Beemer sped forward like it had been blasted out of a cannon, running the tall man over. Now both Natalie and Emily's shrieks pierced the night air. Will stopped the BMW and powered up the windows, then slammed it into reverse and sped backward. *Ka-thump!* He ran over the tall man again. Natalie spoke.

"Will! What if—?"

"What if nothing!" he shouted.

His instincts had been right. Even after being run over multiple times the tall man, an ancient demon, stood up on spindly legs, his jagged broken hipbone jutting out like part of some weird exoskeleton. His neck was broken and his head was hanging, bowed as if in prayer. Blood flowed freely from a hole in his neck. But he righted his head and took a few steps forward, holding up his mangled hands like lobster claws. His wicked face was like a mask that had been tacked to his skull. He could barely move and Will suspected that, at least for the moment, he wasn't a threat. But the tall man did have something to say—his jaws were moving grotesquely—and cautiously Will rolled down his window to listen. The tall man fell toward them, collapsing on the street. He looked up at Will with hateful eyes.

"*Parricida!*" he rasped, as black blood seeped from the hole in his neck. He sucked in a bloody breath and then spoke again, his croaking voice haunting, accusing, condemning.

"*Parricida!*"

Then, with a final death rattle, the old demon disintegrated into sparkling particles of light, tiny red droplets that leached into the asphalt. Natalie and Emily caught their breaths. Will was staring at the spot where the demon had dissolved, his mind going a million miles a second.

"Will?" whispered Natalie.

Will kept staring, thinking. Natalie's heart hammered.

"What language was that?" she asked. "Do you know what he said?"

"It was Italian," said Will. "Or maybe Spanish. *Parricida* means someone who kills a parent."

"Uh, can we please get out of here?" asked Emily. She was pressed as far back into the back seat as she could get, pale and shaken.

"We're gone," said Will, and he stepped on the gas. Ignoring stoplights, they were up the hill and pulling into the mansion drive-way in two minutes flat. Natalie was looking at Will, trying to read him. They pulled into the garage, and when the doors closed behind them and the double security shutters came down as well, Will turned and looked at her.

"He was accusing me of killing one of my parents."

The notion circulated in their brains.

"Does that mean you . . . inside the mountain . . . the battle . . . your . . . father? Could the Dark Lord really be—"

Will and Natalie had never spoken about Will's newfound heri-tage. It was a fact so terrifying in its implications that they had a silent agreement to let it lie. Hearing her say it aloud now was like hearing it for the first time all over again. But that paled compared to the hope that wanted to grow in his chest. What if Will's dream at the rest stop, his vision, had been true? What if the Dark Prince *was* dead? What if Will had killed him in the battle inside Mount St. Emory?

But the Dark Lord was not the only parent whose fate Will was unsure of. April was out there somewhere, having followed his instructions and hidden someplace he hoped was safe. But that night's encounter had just reminded him that nowhere would remain safe for long. Will knew he could not let another day pass without finding her and bringing her to the manor.

"I'm going to need a couple hours of sleep and then I'm taking off," he said, getting out of the BMW. Natalie and Emily followed him into the house, the mood somber, old fears once again creeping into their veins.

Inside, Natalie grabbed Will's wrist, wanting to know if he thought the Dark Lord *could* be dead and where he was going and how long he'd be gone.

"Not right now," Will said, brushing her off as if he wasn't even seeing her, and retired to his bedroom and closed the door behind him. As she stood outside his door, she wondered if there would ever come a night when he would leave it open, or better yet, invite her in and close it behind them. She went to her room. In moments there was a tapping at her door. It was Emily, still looking wan.

"Can I sleep with you tonight?"

"Of course, come on in."

Natalie ushered her sister in and gave her a comforting hug, putting her own problems aside, at least temporarily.

In his room, Will did his best to calm his charging panic. He would accomplish nothing now by fretting about his mother. He used his training to go into a Zen trance, clearing away the mental debris. But one thought persisted, and it was a hopeful one. If by some miracle the tall demon's words held the *good* meaning, the *right* meaning, if indeed he *had* killed the Dark Lord, it might mean the beginning of the end of the demon race. And that would mean that he and Natalie could be together. Will dared not hope; he knew better than to celebrate anything until the deed was done. But he couldn't help but wonder. Was it possible? Was *he* truly dead and gone?

What was left of the Dark Lord's body lay in state 666 cold dark feet under the earth's surface. One by one, various demons filed past, paying their respects in the traditional demon fashion by hissing and spitting on the ground, the rocky earth around the Master burbling with an accumulation of toxins. After the blast at Mount St. Emory, the surviving demons from the surrounding area had fanned out and gathered up their leader's charred and lacerated body parts. They'd located the limbs and organs and bits of flesh by sniffing the air. His scent was, to a demon, intoxicating, what they craved: acrid and foul. Now, like an ancient dinosaur skeleton unearthed by paleontologists, his body parts—all those that had been found—were gathered together and laid out, a hideous-looking accumulation if ever there was one. The gory assemblage was gradually becoming joined together as an evil, sentient, sinewy, fleshy red substance wormed in and around it in a grotesque kind of satanic healing fusion.

A demon approached an underlord, eyes locked on the ground in submission, and whispered: "We are still looking. We are working tirelessly."

"Of course you are," said the underlord. "The future of our very existence depends upon it."

"Yes, we know. I beg your leave."

The demon nodded and backed away into the darkness. The underlord stared again at the remains of the Dark Lord. In the event that they were unable to locate what they sought, and soon, it was possible that the entire demon race would perish.

The Dark Lord's memory was hazy. White. So much white. When a human died or began the first process of dying, they went into the light. For a demon, even the prince of demons, the process was much the same. First came the searing pain, the fire along the spine, then the consciousness tilting like the deck of a boat in a storm. And then the brain melting, like a chunk of ice sizzling in lava.

He remembered being flung backward by the first shockwaves, blasts of powerful steam, Mother Earth hurling huge boulders like grains in a sandstorm. The massive rocks were Earth's shrapnel and they ripped into him, slicing and dicing him like a hunk of meat. It was as if he'd been attacked by a mad butcher with rusty knives. His limbs had been torn from his body and blown to smithereens, his torso chopped in half, then halved again and again as more and more granite projectiles hit him. Mother Earth was angry, and she'd slaked her thirst for vengeance upon his body. He'd felt his neck snap and his head being wrenched from his torso—a shame, since he'd only just reattached it after his own son had beheaded him with the dark holy Triad of Power. As the Dark Lord had rocketed up into the sky, burning, aflame, he tried to move, but with his brain no longer connected to his spinal cord, it made things . . . difficult.

Time passed. Time stopped. A blanket of nothingness fell over his consciousness. Time started again. He held on to hatred, and it kept him from falling any deeper into the void. Only his hunger for vengeance kept him from letting go. So he held fast, imagining over and over again how he would make his young adversary pay. With exemplary pain. And as much blood as possible.

Rumbling along on I-90 in their thirty-two-foot Commander RV, Andrew and Martha Hastings and their three children, Zachary, eight, Ben, seven, and little Megan, four, were weary from the final leg of their vacation. They'd roamed far and wide in the Pacific Northwest, and capped it off with a five-day stay in the Columbia Hills State Park. They'd jet-skied and fished and swum in the Columbia River and were just plain tuckered out, and now the whole family was looking forward to getting home to Coeur d'Alene.

Megan kept whining about having scary feelings, convinced there was a "monster" after them. She had said this for many days on the trip. She said she could feel evil. But her parents didn't believe her. And Zachary and Ben were too busy watching a horror movie on the onboard DVD player to notice anything. Megan was always seeing and hearing things, so this time seemed no different. Martha scolded the girl, telling her to lie down in the back bay, be quiet, and play with her Bratz doll.

Truth be told, Andrew thought he might have been having a case of the heebie-jeebies himself. He considered pulling over—*Rest Stop 1 Mile Ahead*—but he kept picturing sucking down a cold Miller Lite on his own couch. He passed the rest stop going ninety miles per hour, even though Megan was now crying, burbling that there was a monster on the roof. Ben pinched her and told her to shut up. She was always whining about ghouls and ghosts and ogres. And everybody knew there were no such things.

But the Dark Lord—or a part of him—was indeed in their midst. He fumed at the ignominy of his predicament. But he would find a solution. He had a plan. He always had a plan.

At 12:01 A.M., Andrew pulled the Commander into their driveway. At 12:15 they were all asleep in their beds. Then a sickly smell permeated the house, and at 12:42, little Megan bolted upright in her bed and screamed. Zachary was standing in her doorway holding a baseball bat. *Swing away, little slugger.*

The events that occurred over the next seven minutes were horrific: a young mind haunted by an ethereal, commanding voice; a voice entreating a son to punish the very beings who had brought him into the world and nurtured him; a voice whose undeniable power sent the young man into a blind psychotic rage. Megan's keening shrieks were so visceral that both Andrew and Martha were up and moving immediately, their feet propelling them through the house as though it had been rocked by an earthquake. Their veins pumped panic and their vision was blurred by confusion. They didn't see Zachary as he leapt from the shadows. But they felt the bat. Until they could feel no more. Zachary's parents would recuperate, but the local authorities and neighbors would spend many sleepless nights thinking about what had happened in their bucolic town. They kept asking themselves the same question over and over: What could possibly make a child turn so cruelly violent?

It was simple. The Devil made him do it. He was possessed.

It was a signal. A call to arms. The Dark Lord hoped that it was enough; surely his minions would recognize his handiwork and would come for him soon. He had failed in the belly of Mount St. Emory, failed to use his own son to unlock the portal of the damned. But he would not dwell on his failure. He was already formulating a new scheme. He sent out black thoughts to his followers. *Come to me. Rescue me and I will reward you by swinging the Sword of Armageddon and bringing a painful end to all of mankind!*

Chapter Four:
Dreams

Natalie turned over in her sleep, rolling onto her side, clutching the damp wrinkled sheet to her breast. Her eyes flicked back and forth under her lids. There was Will's face, smiling, his teeth straight and white. Then a demon flashing down, then Will whirling and effortlessly dispatching the creature with a wave of his hand. They were on a mountain. He moved closer to her. He was wearing a white T-shirt, black cords, and no shoes. She was wearing a pink cotton sundress and was also barefoot. His muscular arms at his sides, his hands hanging loose, he leaned forward, teasing . . . teasing. She felt ribbons of pleasure spiraling around her body.

Then they were in a room by the sea. The window was open. Billowing in the ocean breeze, the sheer saffron curtains danced in slow motion. The bed was on the floor with no headboard, no frame, a plain white fitted sheet covering it. She was on the bed and Will was next to her. He had his shirt off. The ocean waves crashed outside and she ran her fingertips over his chest, tracing imaginary patterns, her desire for him building up inside until she felt she would burst. She stared at his disparate blue eyes, the one deep blue, the other lighter, crystalline aqua. She fell headlong into his welcoming gaze.

Her lips trembled as she yearned for his kiss. She felt herself wanting to clearly proclaim her love to him, but the words were chunky and jumbled and awkward, and her lips would not move to release them. She was sure she was moaning, but he seemed not to hear as he continued to gaze at her adoringly. Then she tore her eyes from him and looked out and saw something in the distance. The sky was ruby red now, the setting sun a threatening black orb. And riding toward them on a skeletal stallion was Death himself.

A chill ran through her. Will was standing now, his back to the window, his back to Death. She leapt up and tried to pull him away from the window. She screamed as dark fatal hands entered the room and encircled Will, wrapping around his neck. But he was so entranced with her, so in love with her, he barely noticed. Natalie heard crying and woke up. It was Emily, crying in her sleep again.

"Hey, Em, hey, it's okay . . ." Natalie stroked Emily's cheek and, even still asleep, Emily seemed to calm at Natalie's touch.

"Shhh . . . you're safe, I promise. Dream of good things."

Natalie waited until Emily's breathing was deep and regular, and then rolled onto her back and stared at the ceiling, where shadows thrown from the swaying branches outside danced to and fro. She couldn't help but face her fear that by encouraging Will Hunter to love her, she could be bringing about his ultimate demise.

Will was dreaming, too. His mother April was just ahead of him on a busy street, a sidewalk teeming with faceless souls bobbing by. He kept calling to her, but though she would turn and smile at him, she would never answer his pleas for her to stop and wait for him to catch up. He had so much to tell her! He yelled and yelled, but she just kept walking. He ran but made no progress, the sidewalk moving beneath his feet, the pedestrians jostling him, blocking him, now clawing at him as their eyes changed, yellow eyes seeping black, hair and nails growing longer as they shrieked and began to surround him and, yes, up ahead, ensnared April, clutching her, now offering her to *him*, to the Dark Lord, his gaping mouth opening to . . . ? Will reached for his mother and the dream went white.

His heart was throbbing, his jaw clenched tightly as he ground his teeth. Then his breathing became more regular as his dream ship found new routes, changed course, and he was now following Natalie up a long stairway, the world falling off on either side. She was beautiful. She giggled; this was a game for her, a race to the clouds. Will redoubled his efforts, and the stairs crumbled into dust behind him with each precarious step. Finally he caught up to her and took her into his arms and whispered to her, the words like notes from a song. She melted into his embrace. He kissed her, gently at first, then more fully, tasting her, joining her to him. Then the scene shifted rapidly, and they were in his old bedroom, back in Corpus Christi where he'd lived with his mother and her second husband, Gerald, surrounded by Will's childhood artifacts. Model planes hung from the ceiling. Sports posters adorned the walls. But the bed was an adult bed, and in it they did adult things.

White. And more white. Clouds, now a horizon, Will was on wings, drifting, now dropping down slowly, light as air, a spring breeze. Now a church with a towering steeple. The bells were ringing. Will didn't know why, but this made him feel good inside. He looked down. There! Coming out of the church, young newlyweds, smiling their way through the ranks of well-wishers tossing birdseed. Will swooped lower, eager to see the happy couple. He recognized the girl first: Natalie, fiercely beautiful in her white dress, and more in love with her new husband than she had ever imagined possible. And her husband was Will. He saw himself smiling, and Natalie kissing him. And then suddenly his teeth begin to fall out as the church and the guests were sucked into a vortex and went down and down.

The hospital corridor was cold and shiny, the fluorescent lights casting a sickly green light. Will floated down the hallway, seesawing back and forth, seriously out of whack. He heard a young woman's cries and moved faster now, into the maternity ward, pass-ing nervous expectant fathers, nurses, a doctor. Now into the room where Natalie was pushing, pushing, and he was by her side, help-ing her breathe deeply, coaching her, *It's gonna be okay, you're at ten centimeters. . . .* Now the head, it was coming out! What a blessed moment: a child, *Our child, Nat, the product of our love.* But Natalie didn't respond. She wasn't moving. She wasn't breathing. The baby cried. The baby opened its eyes. They were liquid black. They were the eyes of a demon.

Will woke up in a pool of sweat, the certainty that he could never consummate his love for Natalie bearing down upon him, clench-ing his gut, squeezing his heart. The images from his dream still clung to him, made him despair even further of ever being able to be with Natalie the way he wanted to. If there was any chance, *any chance at all*, that he could cause anything even remotely demonic to grow within Natalie—well, he knew he couldn't take that chance. *Ever.*

He got up and took a shower, standing for a long time under the hot water, cleansing himself of the dream, needing a rebirth, needing to recalibrate his system—needing to go from teenager to warrior. He twisted the hot handle to off and balled his fists as the water turned cold, his skin tightening, his resolve steeling. He stepped out of the shower and toweled off, brushed his teeth, pulled on a T-shirt, and stepped into his underwear and jeans. He looked in the mirror. The young man looking back at him wanted to be a lover, but it wasn't worth the risk. It wasn't good for him—it was a distraction—and it was potentially deadly for Natalie. If he loved her—and of course he loved her, more than his next breath—the right thing to do would be to set her free so she could find someone else and have a normal life. As soon as it was safe, he'd send her and Emily away. Natalie would fight it, of course, but someday she'd understand.

Down in his lab he loaded a cache of weapons into a satchel. Rudy, floating in the Demon Trapper, mouthed silent, sorrowful pleas. Will stepped over to the Demon Trapper and read Rudy's lips. *Please*, he was saying, *help me! I won't cause any trouble, I promise. Just please let me out of here. You're my best friend! Let me out!*

"Sorry, buddy, no can do. Not until I create the antidote."

Will shook his head sadly, not knowing if that day would ever actually come. Just before plunging to his death, his father—his *adopted father*—Edward, had told him that his grandfather had discovered a treatment for demonic infection. And it had worked for him for many years. Will just had to find the formula, and he could liberate Rudy from his present state. He owed it to Rudy to save him. It was his fault the guy was like this—the same way it would be his fault if anything happened to Natalie.

As Will backed away from the Demon Trapper, Rudy went ballistic, writhing within the confines of the trap and raking at the Plexiglas with his nails. Will again read his lips, and this time Rudy was not so polite. *I'm going to get out of here! I'm going to kill you! I'm going to rip the flesh from your bones and watch you die!*

"Yeah, I love you too, bro," said Will. Sometimes his whole world was pure madness.

Will turned away from Rudy and zipped up his backpack, picked up the satchel, and exited the lab. One minute later he was backing his Mitsubishi EVO out of the garage. Upstairs, Natalie woke up at the sound of the garage door and rose from her bed. She rushed to the window, parted the curtains, and stared down at Will as he pulled out through the big iron gates and sped away. She wondered if this would finally be the day that he never came back. She didn't even get to say goodbye. She shuddered. *Come back to me, Will, please come back!* Natalie felt arms encircling her from behind. It was Emily.

"He'll be okay. I know he will."

But her words were nothing more than a comforting lie. Because deep down, neither of them knew any such thing.

As they had for several weeks now, hundreds of followers of the Dark Lord gathered at the apex of Mount St. Emory. Among them was Rocco Manelli, an imposing six-foot-four-inch Alpha demon-teen from a Seattle high school. Rocco shouted orders and punched people to get their attention. Also there was a phalanx of girls from the same school, drill team members who had changed out of their uniforms and into black gear. They were wicked and fast and deadly, already high on the crystal meth that amplified their strength and speed. Though they were mind-blowingly beautiful, no boys approached them. They knew better. It was well known that no guy ever scored with them.

The whole gathering of demons proceeded to get high on drugs and booze, and then fanned out in every direction, resuming their tireless search for their master. They covered the same territory repeatedly, leaving no stone unturned. They dug up the earth and felled trees. They searched in streams and rivers and caves. But again and again, after hours of searching, they came back empty-handed and angry. Insults led to fights. They were becoming desperate. If they couldn't find what they needed to save the Prince of Darkness, who would lead them? What would happen to their kind? They drank and smoked and snorted and howled in agony, beseeching their leader to somehow reach out and guide them. A few demons claimed to have heard the Dark Prince's foul curses riding on the currents of the night, but no one could tell from whence they came, and the vast majority of followers, when listening for their leader, heard only the wind. The elite among them lashed out at the incompetence of the others, a brief bloody skirmish ensued, and then the elite flew off into the night to search on their own. But after a few hours, they too gave up, preferring to retreat rather than face the rising sun in defeat.

Exiled in his peculiar limbo, the Dark Prince waited, none too patiently. Where *were* they? How could it be that they had not found all of him yet? Did they not hear him calling to them?

But he knew the answer. He could not communicate with them directly. With those with whom he shared blood, he could easily ride waves of thought into their heads. He could plant explicit thoughts there; he could send them dreams, smells, sounds, and words. He could invade their dreams, invade their consciousness. But the Dark Lord could not do the same with just anyone, let alone his legion of followers.

His disciples were not, as a rule, consistently intelligent and coherent creatures. While many had the capacity for superior intellect, their penchant for indulging in vices often sabotaged their ability to concentrate. They had fury, power, strength, and cunning, but they were easily distracted by avarice, wrath, envy, and a general need to be malicious toward every living thing. They drank alcohol, they smoked tobacco, marijuana, crystal meth, crack cocaine. They were addicts on every level: addicted to food, drugs, booze, sex, and violence. They were easily provoked and brawled frequently. They craved mayhem. They could not be counted on to use their brains. Which meant the Dark Lord would have to find another way to reach them. He proceeded to send a torrent of blood curses into the atmosphere.

DAVENPORT, WASHINGTON

A freak hole in the ozone, that's what some would report. Detective Mears studied the bodies and then glanced at the sky. *Impossible.* But who could say, really, with all the havoc the weather was causing? There were two of them in the field, naked as the day they were born. On a blanket, both middle-aged, their flesh sagging. The man's hair graying, the woman a bottle blonde. Both wore wedding rings, but Mears would bet dollars to donuts they weren't married to each other. They were adulterers, plain and simple. They had to have been having an affair; why else come all this way to do the dirty deed in a field?

Danny Anderson and Pam Mead were in love. Danny was sick of his wife and her constant nagging and her addiction to TV. Pam said she still loved her husband Randy, even though he was morbidly obese and spent all his free time stuffing his face and playing *Demon Hunter* and other online games. But she didn't *really* love him; she just didn't have the heart to ask for a divorce. It would hurt the kids. This way was so much simpler. She could make love in a field with a man like the heroes in the romance novels she devoured when she wasn't working at ValueMart or cleaning up after the kids. So they had started the affair after meeting on church bowling night. Danny had told Pam she had a great toss. And she did, bowling a 212. They all had beers afterward, and Danny lingered, his hand finding Pam's on the bar. He bought her a Cosmopolitan and she got tipsy, and when he walked her to her car, the friendly goodnight kiss evolved into something more delightfully wicked.

They met again in the middle of the day on their lunch breaks. Randy was over in Portland on business, so it went down in the Meads' rec room on the pool table. After that, Danny and Pam couldn't keep away from each other, both reliving those golden high school days when sex was brand new. It was heaven. But today had been different, the guilt of the whole thing finally bubbling up in them both, and they held each other, weeping, deciding that this was the last time, that from now on they would stop sneaking around and honor their wedding vows. Danny wiped the tears from Pam's face. Pam had worn her new jeans, but she didn't stay in them long. They drank some wine, not the usual box stuff Pam kept in her fridge, but an expensive bottle from Costco. Tipsy, they disrobed and began their final adulterous dance, in full view of the universe. The taste of the wine, though, went sour in their mouths. They couldn't identify or articulate the taste, but it tasted somehow . . . wrong. Their flesh heated up, and for perhaps a minute they both thought that it was their passion that was searing them. Then the pain became all too real as the sun's rays intensified. It was as if someone were holding a giant magnifying glass above them, and they burned, their naked white bodies reddening and then breaking out in blisters. No one was close enough to hear their screams as they slowly and agonizingly burned to death.

Chapter Five:
The Pig Demon

Will was on his way to find his mother. He parked two blocks away from the U-Send Postal Annex and looked up at the gray sky as sunlight cracked through the ubiquitous cloud cover. Sunshine. A sign that everything was going to be okay. He walked in a roundabout manner to the small shop, his eyes sweeping the surrounding area. You could never be too careful and he refused to make any mistakes. He was going to find his mother and bring her into the fold, and then somehow make the world safe again.

Reaching the storefront of the U-Send shop, Will looked around for the third time and then went inside and walked directly to box 999. He'd chosen the box number because some thought it was the antithesis of the demon mark of 666. Heavenly 999. He punched in the combination but paused before opening the small metal door. He shot a glance at the friendly looking clerk behind the counter, a tubby guy with an orange T-shirt and a day's growth on his sad chin wearing a Washington State Cougars baseball cap. He was chewing something. It looked like he couldn't decide whether he wanted to spit it out or swallow. He swallowed—*ugh!*—then went on stamping packages with postage.

Again Will looked at the mailbox. Inside he expected to find a postcard from his mother informing him of her whereabouts. He'd given her this address when he put her on the private plane out of Harrisburg and instructed her to send the postcard here. He reached again for the box. But then the skin on the back of his neck prickled.

He jerked his head to the right and thought he saw a flash of black in the clerk's eyes. Bending time, he leapt over the counter. He had a half-dozen Concussion Shockers in the side pocket of his cargo jeans, but he opted to go physical instead. Sometimes it was best to get the job done bare-knuckle style. Besides, more and more often, it just plain felt good.

"Hey, what the hell?" squealed the clerk, rearing back as Will grabbed his shirt, ripping it. Will punched him in the throat. He made frog-like gurgling noises.

"Don't talk," Will ordered.

Will grabbed the guy's hands and checked his palms. Sometimes demons had eyes, or even mouths in their palms. This guy's palms were smooth. But that didn't mean he was clean. There was another way to check for sure, a method Will had stumbled upon while combating demons in the forests surrounding Mount St. Emory. He squeezed the guy's temples and watched his eyes closely. If you forced your thumbs against the temples of a demon, their eyes invariably shaded up to that sickening inky black. But the clerk's eyes only got more bloodshot. This guy wasn't infected.

"Sorry," Will said, releasing his hold. "My mistake."

"M-m-m-m-*mistake*?" the guy stammered, his eyes round with fear as he rubbed his temples. Will took out his wallet, peeled off five $100 bills, and dropped them on the counter.

"Sorry for the trouble. Buy yourself a new shirt."

The guy gaped at the money, then quickly snatched it up and stuffed it in his pocket. *Shirt, hell, I'll buy myself some weed!* Suddenly his temples didn't hurt so much anymore.

Will went and opened the mailbox. It was empty.

He stood for a moment, panic clawing at his stomach, silently admonishing himself for not getting here sooner. Had April gotten the chance to send the postcard in the first place? Or had she sent it, and someone had just gotten here before him? How long had she been in danger? Finding and fortifying a new base of operations before coming to get her had been necessary, but why had he wasted time hanging out with Natalie and Emily, trying to lead a normal life for a few hours? He wasn't normal and he never would be. He just hoped that the mistake wouldn't cost him.

Will exited the storefront, and after a visual sweep of the street, he crossed through traffic to the opposite sidewalk in front of a red brick building. Looking up, he spotted his surveillance camera. It was tiny, the shape and color of a brick. Just as he had suspected, it was still in place and more than likely had gone totally unnoticed. He would know soon enough whether someone—or some*thing*— had beaten him here.

The sun was just dipping down over the horizon when Will rappelled over the side of the building and retrieved the camera. He took it to the hotel room he'd rented for the day and carefully reviewed the data on the hard drive. His laptop was remote-linked to his mainframe, so he was able to access the latest recognition soft- ware programs he'd written.

Tearing open a bag of barbeque chips and popping open a coke he'd grabbed from the vending machine outside, he ate and drank as he fast-forwarded through the surveillance images. It didn't take him long to drill down on a suspect. One porky guy came riding up on his Harley at the same time every day, and every day he went in and then came out empty-handed. Either he was one very unpopular dude or he was waiting for just the right piece of mail. Finally the guy came out tucking something into the pocket of his leather vest. Bingo.

Will logged on to his *Demon Hunter* game-creator program within his mainframe and pulled out a series of characters. He clicked on a couple of the chunkier ones, dropped down a sub-menu, and went into past game versions where those characters had appeared. He copied a section where a pig-like demon moved swiftly across a hallway before turning and snorting, piggy eyes red, snout enlarged, barbed tongue snaking out. Will overlaid the sequence on top of the surveillance clip and his deductive software quickly matched Harley Dude to Pig Demon. Double Bingo. No doubt about it, Will had found himself a three-hundred-pound pig demon in a human suit. It appeared as though the demon had retrieved the postcard—if that was what he'd retrieved—within the last couple of days. That meant Will had time. Not much, maybe, but hopefully some.

Freezing the image of the Harley, Will lifted the plate number, then hacked into the state's database and retrieved the information necessary to find out where Harley Dude hung his helmet. In minutes he had the address and was in his car, ripping down the road.

The city gave way to suburbia, which in turn yielded to a rough-hewn rural landscape. Will found the farm at the end of a long gravel road. A dented old Airstream trailer, dulled to sickly pewter, was moored adjacent to a large pen where a dozen or so hogs wallowed in a trench of mud.

Will stepped out and was just able to take in the silent squalor of the place when the trailer door banged open and the pig demon dove out. He was wearing jeans and a torn Confederate flag T-shirt and came up firing a pump shotgun. Luckily Will was ready for the move, and as the buckshot raked across the Mitsubishi he tucked and rolled, coming up with a small sphere he'd dug from his pocket. With a flick of his wrist he threw the sphere, a Series 111 Cloaker. It hit Pig Demon square in the chest. He grunted, then oinked, then tossed aside the shotgun and resorted to his real weapon, his snout, which enlarged in seconds. Snorting, eyes wild with anger, the demon shot gobs of toxic snot at Will as the Cloaker quickly spread out across his torso and began to envelop his whole body. But the snout was still exposed, and he continued firing off burning goobers.

Again, Will had anticipated. He'd seen the snout move before, so he leapt over the advancing demon, then bounded behind the trailer and waited for one . . . two . . . three . . . four seconds as he activated the Cloaker. The beautiful thing about the Cloaker was that Will could control it, making it cinch tighter or loosen up with the twist of a dial. By the time Will emerged from behind the Airstream, the pig man was shuddering and choking, only one eye and his mouth exposed. The rest of his body, snout included, was shrink-wrapped in the Cloaker.

"Where is it?" Will asked calmly.

"I don't know what you're—*AHHHHHH!*"

Will dialed the Cloaker tighter and the pig man's eyes bulged out. A couple more turns and they'd burst right out of his skull. Will hoped he wouldn't have to resort to that. Pig Demon brains stunk.

"The postcard? The one you stole from my box? Where is it? In the trailer?"

Pig man shook his head violently. Again, bingo. It *had* to be in the trailer because the mere thought of Will recovering it clearly scared the beans out of Porky. He knew he'd be called out by his peers, and what they did to those who failed was not pretty. Will could smell the bacon frying now.

Leaving the pig demon wrapped in the Cloaker, he stepped into the trailer and waded through piles of pizza and pastry boxes and crumpled cans of Red Bull. Will carefully surveyed the lair, then went to the refrigerator and opened the icebox. There it was: the postcard from his mother. As he noted the return address, he heard the faintest sound—it wasn't a sound at all really, it was a feeling, a warning from his seventh sense—and without another thought Will dove through the window above the sink, just as the trailer exploded, flames arcing high in the air.

Will was hurled smack into the pigpen, his face slamming straight into mud thick as peanut butter. He yanked his head out of the muck just as the first angry swine tore into his thigh, its massive jaws shockingly powerful. The rest of the drove attacked as well as Will reached down to un-strap his Megashocker from his leg. As it powered up it made a zapping sound, and then he struck out in all directions, the shocker sizzling pig flesh. In seconds he had blinded, de-snouted, or dismembered the most aggressive of the attackers and earned himself a precious few moments to get to his feet and leap over the pen railing.

His thigh burning with pain, he ran and jumped into the front seat of his EVO and tore open a packet of the healing balm he'd chemically engineered, which sped up the healing process from days to mere minutes. He spread it on the torn flesh of his thigh, applied a bandage over the wound, and waited, catching his breath as the balm did its work. He closed his eyes for a few seconds and let the pain have its way with him; no sense fighting it, better to just welcome it into his body and deal with it.

As the pain started to fade, he opened his eyes and saw that the pigs who hadn't been maimed or blinded were ramming against the pen fence. He figured he could do without any more crap from these swine, so he lifted the Short-Range Obliterator, jacked a multi-shell into the firing chamber, aimed, and pulled the trigger. The wide-range blast blew the pigs off their hooves and backward as the second-stage ordnance ignited and blew them to bacon bits.

Catching his breath and wiping the mud from his face, Will stared down at the postcard. It had a photograph of a kitschy-looking greasy spoon built like a log cabin, a tourist trap called the Squirrel Tree Inn set just off the highway, surrounded by towering pines. It was his ticket to his mother.

He just prayed that he hadn't taken too long.

Chapter Six: Rescue

Will sped along Highway 2, the verdant forest rushing past. He would be reunited with his mother soon. But he had some heavy lifting to do to make it happen. The Squirrel Tree Inn postcard meant that April had taken refuge at the cabin near Lake Wenatchee that belonged to her uncle. Will had spent a couple of summers there during his childhood and had fond memories of the place. He and his mom used to joke about the funky, funny Squirrel Tree Inn, and they'd had more than one meal there. He hoped they'd have occasion to have another.

Will put the pedal to the metal and made the drive in just under two hours, and when he was close to the lake he pulled off the highway into the Squirrel Tree Inn parking lot. All he'd had to eat since that morning were the chips and coke, and he needed to fuel himself, so he went inside to the gift shop. It was tempting, but he managed to resist buying any squirrel nuts or squirrel key chains or squirrel outhouse signs or any of the other stupid "made in China" squirrel junk. He did, however, buy two PowerBars and a carton of chocolate milk that he took outside.

A breeze kicked up, carrying the scent of pine and lavender. Will gazed at the mountains as he ate the bars and chugged the chocolate milk. Then he popped his trunk and loaded charges into one of his newest inventions, the Spearzooka, which, like a traditional bazooka, was held on the shoulder like a missile launcher. However, the Spearzooka was much lighter and fired needle-sharp 200-centimeter spears tipped with paralyzing poison to immobilize the enemy while he interrogated them if necessary. He also powered up a Chaosglobe, another device he'd engineered, which, when lobbed, created blinding lights and a high-frequency radio-wave storm capable of knocking a T-Rex to its knees. With the Spearzooka and Chaosglobe, along with his trusty Megashocker and the Cloakers, he figured he was ready to kick some serious ass if need be.

He knew better than to just drive up to the cabin; he'd have to do some recon first. He tapped information into his computer, then pulled a small drone plane, equipped with a high-definition camera, out of the trunk and sent it skyward. He entered the exact coordinates and it sailed off into the sky toward the cabin where he hoped his mother was safe and sound.

But when he started up his car and took off following the drone, he felt an ugly weight in his stomach. Something told him his mom wasn't kicking back and enjoying herself. He hoped his gut was wrong.

The cabin on Lake Wenatchee sat fifty yards back from the dock, across a broad expanse of rolling green grass framed by wild huckleberry and raspberry bushes. In the small stream that meandered through the property, trout fingerlings darted about in the shallows. Drawing to within a quarter-mile of the cabin, Will pulled over and tracked the drone on his laptop. Controlling it remotely, he had the plane slowly circle the nine-acre lot at six hundred feet. He was looking in the treetops, knowing that if this was a trap, demons might be hiding high in the evergreens. He saw none.

So he piloted the drone closer to the cabin. The HD camera captured images of the two clunky old Chevy pickups parked in the driveway and the small aluminum boat sitting on an unhitched trailer. Laundry hung outside on sagging lines. There was no movement on the small porch or in any of the windows. Nothing seemed out of the ordinary. Will pulled back onto the road and drove closer.

At the turnoff from the highway he slowed, then turned into the driveway, tires crunching on the gravel. Every nerve in his body was on high alert. For him, this was life at its most primitive. The hunt. It got him going, his blood racing, synapses firing, dopamine elevating. He tightened his hands on the steering wheel and drove for fifty feet, and when the gravel gave way to damp earth he slowed, carefully inspecting the ground. He braked to a halt and waited, counting down from five . . . four . . . three . . . two . . . one. Nothing. He sucked in a long breath through his nostrils. The forest smelled of pine and loamy moisture. And something else. A smell that caused Will's nostrils to tighten.

It smelled of *them.*

The earth around him erupted in a series of dirt blasts as demons—they were very good at burying themselves and surviving for hours, even days—leapt up and attacked him from all sides. They were armed with sledgehammers, and he would have been beaten to death had he not spotted the perimeter dig marks and anticipated the trap. Before they could strike, he triggered his own blast, a charge he'd mounted under the rear axle—the kind used by stunt men—that fired a solid steel rod straight down, kicking the Mitsubishi ass-end up with such power that the car hurled skyward, flipped in mid-air, then landed back on all four tires. *Wham!*

Will grabbed the Spearzooka, leaped out of the car, and, setting his sights, fired four shots. *Blam-swoosh-chock!* Four times in quick succession. Perfect. He now had four adult male demons impaled in the bases of four evergreen trees. They writhed and hissed and spit, but soon the poison coursed through their ugly purple veins and they could no longer spit with any velocity.

He approached the first demon. "You think I grow weak," Will said calmly, "but every day I grow stronger."

"You are the walking dead, my friend," slurred the demon.

"I am not your friend. But I will show you mercy should you show enough intelligence to tell me where my mother is."

"And spoil your lesson? I think not, young Will. It's too late for her and too late for you."

The Spearzooka had worked beautifully, skewering and numbing the bastards like Novocain. He interrogated the other three with the same net result. He knew if he left them impaled, the poison would eventually wear off and they would work themselves free. So he turned the tiny dials on the ends of the spears. The beasts had two minutes until the embedded charges exploded. They hurled threats and curses at him with their slack mouths, and then, sensing that further aggression would yield them no clemency, they resorted to pleading. Will ignored that, too.

Will off-loaded his battle pack containing the Chaosglobe, Cloakers, and Megashocker. Though he appeared calm, inside he was a storm of jangled nerves. He looked at the cabin. Nothing. He walked over and stepped onto the porch. He thought he heard a whimper.

"Mom, are you in there?" he called.

Another whimper, this time definite. He couldn't wait a moment longer, so he whipped on some Ray-Bans, kicked open the front door, and lobbed the Chaosglobe into the cabin. It detonated, washing the interior with a blinding light. Will smiled, impervious to the blast flash thanks to the blacked-out Ray-Bans. He had a Cloaker in one hand and his Megashocker in the other and was about to step inside when the floorboards on the porch cracked.

He felt them before he saw them. Hands blasting up from beneath the porch—right through the floorboards—grabbed his ankles. They were so strong, he thought the bones in his legs were going to be crushed like hard candy. He lashed down with the Megashocker and lopped off one clawed hand, then another. Demon blood splattered against the cabin wall, searing it. Once his feet were free, he lunged inside.

And stopped dead in his tracks.

The Chaosglobe's light faded. Will yanked off his Ray-Bans and stared in pure horror.

April was hanging upside-down in a flesh web. A hooded demon stood mute in the shadows. Just then, Will heard three popping explosions behind him. Three of the impaled demons outside had bought it—but what of the fourth? The hooded demon held the answer in its hand: A spear. The fourth one.

Seeing his mother hanging like a side of beef in a butcher's shop made Will's heart thud. He spoke to her softly.

"Don't worry, Mom, everything's going to be okay."

"Will . . . go . . . get out of here!" She shook her head back and forth and tears spilled from her eyes onto the cabin floor. Will's jaw tightened.

"We're leaving together, just you and me."

"That's doubtful," said the hooded demon.

They hadn't cut her that he could see, but her eyes were wild with fear. Another hooded demon revealed himself, and with catlike quickness had a blade to her throat. Will needed to do *something*, faster than fast. He was calculating his moves with the Megashocker when the first hooded demon threw the spear. It zinged through the air like a bullet and sank into Will's left arm, pinning him against the doorframe. The pain was searing, a torrent of agony, and the poison spread like flames through his body, moving from left to right. He could still move the Megashocker, but unless his target was closer, he couldn't use it. The hooded demon holding the blade to his mom's neck barked out a command.

"Put the weapon down."

Everything had gone wrong.

Will had no choice. He dropped the Megashocker. It made zapping noises as it clattered on the wooden floor.

"It's over for you, Demon Hunter," said the spear thrower. He approached Will in a blur, extracting something from his tunic. It was a claw-like torture device with six jagged talons.

"I'm not sure whether I should cut your dear mother to ribbons while you watch, or vice versa. What do you think, Will?"

The poison continued its numbing wave through Will's body, reaching his right hand and rising up into his throat. He spoke in a rasp.

"I'm going to enjoy watching you die."

The demon laughed and looked from April to Will and back again.

"Watch this closely. It's going to be painful. Observe, and let the images burn into your brain for eternity."

It was time for Will to bite the bullet. Or, more specifically, the capsule he had planted under tooth number nineteen, the lower left molar. Biting down hard, Will caused the capsule to burst, and the antidote to the numbing poison shot through his system. He shuddered, then pumped the fist of his right hand as the chemicals spread. The hooded demons had counted Will out and were circling April, chanting demon curses as they waved their weapons, ready to flay her.

Will reached over with his right hand and yanked the spear out of his arm, then flung it, back-handed. The spear rocketed across the room and entered the knife-wielding demon's left eye, killing him instantly. Claw-demon whirled just in time to see the Megashocker in Will's hand come thrusting up under his chin. It was not a pleasant final image, no doubt, and Will finished him off by plunging the Megashocker all the way up through his skull. The creature fell backward, and his body began to shake in a death dance. One half of his face remained intact, his yellow demon eye blinking in mute outrage.

With a dozen more deft strokes of the Megashocker, Will freed April and held her in his arms.

"Come on, Mom, let's get you out of here."

"Will . . . am I alive? Am I really alive?"

"Yeah, everything's okay. We made it."

But Will hadn't paid close enough attention as he'd entered. If he had, he would have seen the charges the demons had placed at the interior perimeter of the cabin at floor level. Half-face managed a horrific, gnarled smile as he stared up at Will with his one eye, and then he pressed a button.

The charges blew in rapid succession and the cabin collapsed with the sickening sound of timbers cracking, splitting, imploding. Will did his best to shield his mother but could not prevent one of the larger, thousand-pound crossbeams from clipping her—just a glancing blow, really, but one with such force that April's world went to black. Her last thought was that for all of her sins, for her part in creating Will and damning him to being what he was, she deserved to be sucked down into the sunless void.

Rising up from the rubble, his bloody, unconscious, and possibly mortally wounded mother in his arms, Will unleashed a holy howl of pain that echoed through the woods. Frightened birds took flight.

As for April, she was far, far away in a very dark place.

Chapter Seven: April's Cosmos

The moment she received Will's text, Natalie loaded up the numbered cases he had requested from his lab and drove them to the Swedish Medical Center on First Hill. She met him in the ICU waiting room. She rushed to hug him—he'd been gone for more than two days, and she was so relieved to see him unharmed—but his body language made her rear up like a skittish horse. It was like he had a force field around him.

"Are you . . . okay?" she asked.

He wanted to tell her everything: that he was definitely not okay, that his mother was in a coma, that it was all his fault for not being 100 percent focused. But he remembered his promise to himself before he'd gone after April all too clearly. He had to cut his losses now. What happened to his mother only made keeping Natalie safe more important.

"Thank you for bringing these. Now go back home and—"

"But, Will, I—"

"Natalie, for once, don't argue with me. Just do it! Drive back home. Fast. And then go into lockdown mode."

The words stung but she saw the urgency in his eyes. Even as the tears welled, she nodded. He wiped a tear from her cheek and she thought he might soften a little and give her a hug, even just squeeze her hand, but if anything, he only hardened more.

"Now, please."

She did as he requested and left.

When she'd gone, Will picked up both cases and moved swiftly down the hallway. He reached a locked door made of heavy steel and used a key card to open it. He was now in a private wing of the hospital, a wing he'd paid for. He set up the wide-beam lasers and armed them, then checked on the surveillance cameras. They were functioning perfectly. Then he went into her room.

He stood motionless before his mother's body, watching the ventilator tube do its job, coaxing her chest to gently rise and fall with every mechanically forced breath. The doctors had said that since she'd been in a coma for nearly twenty-four hours, the chances of her regaining consciousness were very slim indeed and growing slimmer with each passing hour. After two days, the odds of her coming out of the coma without significant brain damage would be roughly the same as winning the state lottery. Medically, the doctors had said, there wasn't anything keeping her from regaining consciousness. But she wouldn't wake up.

Will knew he only had one chance. He had to plant within his mother's brain a powerful desire to reawaken. In essence, he would have to venture inside her mind and bring her out himself. He remembered being face to face with the Dark Lord, remembered how they'd been able to travel at lightning speed in and out of each other's minds, in part because they'd been connected by blood. He now had to do the same thing with his mother. He placed his hand upon hers. Her skin was dry and cool. He closed his eyes and concentrated, and mentally bled his warmth into her through their touch.

Creating an energy stream between their minds was the key. Because her own mind, nearly totally bereft of alpha waves, was so weak, the task at hand was for all practical purposes impossible. But Will would not give up hope. He kept on visualizing an energy stream, a glowing, flowing thing of shimmering beauty, beauty he could ride on as one would ride a wave in the ocean. *Now. Again. Try again.* But he got nothing. Nothing but darkness and the chilly gusts from the air conditioner.

He gently pushed all competing thoughts from his consciousness until his mind was a ball of white energy. And there! He felt a tendril moving, snaking out from his mind, searching. Now! There! He'd caught a hold of something! The tendril grew thicker, brighter, the connection solidifying between them. He wasted no time, mentally getting on board and sailing on the stream.

He was in. Soaring. His mother's mind, her brain, her consciousness, was a vast cosmos, with bubble planets floating in massive random jet streams, each planet a cluster of thoughts and emotions. He ventured into the brightest bubble planet. It was a fortuitous choice. He had come to the place where she held her most salient thoughts, the thoughts of the here and now. As he entered the bright space he could feel her thoughts, her regrets. Then he saw her face.

"I'm sorry." The voice of a bird, an angel, a saint.

"Mother?" he said.

"I'm ready to face my sins," she said.

"You haven't sinned."

"We've all sinned," she whispered. "But mine cannot be forgiven."

"I forgive you."

April closed her mouth and a tear curled down from her eye and crossed her cheek.

"Mother, you have to come back. Please?"

She shook her head. "You don't know—you didn't see what I did." She was wracked with guilt for the Night of Evil—the night Will had been conceived.

"We make choices," she said. "They follow us like ghosts for our entire lives. Only most of us don't see them. But they are always there. I am going where the ghosts are pulling me. Where I deserve to go."

Will tried to reach out to her—but he was suddenly outside the bubble planet he'd just entered. He knew he had to venture further within his mother's mind to a memory of the night of her perceived transgression.

He sailed on, entering another bubble planet. April was twelve years old, crying in her backyard, her dead kitten beside her in a shoebox, about to be buried in a solemn backyard ceremony. She was a beautiful girl.

Will retreated. Searching. Searching. He found the violent jarring memories of her birth, the blissful memories of her wedding day—how handsome Edward looked in his tuxedo in the church in Honolulu!—and a half-dozen other gilded days. He searched memory after memory until he came upon the fateful night, the Night of Evil.

After a brief argument with Edward, April was out the door and in the Mustang, cruising, her high-heeled Nine Wests jamming the accelerator to the floor, the window down, her hair whipping in the wind. She wasn't leaving Edward; deep down inside she knew he was too good a man. She was, rather, trying to flee her own sense of self, to get out of her own skin, if only for a few brief moments. She and Edward had been unable to conceive. She wanted a baby. The thought of not having one made her so angry, it ate at her soul like a poison.

In the Lazy J Tavern she sat on a black leatherette stool at the bar, nursing a whiskey, her eyes going soft as the jukebox pumped out heartbreak blues. Men checked her out and liked what they saw. Two of them tried to send drinks her way, but she declined them. She stared down at her wedding ring, a simple gold band with a proud little one-carat diamond. She twisted the ring on her finger, sliding it up past her knuckle then pushing it back down. She knew she wouldn't take the ring off. It was there for a lifetime. She shook her head. *What am I doing here? Edward must be worried sick.* She made up her mind to leave the bar. She was about to pay when a crisp $100 bill floated onto the counter.

She looked into the mirror. The reflection of the tall man suddenly next to her startled her. The man ordered her a drink, and instead of turning it down immediately the way she had the others, she hesitated. The drink arrived. She looked at the man again. He was handsome in a hazardous kind of way. The bad boy of all bad boys. And she'd let him buy her a drink.

"I'd better go," she managed, in a hoarse whisper.

"It's early," he said.

"Not for me."

She didn't notice his hand—large, with bulging veins that pulsed rhythmically—pass over her drink, changing the color from faint amber to deep saffron.

"At least finish your drink first." His voice was eerily resonant, as though emanating from an ancient cave.

April wanted no more alcohol, was already distrusting her judgment, but something in the man's voice was so commanding that she found herself sipping once again from her glass. *Boom.* The next thing she knew, she was behind the wheel of the Mustang, speeding recklessly through the unforgiving night, the tall stranger beside her.

When they reached April's house, she noticed that Edward's car was gone. He was out looking for her. The thought calmed her. But that was the last feeling of tranquility she would experience for a long, long time. She opened her mouth to protest, but in an unholy flash the stranger was pulling her from the car. She went limp from the potion he'd slipped into her drink and fell headlong into unconsciousness.

When she regained control of her mind, the first thing she became aware of was her throbbing head. Splayed on the bed, her body wracked with pain, April's head turned and she saw first her naked finger, and then her wedding ring sitting lonesome on the nightstand. She rushed to self-hating judgment, concluding that she had taken off the ring herself.

The die had been cast. She would hold this blame within her for years—held it still, in fact—allowing it to gnaw away at her insides, corroding her soul.

Will came out of her mind and back into the hospital room. His mother was innocent, yet had tried and convicted herself. And her punishment would be a one-way ticket away from this life. Will couldn't let that happen.

"Mom? It wasn't your fault. No one could have resisted him. You never took your wedding ring off your finger, he did! Listen to me, you can't go. I won't let you!"

The ventilator kept up its steady rhythm. April's chest continued to rise and fall. But her pallor was frightening, as though the light inside her had already been snuffed out.

"Mom!"

He touched her hands, stroked her face. She was growing colder as, outside, the sun was blocked out and the sky grew dark. He could feel it. She was letting herself fade away. He had to stop her!

"Mom, please don't go. I need you!" He was telling the truth. He did need her. With Edward gone, and his decision to let Natalie go, his mother was his anchor. "Please . . ."

And then Will did something he hadn't done in a very long time. He cried. Tears spilled from his eyes and onto April's wrist. Their warmth spread up her arm until it reached her chest. Will had touched her heart, and it began beating rapidly.

Will felt the energy in the room change. His tears ceased. He looked down at his mother. Her face had regained some color. He moved to the foot of her bed and raked his thumbnail up along the bottom of her foot. Reflexively, it jerked ever so slightly. And then she coughed. Will could hardly believe his eyes. She *had* heard him! She knew he needed her, and she was coming out. He was starting to feel joyful.

But then he heard the Dark Lord's voice.

"We have unfinished business, my son."

Will looked around. The Dark Lord was, of course, not present in the room, only in Will's mind. He closed his eyes as he realized what he'd done. While he had traveled into his mother's mind, he had inadvertently brought the Dark Lord with him. *And now the beast was in there.* He had to get him out! Will wasted no time finding and riding a thought stream back into April's mind. He found a throbbing orb the color of rust and entered. It was a hot, humid cave. The Dark Lord was grinning. But it was only his head, propped atop a stalagmite.

"I knew you would come," his weighty voice rumbled.

"What have you done with her?" Will demanded.

"I have only to let her do what she desires, to become what she wishes, deep inside."

April was wearing the same dress she had worn that fateful night. Her eyes were glazed and she danced as if in a trance.

"Mom? Mom, come with me! Come with me now, please?"

Will reached out his hand. As she twirled, April's eyes swept around the room and she looked right through him, so deep was she under the Dark Lord's control. Will knew he had to act fast. He leapt at the Dark Lord's head with his right foot uplifted, preparing for a death kick. But Will was unable to time-bend here, unable to move with any velocity at all. It was as if he was moving in slow motion.

The Dark Lord's laughter rang off the walls of the cave. "You have no power here, boy!"

Will turned to April and tried to grab her, to somehow shake her from the Dark Lord's spell.

"Mother!"

But she was formless, there was nothing firm for him to grasp. For a deadly second, the Dark Lord became a menacing human shape, ghostly in form, except for his head, which appeared solid.

"You have taken much from me," said the Dark Lord. "More than you will ever know. And now, I will take from you that which is most precious."

The next two seconds stretched into an infinite agony as the Dark Lord swept over, grabbed April's wrists, and, with a malevolent roar, ripped her gauzy being across the cave.

A sword plunged from above and sank into the earth. The Dark Lord lifted it into his hand and smiled triumphantly at Will.

"Take a good look at this sword." The Dark Lord caressed it as though it were his lover. And then suddenly he swiped it threateningly through the air. It made a terrifying crackling, whooshing sound.

"The next time you see it . . . it will be the *last* thing you ever see."

The Dark Lord once again swiped the sword, this time dangerously close to Will.

"I look forward to that moment. Come find me!"

And then he swept April away into the ink of nothingness as Will screamed until his throat bled and the cave plunged into darkness.

Will was back in the hospital room, his eyes clenched shut in pain. The night nurse came thundering in and immediately misunderstood the situation when she saw the brainwave monitors. It appeared as though April had finally taken her leave and was gone forever. And for all practical, medical purposes, she was. The Dark Lord had taken what was left of April's mind: her last thoughts, her will to live, her soul. The night nurse and now the two orderlies that had come running all concluded that the screaming young man was at long last letting go of his comatose mother. They reached to console him but immediately drew back as he stood up and opened his mismatched blue eyes, which were filled with resolve and fire. He was not letting go. He was making a pledge to himself. He would find the Dark Lord and free his beloved mother from the beast's grasp.

Will swore that she would live again.

The doctors, with their long faces and grave expressions, came and went like drones in their white coats. They counseled Will as best they could, again and again advising him that the most humane thing to do would be to terminate her. How he loathed that word! No, there would be no termination. As surely as Will's heart beat in his chest, he knew his mother would open her eyes and smile at him again.

This was his vow, this was his promise. This was his destiny.

THOMPSON FALLS, MONTANA

Edwin Baily and Mary Weiss were at the head of the group, the parade of pious souls who had come to cast rose petals over the Thompson Falls Dam in honor of the teenage lovers who had taken their lives in the roiling waters here exactly one year prior. Edwin's son, Terry Baily, was only seventeen but locked forever in love with Cynthia Weiss, Mary's sixteen-year-old daughter. That was what the suicide page they left on Terry's MacBook had said, that they were now "forever locked in love."

Behind Edwin and Mary were other Baily and Weiss family members and a smattering of brave schoolmates from Thompson Falls High. One of them had brought a CD player. The rose petals had been donated by Emerson's Florist Shoppe.

As the group reached their destination, gathering on the overlook, Edwin cleared his throat and spoke first. He said this wasn't to be a mournful day, but a day of celebration. Yes, what had transpired one year ago was a tragedy, but they'd all forgive and forget on this, the anniversary of their death. With the casting of the rose petals into the water, they would be releasing one year's worth of pent-up sorrow.

"The young lovers are free now," said Edwin, "and we should all pray that they are somehow, somewhere, in each other's arms."

And so the rose petals were disbursed as "Here Comes the Sun" was played on the CD player. When the last ruby red petal had fluttered down and landed gently in the water, the air became cool as a great shadow descended upon the whole of Thompson Falls. Everyone in the group gazed skyward and chattered with amazement at the sudden eclipse. Edwin, an amateur astronomer, was the most shocked and surprised, because he knew there was no eclipse scheduled to occur for another seven months. *What in the world is going on?* he wondered. Some of the kids joked about how they shouldn't be looking at the eclipse because doing so could make you blind.

And then Mary Weiss screamed. Six seconds after gazing up at the eclipse, she *had* gone blind.

Edwin assured her that it was only temporary, even as his own world was growing dark. A teenage girl cried out that she too had just lost her sight, and she began wailing hysterically. The wailing was contagious as the entire group realized in a harrowing moment that they had all been spontaneously struck blind. They could not see, but they all heard a sound that chilled them to the bone. When asked about the sound in the hospital, each and every one of them identified the sound as the Devil laughing.

Chapter Eight:
The Cure

Natalie was peering out the turret window and watched as Will pulled his car into the mansion driveway. She'd been waiting for him, unable to sleep. She was worried about him, worried about his mom, worried about Emily, whose nightmares had been worse while Will was away. Despite the way their last conversation had gone, she was convinced that if Will gave her just one good long hug, a feeling of wholeness would sweep through her body like a magic potion and she would be able to lie down and sleep. And now here he was, her knight in shining armor (his bulletproof Mitsubishi EVO was definitely armor). She turned and bounded down the long staircase and met him as he came through the security garage doors.

"Is she alive . . . ?" Her voice trailed off as she saw the rage behind Will's eyes.

"Barely." Will shook his head, hardly looking at her, clearly in pain. "I almost had her. I was almost able to bring her out, Natalie, out of her coma. But *he* ruined everything."

"The Dark Lord?"

"He's got her."

"He took her body?" Natalie shuddered at the thought, recalling when the Dark Lord had kidnapped her, hauling her into a black hearse drawn by winged horses that flew into the sky, transporting her to a hellish nightmare prison in Mount St. Emory.

"No, he didn't get her body. But he's . . . he's got her mind, her will to live. And if it's the last thing I ever do, I'm going to get it back."

Natalie made a move toward Will, but his body stiffened in response so she paused. He didn't move away, though. He studied her instead.

"You haven't slept."

"I don't need sleep. I need . . ." She wanted to say she needed *him*, needed him so badly she ached night and day.

"You need to sleep. We all do." But as if he'd heard what she hadn't been able to say, Will took her into his arms and held her. She relaxed, melting into him, going so slack that he lifted her up, cradling her into his powerful arms. He carried her up to her room and gently laid her down on her bed.

"I . . ." She wanted to say it, wanted to announce her love for him so badly, but the words caught in her throat—*I love you. I love you. I love you.*

"I know," he said, and then kissed her softly on the cheek, butterfly wings dancing on her skin.

"Now sleep. Please. For me."

She would do anything for him. And so after one long last lingering look into his eyes, she closed hers and fell backward off a cliff into velvet black night. She was asleep in a matter of seconds. He had to pull away from her, and he would. But seeing her standing there, exhausted but obviously waiting up for him, had broken his heart. Will sat and stared at her for a moment. Sweetness and heartbreak. In repose—as when she was up and moving around, eyes alit—she was beautiful. He wondered if there was ever a moment when she wasn't. He closed his eyes to be in that warm place with her for a few precious seconds, then rose and exited her room.

In the laboratory Will first checked the surveillance cameras linked to April's room. No one had come or gone except the private doctors and nurses he had on staff. Her vital signs were stable, but she hadn't improved. Will prayed she would soon. In the meantime, he would turn all his efforts to locating the Dark Lord. He looked over at Rudy gesticulating madly from inside the Demon Trap. In seconds Will had a plan to find the Dark Lord, and it involved Rudy. Finding the cure for demonic infection was key.

Turning from the monitors, he ignored Rudy's frantic gestures and moved to the floor safe. Punching in a code, he opened the heavy steel door and extracted a case, which he lifted onto the workbench. He opened the case and pulled from within it a very special book. Or, rather, half a book. It was the book his stepfather had bequeathed to him, the book Will had waited until his thirteenth birthday to decode and decipher, the book that had at once terrified and emboldened him as he learned of his lineage and his destiny. He was, as he'd learned almost four years ago, an *everto venator*, or Demon Hunter. Since that fateful day when he'd opened the book and began to study it, he had killed over 666 demons. And now, after the Dark Lord's latest abominable deed, he was eager to kill more on his way to finding and rescuing his mother. And after he had done that, after he brought April back to the land of the living, he would perform the coup de grâce. Father or no father, he would kill the Dark Lord himself. He would drive a stake through his heart without so much as shedding a tear.

But before that glorious moment could happen, there was much work to be done.

Will had to find or recreate the antidote for demon infection Edward had said Will's grandfather had concocted. If he did, he could use it not only on Rudy, but potentially on hundreds or even thousands of others so infected, and take the Dark Lord's army away from him. The only problem was, if Edward had known the formula, he had taken it with him to his grave. So Will prayed that the formula for the cure was to be found in the book. He had never seen it there before, but perhaps that was only because he did not know it existed and so was not looking for it. And thus, he began to search. He studied page after page, searching for hidden symbols, coded meanings. But there was nothing. The only mention of any kind of antidote to demonic infection suggested he look to "what lies beneath." And Will knew only too well what lay beneath him. Hell. Hades. The Inferno. The caverns of the damned. He searched for the hidden formula for the cure for two days straight, pausing only to eat the sandwiches and chips that Natalie and Emily brought him. He *had* to find it. It was the key to his plan for defeating the Dark Lord. At the end of the second day, he was so frustrated that he slammed the book closed angrily, and his fingernail caught on the binding and caused a nasty cut. Though the pages were of cabretta leather, the inner cover board was lined with some sort of stiff parchment. He looked closely at the tiny drop of blood on the soft flesh beneath the tip of his fingernail. He sucked on his finger, and then stared at the cover board. The cover board parchment appeared to have been, like almost all books, attached and pressed using some sort of glue. *What lies beneath.*

Using his magnifying loupe, Will illuminated and magnified the book's cover board seams. With a pair of stainless steel surgical tweezers, he gently lifted an edge of the parchment. The magnification on the loupe wasn't powerful enough, so he swung a microscope over and peered through the lens. He could see the miniscule crystals of the glue. On a hunch, he extracted a few tiny particles.

Moving slowly and carefully, he dropped the particles into a Petri dish and mixed them with a neutral solution, then began a series of tests to determine their chemical composition. Once he had that in his computer, he cross-referenced it with the chemical composition of a variety of glues and other glue-like substances. He Googled a book binder and emailed the older woman, who lived in upstate New York, offering her an absurdly high cash advance in exchange for her expertise.

She wrote back right away, saying she was eager to help him, and sent him a long list of types of glues and other adhesives used to bind ancient books. Will thanked the woman and entered the information into his mainframe. The most likely candidate, given the age of the ancient book, would be a glue made from the animal protein colloid, most likely from a horse. *Bingo.* The crystals from the binding matched. But there was something else within them as well, and Will's heart began beating faster as he extracted the superfluous chemical compound formula and found it to be complex in nature.

His senses told him that he had found the antidote, that his grandfather had left it within the binding of the book. He set about replicating the substance.

As the cure was cooking, Will again examined the book's binding. He had intended to re-glue it, but when he went to do so, he saw something underneath the lining. He gently began to peel it back and discovered a thin sheet of parchment tucked within. So his grandfather had hidden *two* secrets here! Will extracted the parchment and saw that it was, like the book itself, written in code, using symbols. He quickly discovered that the code system was the same as the one used in the book, so the message was easy to decipher. His father, or perhaps his grandfather or even his great-grandfather, had entered a series of numbers: 26–7, 68–114, 113–79, and so forth. It took Will a while, but he finally concluded that the first number in each pair corresponded to a page number and the second to the precise word on the page. When he put all the words together, however, they made no sense. So he tried the first letters of the words, but still came up with nothing that made any sense. Then he plugged in the last letters of the words, and from them constructed the following simple warning: *Beware the Sword of Armageddon.*

Will's spine felt icy cold. He remembered how the Dark Lord had appeared to him as he'd journeyed into his mother's mind and had threatened him with a sword—a sword he'd called the Sword of Armageddon. What did he have to fear from this sword? And why had the warning been hidden in the binding of the book? There were no details on how to find the sword, or even how to use it. It must have been hidden for the same reason the formula for the demonic antidote was hidden in the chemical makeup of the binding: it would take someone with superior intelligence to find it. Someone like him. But what good did such a vague warning do him?

He put the question aside to worry about later. He'd solved one problem already today—and now it was time to put his plan into action.

Natalie and Emily were in the workout room, going at it with the bamboo staffs.

"Ow!" yipped Natalie as Emily barked her shin.

"That's what you get for cheating," said Emily.

"There's no such thing as cheating in stick fighting, Em. Will said so."

"Speaking of Will," said Emily. She pointed at the door, where Will was now standing. When Natalie turned to look, Emily tapped her on the shin again with the staff.

Natalie laughed. "Hey! Cheater."

"No such thing as cheating," said Emily. She was smiling.

"You guys are looking good," Will said.

"One, we're not guys," said Emily, as she peeled off her pads and headgear. "And two, nobody can look good wearing this stuff."

"Break time?" asked Natalie.

At first, every time Emily got hit it was a not-so-subtle reminder of the torment she'd endured while captive. She couldn't wait to get the pads off and put down her weapon. But as she'd improved, she grew to appreciate feeling like she could defend herself if something came after her again, and tended to push herself even harder than Natalie did. Still, they'd been sparring for over an hour. A break sounded like a good idea.

"Yeah. I'm getting something to eat," she said. She looked at Natalie and then Will, and added, "I'll eat slow," before she left.

Will hadn't said anything but Natalie could tell he was happy about something. "What's going on? You look like you just won the lottery."

"I found it," he said. "At least, I think I did."

"Found what?"

"The antidote, the cure my grandfather created. For demonic infection."

Natalie's eyes lit up. "Will, that's fantastic! Did you give it to Rudy?"

"Not yet. I felt like sharing the good news with someone. And here you are."

"Here I am."

They stood facing each other, awkward as seventh graders at their first dance, fearful to tread forward. Natalie thought she was going to crawl right out of her skin if she didn't do something, so she sort of lurched forward and gave him a sisterly hug and a pat on the back.

"Well, uh, congratulations."

"Thanks."

Will took her face in his hands. Natalie thought, *This is it; this is the moment where he kisses me again!* Will wanted to hold her longer, to linger close to her, to breathe in her smell, to touch his lips to hers, just for an instant. But he couldn't. Not anymore. He'd almost forgotten. He released her.

"You're . . . swell. Just terrific. I . . . I gotta go. I'll let you know how it goes with Rudy. Stay in until I tell you different, okay?"

"Okay . . ."

Natalie watched as he left the room and let out a sigh, confused. Again.

● ● ●

Will entered the laboratory. Had he really just told her she was "swell"? He felt like an idiot. But he had to restrain himself, he just *had* to. They could never be together in the way that they both wanted, and to act like that wasn't true would just make it worse for both of them in the long run.

Rudy was pressing his eyes up against the Plexiglas of the Demon Trapper and clawing it with his fingernails, looking wretched and frightening. He was imagining living outside again and yearned for freedom. When Will approached the trap, Rudy turned himself upside-down, his hair hanging down like a kid on a jungle gym. He attempted a smile, and once again, as he had done with the twins, he held his hands together in prayer. Will got it.

"I hear you, little buddy, and this is your lucky day. You're coming out."

Rudy blinked in disbelief. Had he read Will's lips correctly? Did he just say Rudy was coming *out*? The thought made Rudy's brain do cartwheels. He watched as Will lifted the Demon Trapper up and connected it to some sort of contraption with a tangle of tubes and wires attached to it. Then the colors inside the Demon Trapper changed from orange to blue to green, and then the liquid around him went clear and he could no longer keep his eyes open. And then . . . nothing.

An indeterminate amount of time later, Rudy opened his eyes. They stung from the bright lights glaring down at him from the ceiling. He tried to rise but couldn't because he was strapped down with metal bands on his ankles, knees, wrists, and elbows. This wasn't what he had in mind when he asked to get out. He whipped his head around and saw Will standing with his back to him. He couldn't help himself—he was a demonteen after all—and the rage exploded from within him.

"Will Hunter, you scum! I'm going to kill you!"

Rudy jerked against the metal bands, his body convulsing, frenzied. "I'm going to rip your face off! I'm going to tear you open and eat your heart!"

Will turned around slowly, a syringe in his hand.

"Hi Rudy, what's up?"

Rudy froze, his body stiffening, his eyes glued to the syringe. Still, he kept talking. "You ruined everything, Will! And we're going to make you *pay!*"

Again Rudy struggled violently against his bonds. His wrists and ankles were wracked with pain, but it only made his body surge with even more anger. His eyes flashed black. "We're going to kill you! You son of a bitch!"

"Don't you mean, son of *somebody else*, Rudy?"

Rudy snarled, then hissed, then spit at Will, who deftly ducked out of the way.

"Do that again and I'll staple your mouth shut, got it?" Will said calmly.

Rudy thought about that and slowly nodded his agreement. Again he eyed the syringe. "What . . . what is that?"

"This, my friend, is your salvation. This is the cure for what ails you."

"Nothing ails me!" Rudy screamed.

"We both know that's not true. We both know you're infected, you're a demon, and you need help. You may not know that you need help, you may not feel like you do, but believe me, you do."

Rudy began breathing as rapidly and as deeply as he could, inhaling the good air, polluting it with vile thoughts, and then forcing it out, a demon mantra technique. He was building up anger and venom because he was planning to unleash a burst of energy, which would enable him to break free and crush Will's skull with his bare hands. Will was more than just his captor, he was the ultimate traitor, the son who had turned on his father and betrayed the entire demon race. Will must be killed, and Rudy planned on snuffing him out like the flame on a candle. *Poof!* Gone. Slain. And Rudy would take Will's slack body and present it to the Dark Lord as a gift! He could hear the accolades now.

"This might hurt," Will said. "You might feel a pinch. Well, actually, most likely more than a pinch. Who knows what this might do? I mean, it could be like shooting holy water right into your veins."

"*WHAT IS IT?*" screamed Rudy as the tip of the needle pierced his flesh and sank into his vein.

"A formula created by my grandfather. It kept my father—"

"Your father is the Devil!" screamed Rudy.

Will forced himself to smile sadly at Rudy.

"My real father was Edward, and this medicine kept him clean and sober, if you will, for many years. I'm hoping it works on you. It should purge you, Rudy. It should counteract the toxins running through your body, polluting your thoughts, your feelings, your soul."

Rudy writhed and shrieked and looked down at his arm as he felt the drug moving from the syringe into his body. It stung, but the sensation wasn't overwhelming. He wondered what it would feel like to be *human* again. He closed his eyes as the drug made him feel . . . weird.

Will was at his computer, updating his online game, *Demon Hunter*, while he monitored Rudy's vital signs. He was inputting his recent hunting activity, integrating it into the ongoing "gaming" experience that only he knew was real, not just a video game. As he checked in on the real-time online game, he noticed something strange happening. A new player with a green fox avatar had entered the game arena. "Jade16" was blasting through the game and racking up kills with astonishing speed and skill. Will had never before encountered anyone who could navigate the perilous landscape of *Demon Hunter* with such apparent ease.

"Will?"

Rudy was awake. Will went over and looked down at him. He looked normal.

"I'm right here, Rudy."

"What h-h-happened?" Rudy asked. His voice was shaky, the bravado he'd displayed previously a thing of the past.

"I gave you a drug."

Rudy blinked and craned his head up so he could look around the room. "Where am I?"

Will ignored the question. "How do you feel, Rudy?"

"Like . . . like I just woke up from the worst friggin' nightmare ever. You wouldn't believe the freaky dreams I've had, man! They'd blow you away!"

"How do you feel . . . about me, Rudy?"

"You? Man, you know how I feel about you, Will! You're the coolest dude I've ever met in my whole life!"

Will allowed himself a slight smile. Rudy looked down at his hands. "My wrists hurt. So do my ankles." He wiggled his fingers and moved his feet. "And I am *starving*! Man, I am *so* craving a cheese-burger and fries and a chocolate shake right now."

Will studied Rudy, getting right in his face. It looked like the memories of the past several weeks were flooding into his brain.

"Oh, man, I'm starting to remember everything now. And I have been such an a-hole! I can't even imagine what you wanna say to me, Will."

"I've got just one thing to say to you, Rudy." Will paused for effect, then hit a switch and the metal bands restraining Rudy's arms and legs retracted. Will held out a hand to help him up.

"Welcome back."

Tears flowed from Rudy's eyes as he sat up and hugged his best friend.

NOXON, MONTANA

Four friends were out rafting on the Clark Fork River. They had plenty of beer, though not so much sunshine; it was mostly gray skies, the air cold enough to raise a flush on your cheeks. But the beer buzz made it all good, at least for Jimmy Varnes and Kris Hoffman, boyfriend and girlfriend, still in the honeymoon stage of their relationship, constantly kissing, holding hands, giving each other googly eyes. Todd Hepper and Susan Townes were a year older and had been going together so long that handholding was pretty much a thing of the past—unless Todd had done something stupid (a frequent occurrence) and had to make up for it by kowtowing to Susan in order to get back into her good graces and, therefore, her Levis. The foursome had had a long, lazy day just cruising on the river, not riding rapids or anything like that, drinking plenty of beer and shooting the shit, the guys jawing about the Seahawks and Steelers and the girls going on about Brad and Angelina. It was just another day of post–high school fun. But then Todd and Susan had gotten into it, arguing about if and when they ever got married and if and when they ever had a baby and if that baby was a boy—would it be circumcised?

Jimmy thought it was the stupidest fight anyone could have. Nonetheless, Todd and Susan weren't speaking now, and it cast a pall over the trip. Jimmy wasn't paying attention and they took a wrong fork in the river and wound up drifting along. Now they had something else to argue about: Jimmy having taken a wrong turn, and whose fault was that anyway? Susan started digging at Todd about him not paying attention, and Todd responded by drinking the tipping-point beer, the one that sent him over the edge into belligerence. That was why he used the F word with Susan, and she responded by standing up in the raft and slapping him. He was so shocked he used the F word again and shoved her, and she lost her balance, her arms pinwheeling like a circus clown.

"God damn you, Todd!" she screamed.

In this frozen moment, with time expanding, a wave of real-ization washed over Todd. He realized how much he really loved Susan, how he wanted to be with her forever. And it was at this moment that he decided he would ask her to marry him. He reached for her, smiling now, but as he grabbed at her, he missed and she fell over backward, off the raft. Jimmy laughed. Kris shook her head: boys will be boys. But then Susan began screaming, and it wasn't a normal scream, it was the kind of scream that raises the hair on the back of your neck.

When all three reached over to pull her back into the raft, it took several seconds for them to process the sight. Susan was thrashing around in the dark water, surrounded by dead fish. The fish were floating on the surface of the water just like they did when someone was stupid and cruel enough to go dynamite fishing. But that wasn't the reason the fish—and there was a dead beaver, too—were floating like that. Stunned, still uncomprehending, Todd and Jimmy pulled Susan into the boat. The gaped silently because they had no words for what they were seeing. Susan gasped for breath and then started screaming again, and this time, so did Kris. They screamed because what they were witnessing wasn't just a flotilla of dead fish and other creatures. What they were witnessing was true evil: the river had turned to blood. They held their noses as the smell became over-powering. It was the smell of Hell on Earth.

Chapter Nine:
The New Breed

Will and Rudy stood before a mirror in Will's laboratory. Rudy shook his head.

"Man, I can't believe how I look. I mean, I like the fact that I'm ripped and everything, but these clothes! Geez, I look like I'm in an Iron Maiden tribute band or something. And the tats . . . a rattlesnake coming out of a skull? Seriously?"

Rudy was examining all the ink he'd had laid down, along with the piercings. "How can you ever forgive me, dude?"

"Already done," said Will. "You made one incredibly stupid move, and then you couldn't help yourself."

Rudy grabbed Will in a hug again and Will hugged him back, then playfully shoved him away.

"Hey, enough already."

"I'm soooo starving! You got anything to eat?"

"How about we cruise up to Dick's Drive-In and get some burgers?"

"Oh man, are you kidding me? Let's go! I am all over that!"

Rudy did his signature crazy-as-a-loon dance and Will smiled again. It sure looked like his little friend was back and in fine form.

"One thing, though," said Rudy. "Can you loan me some, like, not quite so death-goth-blackness-evil-ish clothes?"

"Sure thing. And there's somebody I know who will be psyched to see you."

Ten minutes later, they emerged from Will's room with Rudy wearing some cords, a Jimi Hendrix T-shirt, and an army jacket. Rudy's face lit up as he saw Natalie.

"Rudy! I can't believe it!" shrieked Natalie as she ran down the hall and grabbed him into a hug. And then she quickly backed off.

"Are you . . . ?"

"I'm cool," said Rudy. "I'm back among the living."

"The cure worked," said Will.

"Will, that's fantastic!" Natalie exclaimed. Then, turning to Rudy, she said, "Rudy you . . . you were such a . . ."

"I know . . . I know, I was a total scumbag punk idiot."

"But all is forgiven," added Will.

The three old friends stood smiling at each other. Then Emily's voice cut through the air like a knife. "I so do not *believe* this!"

They turned. She was standing in the doorway of her bedroom with her arms folded over her chest, eyes reproachful. "What did you do, Will?"

"I cured him."

"Oh, so now he's just gonna skate? You're just gonna forget all the horrible things he did? He was one of *them*!"

"Calm down, Emily," said Natalie.

"I'm not gonna calm down! He should be toast! Give me a sword or a phaser or whatever you call it, or one of your other crazy weapons, and I'll do him! I swear it, I'll do him!"

Her eyes narrowed with loathing, Emily took a threatening step toward Rudy, but Natalie stepped between them.

"Em, stop it. It wasn't his fault."

"No, Natalie, she's right," said Rudy. "I was out of control. The things I did . . . I don't even want to remember them. They're gonna haunt me forever."

Will stepped over and took Emily by the shoulders.

"Listen to me, Emily. He's cured. He's one of us now. End of story, got it?"

She stood trembling with anger for a few more seconds, and then reluctantly nodded. She wasn't going to turn her back on him, but she owed Will. If he wanted her to let it go, then she'd try.

"Yeah, sure . . . I got it."

"Good," said Will. "Now, who's up for cruising out to snag some burgers?"

They took the Beemer, and with tunes cranking they sped up to the Dick's Drive-In in Wallingford on N.E. 45th. The place had a history, going all the way back to when burgers cost nineteen cents. The burgers hadn't changed much over the years, which was one of the reasons they tasted out of this world. The parking lot was packed with cars, full of teenagers hanging out, along with a smattering of old-timers who had grown fat wolfing down Dick's double cheeseburgers. An old Elvis Presley song was playing on the outdoor speakers. Will parked and got out and gestured for Rudy to do the same.

"How about we go get the food for the girls?" he asked Rudy.

"*Soitenly!*" chirped Rudy as he got out. He smiled at the lights, smiled at the cars going by, smiled at everything in sight. He looked like he'd just been released from prison. He turned to Natalie and Emily and smiled wider as he pretended to whip out a pad and paper.

"Good evening and welcome to Chez Dick's, ladies. May I take your order?"

"Double cheeseburger, fries, and a coke," said Natalie.

Emily was still in a funk. "I'll have the same," she said, refusing to look at Rudy. "Just don't touch it, okay?"

"Gotcha. No touching the food. I might lick it, but I won't—"

Emily turned and glared. "Just tell them to double bag mine, got it, Diablo?"

"Okay, okay, I'm just messin' with you. I won't touch your precious food. It's no problemo," he said, but he looked a little hurt.

Will and Rudy went up to the window and placed their order. The food wasn't called "fast" for nothing, and in just a couple of minutes they had six burgers, six orders of fries, two cokes, and two chocolate shakes in hand. As they walked back to the car, Will gave Rudy a searching look.

"How you doin', my man?"

"I'll be better once I dig into these double cheeseburgers," said Rudy.

"How do you feel—I mean, physically?" asked Will.

"I feel, like, normal, I guess. You know. Hungry, horny, and ready to rock and roll."

Will chuckled. They climbed in the car and Rudy started eating ravenously, moaning with pleasure every few bites. The old habit of his had Natalie giggling, but Emily was annoyed.

"You're gross," she said. "That's disgusting. It sounds like you're going to the bathroom or something."

"Ewww! Now who's being gross?" asked Natalie.

Rudy ignored the insult and kept shoveling the burgers and fries into his face and gulping down his chocolate shake.

"This is the best food on the face of the earth," he declared. And then, after polishing off his last few bites, he cut loose with a long, loud burp. The girls shook their heads. Rudy looked over at Will.

"Will?"

"Yeah?"

"Thanks, man. I mean it. Just . . . thanks so much."

"No problemo."

"Riiiight," said Natalie. "As if discovering, replicating, and concocting the most important antidote ever was 'no problemo.' Modesty, Will Hunter is thy name."

Natalie was proud. *Really* proud. But more than that, she was happy for him. She knew how much responsibility Will carried on his shoulders, and how much he wished he could live a normal life. This new discovery and the ability to cure the infected could change so much for him—for *them*.

Rudy was moaning again, only this time it wasn't because he was hoovering cheeseburgers. He was holding his stomach.

"Ohhhhh, man. My gut feels like I swallowed a bowling ball."

"That's what you get for being such a disgusting, gluttonous, pig freak hog boy," said Emily.

"I gotta hit the head," said Rudy. He looked at Will. "Seriously. I think I'm gonna blast—"

"Would someone please shut him up?" said Emily.

"When you gotta go, you gotta go," said Will. "So go already."

The threesome watched as Rudy got out and loped awkwardly toward the bathroom, looking like he was ready to either throw up or explode—possibly both.

"Could you try to be a little nicer to him?" Natalie asked Emily as soon as Rudy closed the bathroom door behind him.

"It just sucks, letting him off like that, like he isn't some kind of criminal," said Emily. "He's a *demon*."

"Correction: he *was* a demon, right, Will?" said Natalie.

Will said nothing as he stared at the bathroom door.

Rudy was in the toilet stall, but he wasn't sitting down. He was on top of the seat struggling to open the bathroom window.

"Come on, you stupid thing! Open! I said, *OPEN!*" Rudy's eyes flashed an angry black and the muscles in his arms flexed, tense and powerful. The window's steel frame bent and the opaque, wire-reinforced window cracked. Rudy snorted like a horse and yanked again, ripping the window off its hinges. Then he hopped out and down into the back parking lot, terrifying two girls in a VW Beetle. He ignored them, and without so much as a backward glance he took off running, quickly disappearing into the dark night.

Out front, Will watched calmly as the frightened girls came around and reported what they'd just seen to the manager, who grudgingly walked over and unlocked the men's room door and stared in disbelief at the mangled window. Natalie and Emily drew in sharp breaths.

"He took off! I told you he sucked!" said Emily.

"Will, the cure, it must have . . . worn off or something?" It was more a question than a statement, and Natalie was looking to Will for answers.

"What are you waiting for?" snapped Emily. "Go get him! Go blow his brains out!"

But Will remained cool as a cucumber. He just started up the BMW's engine.

"Will? What do you think happened?" asked Natalie.

"I think," said Will, "that Rudy took the bait."

"What do you mean 'took the bait'?" Emily demanded. "He just freakin' escaped! I swear to God, Will, if he comes after me . . ."

"He's not going to come after you," Will said. "I promise."

"Yeah, well, he could be out there right now terrorizing someone else!" said Emily.

"It's too soon for that. He'll run for a bit, put some distance between us, and then he'll seek out a pack," said Will.

Natalie's eyes narrowed as she studied him. He switched on his phone and used a cable to connect it one of the BMW's four USB ports. Then he switched on the car's large GPS screen. She asked, "Will, what's going on?"

"I injected him with a placebo."

"A *what*?" asked Emily.

"A placebo. A little caffeine mixed in with some saline."

"And why would you do that?"

"So I could track him. If there's a local demon population, he'll find them faster than I could on my own. I planted a subcutaneous tracking chip on him."

"You put a chip in him?" asked Natalie. "Where?"

"On the back of his arm, just above the elbow, so he can't easily examine it."

"You planned this whole thing?" asked Emily. "I was sitting right here in a car . . . with a *real demon*?" She looked furious.

"Yeah. I had to have everybody come, I didn't want him to get suspicious. Now see . . . there he is." Will pointed at the GPS screen, where a small blinking blue dot was moving down a nearby street.

"I'm going to take you two home, and I want you to lock down and stay that way until you hear from me. If for some reason you don't hear from me, then go to Plan B."

Both girls knew that Plan B meant they were to get the heck out of Dodge, fleeing the mansion through the underground tunnel that let out onto a side alley. A getaway car, packed with essentials, was parked there. They'd drive to the Edgewater Hotel on the waterfront and wait forty-eight hours for Will to contact them. If he didn't, it would be on to Plan C, which was essentially them fleeing with a ton of cash and new identities and starting a new life somewhere. Natalie hated the thought.

"Okay," she said. "But you'll be back." She said this not because she was certain but because she wanted to believe it, *needed* to believe it. The concept of losing Will forever was so painful she would not even entertain it.

"I'll be back," said Will, using his best Terminator voice.

It made Natalie feel better. If he was making jokes, he must not have been very worried.

Will drove them home, waited until they were safely inside, and then got back in the Beemer and gunned it out through the huge iron gates. It was time to do a little demon hunting.

Will drove back in the direction of Dick's Drive-In, but a quick glance at the Beemer's GPS told him that Rudy was headed north. Will turned down Aurora Avenue, keeping an eye on the screen.

Rudy was walking down the middle of a residential street when he felt the headlights hit him. He turned and put on his best smile. Apparently it wasn't good enough, because the car—a brand-new silver Taurus—sped up, intending to go around him. But Rudy was having none of it, and he stepped directly in front of the car, causing the driver, Byron Sneedecker, a balding, middle-aged tire salesman, to slam on the brakes.

Sneedecker powered down his window and glared at Rudy. "Hey! What the hell's wrong with you? Are you some kind of moron?"

Rudy moved so quickly around the side of the car that the driver began to shake as he rolled his window back up, made sure his doors were locked, and put his foot on the gas, intending to stomp on it as soon as Rudy opened his mouth to speak. But Rudy had other plans. He slammed his fist through the window and locked his hand around the guy's neck. Byron Sneedecker promptly wet himself.

"Listen," said Rudy. "I was wondering if I could borrow your car."

The guy gurgled as Rudy yanked him out and threw him down on the pavement. Sneedecker was so scared that, just in case, he pulled out his wallet and threw it at Rudy, who caught it in mid-air.

"Hey, thanks, I appreciate it. You have a nice night."

Rudy got into the Taurus and took off. He was thirsty, but not for chocolate shakes. He needed something stronger. He turned onto the highway, and spotted the Lion's Mouth Tavern after just a couple of miles on the road. He pulled in, parked, and went inside. The bartender, a big guy with massive forearms stuffed into a Seahawks T-shirt, moved toward him, fully intending to give Rudy crap about being underage and toss his butt out. But once he got close enough, it was like he could smell the danger coming off Rudy. He stared down at the bar and spoke in a hushed voice.

"What can I get you?"

"A bottle of Johnnie. Black."

Without hesitation, the bartender nodded, reached up, grabbed a bottle of Johnnie Walker Black Label, and set it on the bar in front of Rudy, still avoiding eye contact.

"You want a glass?"

In response, Rudy popped off the easy-pour nipple and started drinking right from the bottle.

The bartender walked away. He was going to mention that the bottle was on the house, but he didn't want to risk even the briefest of exchanges with the likes of Rudy. He'd seen his kind before. So he retreated to the far side of the long wooden bar and busied himself polishing tumblers.

With a good buzz on, Rudy got back in the Taurus, smiling as a cop car passed him going in the opposite direction. *Looks like the schmuck called the cops*, he thought. He wasn't afraid of the cops. In fact, he wasn't afraid of much of anything, except for the Dark Lord himself and maybe Will Hunter.

And he was going to please the former by killing the latter.

He headed north and over a bridge, then cut down toward Lake Union and drove into Gas Works Park. It was a bizarre sight, the sprawling lawns surrounding the ancient rusting monster, the remnants of the last coal gasification plant in the United States. Someone on the city council must have thought it was cute or quaint or something, because instead of tearing the place down, they'd turned it into a park. It was a terrifically ugly place for lowlifes to hang out after dark. Rudy got out of the Taurus and walked toward the weathered, rusty tanks and connecting pipes. Surely there was some fun to be had here.

Will had bird-dogged Rudy to perfection and was now looking down at the gas works. Wearing his night-vision contacts, he could see Rudy clearly as he entered the park. Minutes passed. Will listened to the blustery winds. A storm front was approaching. Rudy sauntered cockily up to a group of teens hanging out, drinking and smoking. Rudy took a cigarette when it was offered, lit it, and sucked in the smoke. Will couldn't help but wonder what would possess a human being that they'd think burning leaves and sucking the smoke into their lungs was a good idea. He knew all about the drug nicotine and how it worked on the brain, raising dopamine levels, but still. How insane did you have to be? Though, if you were a demon, what did it matter? Will watched as the group moved to the central part of the gas works within the tangle of tanks and pipes.

Will wanted a closer look, so he got out of the BMW and walked toward the park. He felt movement to his left and ducked and scanned. A dark figure rushed from the tree line into the gas works as the tanks and pipes started making creaking sounds in the wind. The figure looked slight enough to be a girl. Will kept watching, then rose as four more figures dashed out of the trees. All female, but moving incredibly fast, like phantoms.

It was time for Will to act. He checked the Megashocker strapped to his leg, flipping a switch to power it up. He entered the gas works and ducked under a long connecting pipe, his eyes open wide, his senses on the alert. A girl's scream propelled him forward. He ran with inhuman speed, only to stop in the darkness as his nostrils picked up the acrid scent of demons. He heard the scream again— more of a shriek, really—followed by another, then another.

One of the phantoms shot out from behind a tank and flew at him. She was incredibly fast, but Will was fast, too, and he whipped out his Megashocker and swung it in her direction as she flew at him. In mid-air she jerked her body, cartwheeling, so that the Megashocker blow, which should have caught her full on in the face, only glanced across her knee. It was an indirect hit but it was enough to cause searing pain, and she cut loose with an unholy howl, then landed on the ground and limp-ran around a tank. Will was in hot pursuit, intending to wound her again, then hold her down until she gave up some kind of information. He didn't even know what he was looking for yet, but he knew that he had to keep probing. The Dark Lord was out there somewhere, and these creatures were his best hope of finding him. If they suffered pain in so doing, then it would be all the sweeter.

He ran around the tank and stopped cold, locking on the figure in front of him. It was the dark phantom girl he had wounded— only she looked no worse for the wear. In fact, she was smiling, her teeth sharp, her eyes blazing. And not only that—four of them were now surrounding him. *Very clever*, Will thought. They hunted in a pack like coyotes. One would "attack," then act wounded and attempt to "escape," leading the prey—in this case, him—directly into a trap.

He rotated, trying to keep an eye on as many of them as possible. They were all wearing tall boots and black jeans and some kind of hooded ponchos, and they all had voluminous hair that whipped in the wind. They were just high school girls, demonteens, but something about them was different. They were faster, for one. *Shedemons*, Will thought. He wasn't sure why the name came to him, but it sure stuck. Shedemons. The whites of their eyes glowed. They began to keen together in unison, an unholy chant of some sort, a prelude to malevolence.

The tallest of the four raised her hand and tossed her hair back coquettishly. She was beautiful in a mean-looking way and had a blue streak in her hair. As the wind died down and the night went quiet, she crouched low, her scarlet fingernails extending. The others followed suit, and Will was faced with forty deadly little red knives, as sharp, no doubt, as scalpels. *Good thing*, he thought to himself, *that I brought the Cloakers*. He reached for them in his jacket pocket. His hand made it into his pocket but didn't make it back out before the pack attacked in a flurry. It took everything Will had to drop and swing his legs and the Megashocker in a circular motion. They flew past him, getting close but not making contact.

As the attack continued, astonishingly, Will didn't hit a single one of them. He finally managed to get the Cloakers out, but when he threw them, the shedemons were able to feint and duck and avoid them entirely. Meanwhile, their keening grew in intensity. They climbed the tanks and pipes alarmingly fast, racing to and fro. Just like Will, they were masters in the art of *Parkour*, or *l'art du deplacement*, a physical discipline of French origin wherein one climbed and ran rapidly while negotiating obstacles like rails or columns—or, in this case, tanks and pipes and each other.

Will felt a pain in his back and realized he'd just been deep-clawed by one of them. Blue Streak. He whirled and kicked and managed to catch her under the chin, sending her screeching skyward. She slammed into a tank and dropped to the ground. The blow would have killed a mortal and badly wounded any other creature. But Blue Streak wasn't done yet, not by a long shot. She leapt up and—much to Will's astonishment—began braying with laughter. He was distracted by the shedemon's bravado, so when the other three struck, he was caught off guard. They hit him hard. Their fists were like hammers, their fingernails like box-cutters. They pummeled and slashed at him, and he staggered on his feet. As their fists found the bones of his face, he caught glimpses of the rings they wore. They were imprinted with the image of a winged creature.

The whoop of a siren pierced the night. Three blue-and-white Seattle Police Department Crown Victoria cruisers pulled into the gas works parking lot. They blocked the stolen silver Taurus in, front and back. This was in the event that the perp—who was not visible but could easily have been ducking down—decided to make a break for it. Six officers emerged from the cars with weapons drawn. But they quickly saw that the vehicle was empty and began a foot search.

"Do you hear that?" one of the cops asked. "It sounds like . . . like some kind of weird bird or something." He was hearing the shedemons' protracted, shrill screams as they were about to go in for the kill.

* * *

Will's brain was scrambled. He was seeing double, watching with amazement and more than a little respect as the eight—of course there were only four, but he now saw eight—shedemons criss-crossed past him, slashing and punching and kicking. He realized that he had met his match. There was no way he was going to survive these beasts. They were insanely fast and deadly. Demons were fast, demonteens often even more so, but Will had never seen anything like these shedemons. They were a whole new breed. And they were going to bring his life to a very painful end.

Will thought about Natalie and his mother and how he'd ultimately let them down. He shook his head again and again, trying to clear his brain. But he'd been had. They'd lured him and trapped him, and their punishment would be exacting and deadly.

Anger began to build inside Will. Anger tinged with red. He used to call it the red curtain, because once upon a time it would fall in front of his eyes and turn the world into an ugly place, a place where he wanted only one thing: to inflict pain. As the red malice surged through him, he flipped over and fought with renewed ferocity, managing a couple of powerful blows to the shocked shedemons. But they still overwhelmed him.

"You're going to die," said Blue Streak.

This was it; this was Will's Waterloo. He was going down, and going down hard. The air was thick with evil and Will's head felt like it was going to explode. He reached to his Power Rod retrieval patch in one last-ditch effort to save his life, but he wasn't sure he'd be able to call it down in time.

Will saw a quick movement to his right, then heard a small explosion. He saw a flash of light and was enveloped in a cloud of intoxicating gas. He began to cough. One of the tanks must have exploded, he assumed, flooding the area. Will's head was spinning, but the shedemons reacted to the gas too, coughing and regrouping.

Blue Streak spit some commands at her cohorts and they advanced, coughing more violently now. Will knew he should use their distraction to escape, but he was powerless to do anything but breathe in more of the heady gas. He was certain that the shedemons were going to finish him off.

Then he heard footsteps. Voices. Beams of light slashing across the gas works.

Blue Streak came over and kicked him in the head and hissed, "We'll meet again."

And then, as quickly as they had appeared, the pack was gone, swallowed up by the surrounding darkness.

Now that the immediate threat was gone and the gas was starting to clear, pain rushed into Will's body. He felt like he'd been stung by a thousand killer bees. He rolled over and clawed at a zipper on his coat, pulling out a packet of chemical patches he'd pre-soaked with his special healing salve. He went for his face first, smearing on the salve. In seconds, his flesh began to repair itself. He lay still. And then he heard a voice.

"Hey, you! Are you alive? Can you hear me?"

A girl appeared out of the night. She was dressed in a long duster coat and wore a bandana to cover her mouth and nose against the rapidly dissipating gas. Her hair was strawberry-blonde and her eyes were a disarmingly beautiful shade of green so clear he could see them even there in the dark. They glowed like jewels. She pulled her bandana down and he could see her face. She was amazing.

"They messed you up pretty good," she said.

"I'm okay," Will lied. He was about as far from okay as humanly possible. But he was alive. He was going to make it; he wasn't going to die after all. His attackers had somehow been frightened off. He sat up.

"Who were 'they' anyway?" he asked the girl.

"Trust me, you don't want to know."

"Trust me, I really *do* want to know. I want to know badly. Where are they from?"

She paused, as though deciding between telling the truth and being evasive. "Let me give you some advice. If you know what's good for you, you'll stay as far away from them as possible."

"The thing is," said Will, "I never seem to know what's good for me. How do you know them?"

"They're—" She stopped speaking as the cops' flashlight beams moved closer. Her eyes widened to full alert.

"I gotta go."

"Wait. What were you doing here?" Will asked.

"Listen to me. Forget this night. Forget you ever met me."

One look at Will's burning, intense eyes would have told her that he would do exactly the opposite. He would not forget this night, and he would definitely not forget her.

"You over there! Freeze!" a cop's voice rang out.

Will turned to look at the advancing cops, so he didn't even see the girl with the emerald eyes leave. Their .45s drawn, the cops surrounded him and made him lie facedown as they circled him, cuffed him, holstered their pistols, and took his I.D. from his back pocket.

He wasn't in the database, and when they asked him about the Taurus, he said he had no idea what they were talking about. When they saw how badly he'd been roughed up, they un-cuffed him. They wanted to call an ambulance, but Will told them to forget it.

"Who did this to you?" one of them asked.

Will couldn't think of any reason not to tell them the truth. Or at least part of the truth.

"Four girls."

The cops took a moment to process.

"You're telling us that four *girls* did this to you?"

"That's right."

"Did you get a good look at them?"

"No. I hardly saw them at all. It's dark."

"Four *girls*?" muttered another cop, shaking his head.

"And that's why you don't want the ambulance."

The cops all exchanged knowing looks. Sometimes it was good to be male. Will let the cops assume that he didn't want to report the crime because he was ashamed that some girls had beat the holy crap out of him. Since he'd come up clean on their database, they weren't inclined to arrest him for the theft of the Taurus, a decision that was reinforced when he showed them that he had driven his own BMW.

They let him go, but not before one of them lobbed a macho jab: "Maybe you should think about staying away from the ladies for a spell." His cohorts chuckled.

If they only knew, Will thought. *If they only really knew*. And for a brief moment, he wished the four phantoms would show up and put the merciless toes of their boots to these cops. But such thoughts were pointless and distracting, so Will swept them out of his mind as he climbed into his BMW and drove away.

Rudy had followed the script and performed as Will had predicted. He'd gone straight to a pack of demons. Now it was time to recapture him. Will switched on the tracking screen to see where Rudy was.

But there was a problem. No blinking light. No Rudy. The subcutaneous chip must have malfunctioned. Or maybe Rudy had found it and ripped it out. Either way, he was gone. Will's heart raced. He'd lost Rudy! He should have cured his friend for real, instead of using him as a pawn.

He tapped his fingers and wondered how he could have blundered so badly. Then he calmed down. Because he had a sudden hunch he knew just where Rudy would go. As he steered the BMW up onto Queen Anne Hill, he prayed that his hunch was right.

Chapter Ten: Pursuit

Will drove back to the mansion and slipped into his laboratory without making a sound, passing right by the gaming room where Natalie and Emily were dutifully practicing again with their staffs. But he couldn't help himself from backtracking a bit to glance in at them. They were both getting better. Soon he would introduce them to their real weapons. He only hoped that they would never have to use them.

Once in his lab, he took off his jacket and pants and covered his myriad wounds with the healing salve. He looked at the hundreds of little stab marks the shedemons' talons had made. He remembered how freakishly fast they had moved. This new breed was something he would have to reckon with. But first he had to get Rudy. He stripped, used a spray can of the healing chemical to coat his body, then carefully pulled his clothes back on and lay down, meditating while the chemicals did their work. In thirty minutes he got up and zipped the Demon Trapper into its case and slung it over his shoulder.

Out in the garage, he eschewed the Mitsubishi and the BMW, figuring Rudy would spot him immediately if he was prowling around in either of them. So he chose his jet-black Suzuki Hayabusa

GSX 133R, the fastest motorcycle in the world. The machine was a beast, a veritable crotch rocket that would blast him around like he was riding lightning. Not wanting to have to explain what was going on to the twins, Will silently coasted the GSX out of the garage and down the driveway. The iron gates made a slight noise when they opened, and five seconds later, after kicking the Suzuki to life and twisting the throttle, he was gone like a shot fired out of a cannon.

He parked the GSX on the hillside looking down at Dick's Drive-In and waited. The helmet he wore he'd built himself. It was equipped with a visor that could pick up heat sources at two hundred yards. Will hadn't used it before, but he was confident it would work. Demons ran six degrees hotter than humans, so if Rudy showed up he should be easy to spot, no matter what direction he came from. So far the area was pretty quiet, the only noise coming from passing cars and a pissed-off pit bull barking his head off in a nearby alley. Will's helmet also played MP3s, and he settled in for what he figured might be a long vigil.

Rudy had been a skinny weak kid when Will first rescued him from being dunked in the toilet in the boys' room. But that changed when he succumbed to temptation and went to the dark side. It was a tragically simple process, though you had to be sixteen—like he, Natalie and Emily, and Rudy were—for it to work. If you were in the right frame of mind—feeling mad at the world, like you didn't belong anywhere, like nobody gave a damn about you—you could hear *his* voice, the voice of the Dark Lord. He would say your name three times. And then, if you let yourself be overcome with malicious thoughts, evil thoughts, about things like bringing harm to other people, and if you cut yourself so that your blood was exposed to the air—one drop was all it took—then *boom*, you'd be infected. Then you would slowly morph from a normal human into a demon. It had happened to Rudy on Will's watch, and Will still felt guilty about it. This time, he promised himself, if he was lucky enough to recapture Rudy, he'd cure him right away—no tricks.

Rudy had a powerful craving. What he'd just seen had shaken him to his core, and he'd attempted to calm his nerves by chugging a half bottle of Jack Daniel's whiskey with some sleazebag demon-teens from an Edmonds cell. But it only seemed to jangle his nerves as the alcohol ripped straight on up to his brain. The feel-good buzz that Rudy had felt when he first gulped down the JD had turned ugly, and now he felt like someone had driven rusty spikes into the back of his skull. Every time he closed his eyes, the world was sucked into an explosion of spinning stars, and when he kept his eyes open, the pressure in his head built up so bad he was sure his eyeballs were going to pop out. He needed a fix. He needed salvation. He needed some Dick's double cheeseburgers. He pulled out the wallet he'd gotten from the terrified owner of the Taurus. There was $128 in cash, which he pocketed, and then he tossed the wallet in the gutter.

Will's visor enabled him to see Rudy approaching from half a mile away. The visor optics were even better than Will had hoped for. Rudy was coming up an adjacent alley, moving fast on foot. His signature "playful" dance had turned into an animal thing, and he was not so much rhythmically rejoicing in the air around him as he was slashing at it with hot malice. When he passed the snarling pit bull, the dog wisely cowered, his animal sense telling him this was a creature that shouldn't be messed with. Then Rudy stopped abruptly, as though a bell had gone off in his head, and began to search the area with his eyes. For a moment, Will worried that Rudy could smell him (demons had wild senses that were sometimes insanely acute and other times were dulled to the point of being ineffective). Rudy's head jerked around as his eyes searched. But Will was wearing black on black and he blended into the shadows, and Rudy didn't find him.

There was a long line at the order window at Dick's. Rudy didn't feel like waiting, so he shoved his way past a dozen shocked people. But like the pit bull, they quickly discerned that Rudy was someone you just didn't confront, no matter what the transgression. A few of the customers were so scared that they jumped out of the line and decided to go grab a burger somewhere else. At the window, Rudy tossed a twenty on the counter and ordered his double cheeseburgers. When they came up, he pulled them out of the bag violently, and without even bothering to remove the flimsy yellow wrapping paper, he ate two of the burgers quickly, tearing at them like a wolf mauling a lamb.

Will put the Suzuki in neutral and coasted down the hill. This had to be done just right. Smooth and quiet. Once Rudy had polished off his four burgers—wrappers and all—he turned and, spotting a couple of big guys at a picnic table digging into their own burgers, rushed over, ripped the food out of their hands, and gobbled it down.

"Geez, man! What's your problem?" the larger of the two growled.

"Do I look like I have a problem?" asked Rudy, his eyes blazing. But the guy was a lineman for the UW Huskies, the kind of guy who would stand his ground no matter who he was facing off with. Coach Sark had taught him that. He stood up.

"Yeah, you sure as crap do, dude! You owe me a burger!"

Rudy's stomach was rumbling, the demon acid collecting, doing its job. Demons digested food at five times the rate of humans, so the chow in Rudy's gut was already liquefied. He opened his mouth and emitted the longest, loudest burp either of the big dudes had ever heard. The guy sitting down smiled.

"Awesome!"

But his smile disappeared just as quickly, as Rudy projectile vomited right at the Husky lineman. Though he was caught off guard, he still had the presence of mind to raise his arms in self-defense, a

move that surely saved his eyesight. The toxic demon puke immediately seared through the arms of his hoodie and burned his flesh,
and he screamed like he'd never screamed before. Will couldn't coast
any longer. He kicked the Suzuki to life and blasted the last twenty
yards, streaking right at Rudy, whipping the Demon Trapper around
and aiming it.

But Rudy saw him coming. In a flash, he leapt onto the picnic
table, then onto the top of a car, then onto the roof of Dick's. Will
couldn't let the lineman suffer, so he stopped long enough to toss
the guy's buddy a packet of his healing balm.

"Rub this on his wounds, *now!*"

The guy was a pre-med student who knew trauma when he saw it,
and he wasted no time pulling his friend up onto the picnic table and
applying the salve. The lineman had gone into shock, but the salve
started working swiftly, ensuring that he would not only keep the use
of his arms, but would still be able to play football. Only trouble was,
after this night, he would never feel like hitting anyone again.

Will spotted Rudy running down the sidewalk and gave chase
on the Suzuki, quickly catching up. He aimed the Demon Trapper
but couldn't draw a bead on Rudy because of the way he was weaving back and forth. But then he had a shot! He was about to take it
when Rudy leapt into the street and started running down the middle of 45th Avenue, accompanied by blaring horns. He was purpose-
fully zigzagging through traffic, causing as many fender-benders as
possible in an effort to distract Will. The kamikaze tactic worked as
a 2006 Blazer swerved and clipped the back of the Suzuki, sending
Will into a dangerous skid. Will left the bike to pursue Rudy on foot.
Rudy hauled butt, cutting up through an alley and into a backyard,
and Will followed, hearing screams as Rudy kicked open the back
door of a house and ripped through it.

Will stopped and had to guess. Would Rudy go left or right?
Will chose right and ran through two backyards, hopped a picket
fence, ran out to the sidewalk, and dropped down behind a hedge.

The people in the house were watching a reality TV show about who could eat the most garbage. Seeing Rudy, they all screamed, and the man of the house, Saul Risher, grabbed for a fire poker. Bad move. Rudy kicked him in the kneecap and clawed a hunk out of the side of his face, then kicked down the front door and ran out onto the sidewalk, looking left and right. The coast was clear, and he ran right. He was just starting to gloat about how he'd escaped the great Will Hunter when the shimmering lime green beam caught him. The next thing he knew, he was back in the place he hated most in the world: inside the Demon Trapper.

Will was winded and his heart was pounding. He shook his head.

"Come on, little buddy, let's go home."

Rudy pounded on the Plexiglas and shouted silent curses as Will slung the Demon Trapper over his shoulder and walked back to the Suzuki.

When Will got home to the lab, the first thing he did was check on April, as was his custom. No change.

Then he once again strapped Rudy down to the table like Frankenstein's monster. Only this time, there was no ruse, no play-acting, and Rudy let his full demon self out as he raged against his bonds, straining his wrists, trying to pump his legs.

"Let me go! You'll regret this, I swear it! You have no idea what I'm capable of!"

"I know exactly what you're capable of," said Will calmly. "That's why I'm going to inject you. That's why I'm going to *cure* you."

Will held up a vial of amber liquid. The cure. There were four more identical vials in a tray nearby.

Rudy stared at the vials, trying to concentrate his hate upon them. Then he yelled at Will. "You already tried 'curing' me, you scumbag loser! It didn't work!"

Rudy's body was taut with anger, his muscles bulging, his blood pumping. He was snapping his teeth at Will, trying to bite into his flesh. He spit at him over and over, but Will dodged it every time. "Are you listening to me? I told you your stupid cure didn't work!"

Will pulled on some latex gloves and snapped them tightly into place.

"But you see, I haven't actually tried anything, Rudy. I injected you with a placebo because I needed you to do some recon for me, which you did. Now it's time to put your bad self to bed, and find out what you learned."

"Arrrrgh! I'm going to tear your eyes out and feed them to crows!" screamed Rudy. "If you let me go right now, I promise to kill you quickly. If you don't, then I'll make sure you suffer!"

"If you can't say something nice, then don't say anything at all," said Will, as he pulled out a thick rubber mouth guard and stuffed it into Rudy's mouth. "You'd better bite down on this."

"Why?" asked Rudy, garbling around the rubber piece.

He got his answer as Will injected him with the cure. Rudy's arm felt like it was on fire, and the flame spread quickly. Soon his whole body was burning as the chemical concoction surged through him. Rudy spit the mouth guard out and began howling as his body shook and his eyes rolled back in his head. He growled and shrieked his throat raw. And this time it was all for real.

Emily had heard sounds like this before, back when the demons had held her captive. The caves of Mount St. Emory had echoed with these sounds as demons fought among themselves and tortured each other, the strong preying upon the weak, in the ultimate sadistic macho society. The screaming coming from downstairs sent a shiver of fear up her spine and then took hold of her. It was as though the Dark Lord himself had her heart in his clutches and was squeezing it. She closed her eyes and gritted her teeth, but she couldn't endure the harrowing screams of agony. She got up and ran down into the lab.

Rudy's body was convulsing and green foam was frothing from his mouth. Will jammed the mouth guard in again and Rudy gladly bit down on it, grateful for the momentary distraction. The pain was horrific, worse than anything he'd ever experienced. His eyes bulged out, bloodshot, then bleeding. His body continued to shake. He spit the mouth guard out and it ricocheted off the ceiling as he exploded with more shrieks and howls and snarling sounds.

"Ahhhh! No! Just kill me!" he screamed. "I'm begging you, just kill me!"

Rudy's eyes were pleading, but Will simply studied him, noticing how his eyes, which had been flashing black, now had ceased doing so and were only horribly bloodshot. And Rudy's skin, which had been thick, with a pebbly texture, was beginning to appear more normal. But he continued howling.

Emily burst into the lab. "Make him stop! For God's sake, Will! Do something!"

"I am. Go back upstairs."

But she was brittle with fear and stood trembling. "I . . . I can't! I can't take this anymore!" She backed up until she hit the wall, and suddenly she was sobbing.

Helplessly, Will watched her cry. If this were Natalie, he could at least hold her. Emily was so fragile, he was afraid to even touch her.

"Emily, I'm sorry. You shouldn't have to hear this." She shouldn't have had to be there at all. She'd suffered enough already. And that's when the idea came to him. How he might be able to convince Natalie to leave without a huge fight.

Behind them, Rudy's howls subsided as his head went slack. He emitted a low guttural growl as he passed out. Will turned away from Emily to check on him. When he looked up again Emily seemed to have gotten herself under control, and was furiously wiping away tears.

"Is he . . . dead?" It was hard to tell what she wanted the answer to be.

"No, he's going to be okay. But Emily, things are only going to get uglier and more dangerous from here." Will took a deep breath. "I think it would be best if I sent you away."

From the look on Emily's face, he could tell the idea hadn't occurred to her, but that now that it had, it was a tempting one.

"It's for your own good. You can go to any one of several places in the world. You'll be completely taken care of financially. You won't have to deal with any of this. You'd have the chance to really heal."

Even as Will said the words, he fought against the wave of grief that moved through his body. Because Natalie would never let Emily leave without her. Natalie loved him, but her first loyalty was to her sister. As long as Emily still needed her, Natalie wouldn't be able to let Emily leave alone.

"I think Kauai is the place for you. It's beautiful. Quiet. Peaceful. I'll make the arrangements."

"We're not going anywhere." Natalie had come into the lab and now stood beside Emily, holding her hand. Part of Will was relieved. *She won't go! She won't let me make her.* But he couldn't give in so easily. If he had to push her away, this was the least painful way, for both of them.

"I don't want to argue about this," said Will.

"Good. Neither do I," Natalie said. "You can't send her away without sending me away, and I'm telling you right now, that's not going to happen. I'm not going anywhere. So neither is Em. We're a package deal, Will. You know that."

Natalie turned and looked at her twin.

"Right, Em?"

"Thanks for the offer, Will," Emily said. "But we're staying."

"Well, there you have it," said Natalie.

Will knew she meant business. It was one of the things that he adored about Natalie: her unfaltering loyalty. But he steeled himself.

"Natalie, it's not safe. And it's hurting Emily to be here."

"It's *helping* Emily to be here, learning how to defend herself. And just exactly when and where *will* it be safe, Will? Can you tell me that?" demanded Natalie.

Will hesitated, and Natalie swooped in.

"I didn't think so. We all know *he* won't stop until he unleashes Hell. And you're the only one who can stop him. How could you think for a moment we would even consider running? Will, we met for a *reason*. You rescued Emily and me for a *reason*. And that reason is that we're meant to fight by your side. Don't forget, he killed our parents, Will. We want him to pay, too. And if there's any way at all we can help you, we're not going anywhere."

Will sagged, defeated. He should have known it wouldn't be so easy to convince Natalie to leave. Not in the middle of a fight. If she hadn't come in when she had . . . But it was too late now.

"If I thought I could make you, I would."

"You can't." Natalie had never sounded more stubborn. "Like it or not, we're yours."

His. If only she really could be.

Rudy started to buck on the table again, pulling Will's attention away. When he started howling, Emily tensed.

"Natalie, get her out of here," Will said. He heard the door shut behind them as Rudy started going wild, every muscle in his body contracting. And then he went deathly still. One of the vitals monitors began beeping, and Will knew that Rudy was going into cardiac arrest. He wasted no time charging up the paddles as Rudy began to flatline. Will zapped him once, twice. And then he waited, holding his breath. The monitor beeped. Rudy again had a pulse. He moaned, spittle sliding from his mouth. He opened his eyes. They were crazy with fear.

"I . . . I can't see!"

"Calm down . . . Look at my finger . . ."

Will was moving a finger back and forth in front of Rudy's eyes. But Rudy wasn't tracking. He was overcome with panic.

"I can't hear!"

He was shaking his head back and forth. Will didn't know what to do. Rudy's heart had stopped momentarily, and now he was deaf and blind—maybe permanently. Had Will gotten the formula wrong? Will placed a hand on his forehead. Rudy was drenched in sweat and smelled like a wet rat. Finally his eyes seemed to focus.

"Will?"

"Yeah. Can you see me? Can you hear me?"

Rudy nodded. "Yeah. I can see you. I can hear you. My head . . . my body . . ."

He was exhausted.

Relieved, Will took Rudy's temperature and blood pressure. He was stable. It had been a hell of a ride, but it seemed like he had pulled it off. The serum seemed to have worked. If only he knew whether it would last. *Your grandfather developed an antidote, so I was safe as I raised you. But . . . when he kidnapped me I . . . succumbed,* Edward had said. Did that mean he needed to have regular doses? It wasn't as if Will had gotten the chance to question him. Will never wanted to subject anyone to such an ordeal again. But if that was what it took to keep Rudy clean, he would do it. In the meantime, he would just have to keep an eye on him.

"You're going to be okay now, buddy," he said, gently placing a hand on Rudy's shoulder. Minutes passed. Then Rudy spoke in soft voice.

"I just had the weirdest dream."

"Rudy," said Will, "if I let you up, will you behave?"

"Every bone in my body hurts. I couldn't misbehave if I wanted to."

Will stared long and hard at Rudy. Then he grabbed Rudy's head in his hands and applied pressure to his temples with his thumbs.

"Hey! You're hurting me!"

Rudy's eyes remained normal. No flash of black liquid, just . . . bloodshot. Will released him.

"What was that all about?" rasped Rudy, shaking.

"Just being careful," said Will.

After Will helped Rudy clean up, they went upstairs into the kitchen. The house was stocked with plenty of food, some of it actually healthy. Rudy stayed away from that. He was ravenous and chose chocolate milk poured over Fruit Loops. He ate three bowls. As he set the spoon down and burped, he smiled at Will.

"Thanks, man."

"No problem. Welcome back. And this time I mean it," said Will. He wanted to give Rudy more time to readjust, but he couldn't wait to ask any longer. "Did you find the other demons after you left Gas Works Park?"

Rudy looked like that was the last thing he wanted to think about, but he nodded. "Yeah."

"I want you to tell me everything you remember from the last twenty-four hours."

Chapter Eleven: Rudy's Ordeal

After the cops had come to Gas Works Park, the shedemons had whisked Rudy away along the shore. *Come with us! Join us! Do as we say!* They laughed and hissed and danced as they ran, surreal creatures who held an immediate power over him. He'd always been a sucker for a pretty girl. They led him to a van. He had no idea where he was. They opened the back doors of the van and kicked him into it, then slammed the doors shut. They drove. He was kept in the back like a dog and he *liked* it. He knew he would do *anything* for them. When he reached out to touch one, she whirled and kicked him in the face. He read her eyes. They were deadly. They said, *No one touches me, ever!* He wondered if that rule only applied to boys and figured it probably did.

They ordered him to lie face down and drove for approximately ten minutes. When he had landed in the van he'd landed on his elbow, which now began to throb. He scratched at it until he felt something hard under his skin, and in the inky darkness he began to imagine that some kind of nasty insect had somehow burrowed into his flesh. He extended his claw-like fingernails and dug at his elbow until it bled, then pulled out the small chip and peered at it. It could only have come from Will Hunter. So Will was tracking him like some animal. He'd show him. He'd show him good. He crushed the chip.

The shedemons parked the van. They pulled him out of the back and shoved him into a tunnel. Down they went, Rudy struggling to keep up as they descended staircase after staircase. Bare bulbs hung from the ceilings as they swept through a subterranean city—the Under City—teeming with rats and bats and demons coming and going.

The most beautiful of the four shedemons, the one with the bright blue streak in her hair, moved close to Rudy, licking her lips as if she were about to kiss him. His eyes widened, and though he was scared after being walloped, he still opened his mouth a little in anticipation. He had no idea what to expect. When she drew even closer to him, she spit in his face and he was momentarily blinded.

They herded him down a long flight of crude stairs cut into bedrock, and by the time they reached the bottom his vision had started to clear again. The air became thicker and hotter, the stone walls sweating. Finally they came to a cavern. Hundreds of demons were filing in. The mood was funereal, and in moments Rudy discovered why. This was a viewing room, a vault where demons from all over had come to see their leader—or what was left of him.

The Dark Lord's partially assembled body lay on a large flat raised marble stone and was guarded by a dozen female demons like the four that had come there with him. Rudy's body shook. It felt like a jillion tiny bugs had found their way into his spine. He was terrified by what he saw. The Dark Lord's body was lifeless, in some kind of state of "repair," his tissue being melded together by a worm-like creature. There were urns full of blood all around the stone table. The Dark Lord wore a golden battle helmet and was totally motionless, like a corpse. Like the other demons in the cavern, Rudy filed past and hissed and spit with respect, and then he was roughly grabbed by a shedemon—*What was that, on her chest, something on her chest, her sweatshirt?*—who turned his wrist and punctured it in one swift move. She squeezed and drained off a cup of his blood and put it alongside others, then used a red-hot poker to cauterize the wound. He howled in agony, but no one cared.

He was shoved into a chamber and sucked upward, riding a foul blast of air up and up and up, out of the Under City. He found himself at a door and stumbled out into an alley, and then he was thrown into the same van that had brought him there. Minutes later the she-demons dropped him off downtown. He wandered the streets in a daze until he finally met up with the demons from Edmonds, and then he got blind drunk trying to forget what he'd just seen. He was repulsed and stricken with fear. What would the future hold for him if the Great Leader was dead?

Will sat quietly, contemplating all that Rudy had just told him. If the Dark Lord was indeed lying close by, near death, in this Under City, then that might explain how he had traveled with Will into April's mind. What if he was in some kind of limbo between life and death? If Will was somehow able to find the body and destroy it, maybe, just maybe, in so doing, he could rescue his mother and vanquish the Dark Lord for good. But where was this Under City, and how could he find it?

"How far down were you when you saw the body?" he asked Rudy.

"I dunno, way down. Probably like . . . I dunno, if you turned the Space Needle upside down. Those stairs went on for*ever*."

Will thought about it. The Space Needle was 605 feet tall. Another sixty-one feet would put the body at 666 feet below the ground. That had to be it. But who could lead him there? He had a gut feeling that the shedemons who had attacked him might be a link. The way Rudy described the female demons surrounding what was left of the Dark Lord's body, Will figured they were of the same ilk who had kicked his ass at Gas Works Park.

"You said the female demonteens had a symbol on their clothing," he said to Rudy. "What did it look like?"

"I don't know . . . I wasn't really focusing on that, you know, not with the body of the freakin' Prince of Darkness lying there! And it was in parts, you know, kind of stitched together, but not with string or anything, more like . . . thin strips of human flesh. Oh, man, just talking about it is creeping me out!"

"Here's a news flash for you, Rudy. The Dark Lord is . . . somehow alive, or at least his spirit is. And if he gets a hold of us . . . of you . . . it's going to get a whole lot creepier. If you help me, maybe I can find the body and destroy it. So do you think you can remember for me?"

Rudy thought hard, forcing himself to revisit the cavern.

"Birds. I think they were birds."

"What kind of birds?"

"I don't know! I don't know diddly-squat about birds!" whined Rudy, until Will shot him a withering look.

"Okay, I'll try. Um . . . they weren't stupid-looking birds, like chickens or turkeys or dodo birds or something. They were more, you know, kind of cool, kind of like, I don't know . . . majestic."

"Good. Okay. Let's go to the computers."

Will led Rudy over to his computer station and began tapping keys. Soon, images of birds came up.

"Recognizing anything? Anything ringing a bell?"

"Not really. I mean, they weren't really pictures of birds, I guess, more like symbols."

"Got it. Of course. A symbol. Like a school symbol, a mascot sort of thing?"

"Yeah, maybe," said Rudy.

Will typed some more, and now they cycled through a series of school symbols that included birds—hawks, ducks, seagulls, condors, ravens, eagles, falcons.

"Wait a second," said Will. "I have an idea."

He then tapped into the Seattle School District's database and skimmed through the high schools and the symbols for their athletic departments. He stopped at one when Rudy gasped. "That's it," said Rudy.

Will read the information.

"Lyndon Baines Johnson High School. The Fightin' Falcons."

On the screen was the school symbol: a graphic artist's rendering of a falcon, wings spread, talons extended, beak open, ready to strike. One mean-looking bird.

"Yeah," said Rudy, "that's it. How did you know?"

"I've seen that symbol recently myself," Will said. "It was on a ring. I saw it just before it hit me in the face."

That evening, Will, Rudy, Natalie, and Emily all ate at the grand old oak table in the formal dining room. It was an elegant setting fit for royalty. Emily looked better than she had earlier that afternoon, but she took care to sit as far away from Rudy as possible. The menu was pizza, nachos, and buffalo wings. As usual, Rudy ate too much, and when he was done, he leaned back in his chair, groaning and patting his stomach.

"You're such a pig," said Emily, her nose wrinkling.

"I'm supposed to feel guilty because I like food?"

"You're supposed to act like a civilized human being. That is, if you actually *are* a human being," Emily said.

Before Rudy could reply, Will stood up. "Everybody get a good night's sleep tonight. Tomorrow's a big day."

"Let me guess," said Emily, doing her best to sound particularly snarky. "We get to be cooped up in the haunted mansion all day again?"

"No," said Will. "Tomorrow's different."

Natalie looked at him in anticipation. "What's so different about tomorrow?"

"We're going to school."

Rudy lit up with a smile. So did Natalie. Emily thought about it, and finally decided it wasn't the worst idea she'd ever heard. Anything to get some semblance of normalcy back into their freakishly disjointed and dysfunctional lives.

"Oh, Will, that's great. That's fantastic," said Natalie.

"Pinch me," said Rudy. "I think I'm dreaming. For real?"

"For real," said Will. "Since you two have vowed to stick around like a couple of bad pennies, and since I have to keep an eye on Rudy to make sure he's completely cured, we're all going to enroll at Lyndon Baines Johnson High School, home of the Fightin' Falcons."

Then it hit Natalie and she smiled broadly. "Will," she said. "We're going to be . . . the New Kids."

That night Will made Rudy sleep next to him, just to make sure the cure was was sticking and Rudy didn't engage in any kind of weird sleepwalking, a habit most demons were guilty of. Rudy grumbled about Will not trusting him, but he was exhausted and nodded off quickly, sinking down into a deep sleep. Will wasn't so fortunate. He couldn't stop thinking about his mother. So he slipped out of his bedroom and went down to the lab to check the surveillance tapes of her room. They were clean. No one had attempted entry, save for the requisite medical support staff. Nothing out of the ordinary had occurred. He felt better, but it wasn't quite enough to ease his mind. He wanted to actually see her. So he shot down to the hospital on his Suzuki.

At the hospital, he entered her room and sat down and held her hand.

"I'm so sorry, Mom," he whispered as he sat with her. "I won't let you down again. I'm going to find you. I promise."

He closed his eyes and felt her pulse. He tried to enter her mind the way he had before, if only to make sure she knew he was there, but he could not. He opened his eyes and gazed out at the city lights. Where was she? In what world? Will's eyelids grew heavy and he drifted off to sleep. And then he was dreaming.

Images came at him in waves. Natalie. Emily. The mysterious girl with the emerald eyes from Gas Works Park. The phantom she-demons, attacking like falcons, their ruby red claws slashing at him. And then he heard laughter. The deep husky laughter of the Dark Lord.

The dream shifted and he was in a tunnel with wet walls. His vision was blurry. He touched a wall and looked at his fingers; they were covered with blood. He squinted and his vision cleared, and he saw that the walls of the cave were made not of stone but of flesh. He was somewhere inside a body. Then he entered a cavern with an opening to clouds above. Rain came down in sheets. But it was no normal rain: the droplets weren't water, but blood. Will's mouth opened, but no scream came out. He saw movement out of the corner of his eye: a woman with long hair was sitting on the floor of the cave with her back to him. He moved toward her, floating, his feet not touching the ground. He was afraid of who the woman might be; she looked familiar.

He heard laughter. The cave turned into a bedroom in a house Will had never been in before. Pictures of children he'd never met hung on the walls in oval frames.

The woman was still sitting on the floor.

"Mom?"

She would not turn to face him, so he had to circle around. Her hair hung down over her face. She lifted her head. It *was* April.

"Hello, Will," she said, her voice a spooky monotone. She was not the one laughing. It was deeper, a man's voice. She said, "I have something for you."

She was holding an object in her lap. Will looked down and his stomach dropped.

She was holding the Dark Lord's laughing head.

Will woke up. His shirt was damp with nightmare sweat. He watched his mother breathing for a few moments, then kissed her hand and left. He drove the Suzuki home, then he went up into his room where Rudy still slept, snoring. Will flopped down on his bed and stared at the ceiling. He did not sleep the rest of the night.

POTLATCH, IDAHO

In a barn out on Onaway Road, a group of high school kids from Potlatch were gathered to take a group celibacy pledge. Not one tattoo scarred this group, but they each wore a mark, as upon entering the barn they'd had the backs of their hands stamped with a rubber cross, the ink a deep purple. Punch was served, along with homemade chocolate chip cookies. The boys wore jeans and button-down dress shirts, the girls a mix of pants and skirts with blouses. Rock music from the local praise station was playing, and some kids danced. Many of the kids were coupled up, boyfriends and girlfriends already going steady. The remaining kids were single but had been tempted, and they all had decided to wait until marriage before engaging in sex.

A hand-painted banner read, VIRGINITY IS THE GREATEST GIFT YOU CAN GIVE YOUR FUTURE MATE. Three-by-five pledge cards were distributed and signed and placed into a huge pickle jar sitting on a stool on the makeshift stage. The jar had a cross on it. In a group service, the couples who were going steady exchanged purity rings, vowing to remain celibate because true love waits. The chaperones, locals Hanna Gaines and Larry Lebbert, were proud of these kids. Privately, they wondered if they would have had the strength to be pure when they were teenagers.

As the celibacy pledge ceremony came to a close, the teens gathered in a circle, linked arms, and sang along to an updated version of an old Connie Frances song: *"If it takes forever, I will wait for you."* At the song's climax, the group burst into applause and hugged each other.

Just then, one of the girls yelped. She swore she'd felt something on her neck. She said it felt like a claw. And then the pain began.

Hanna and Larry were perplexed as they watched the teens, who were now all scratching and then clawing at the skin on their necks and faces. It was a spontaneous outbreak of some malady much worse than herpes: the kids' skin was breaking out in inflamed pimples, blisters, pustules, chancres, and carbuncles. Their collective, rising wall of screams could be heard for miles.

Chapter Twelve:
The New Kids

Lyndon Baines Johnson High School was perched high on a ridge on Capitol Hill with a view overlooking the city. It was an imposing three-story masonry building with four Tuscan columns flanking the main entryway and ornate cornices topping the elaborate brickwork. An American flag hung limp on a flagpole. On the west wall of the gymnasium was painted a thirty-foot blue falcon swooping down in attack mode. The school was home to some 2,400 students, a balanced mix of Caucasians, Asians, African Americans, and Latinos. The kids were just like high school students everywhere: cliquish and suspicious of perceived "outsiders." So when Will, Natalie, Rudy, and Emily ventured onto the campus as the New Kids, climbing the concrete stops leading to the entrance, they were greeted with the usual stares from leery students. There were Fightin' Falcon T-shirts and sweatshirts in abundance. It was just before first bell, and dozens of teens were lingering outside, socializing, sipping their Starbucks. It was cold as a coffin in winter, and the students' breath was visible as they spoke to one another. Not one of them spoke to Will, Natalie, Emily, or Rudy. But their eyes . . . all their eyes were upon them.

"So this is what it's like being the New Kid, huh?" asked Natalie, speaking low to Will.

"Yeah. Pretty much the same with every new school. You get used to it."

"I think it's awesome!" said Rudy. "I mean, this is a fresh start for me. Nobody knows I'm a dorky screw-up here!" Rudy did his little dance and waved at a Korean girl with braces.

"Hey, how's it going? I'm Rudy," he said, brightly. The girl turned away and whispered to one of her friends, no doubt dissing the new weirdo.

"Nice going, Rudy," hissed Emily, smacking Rudy on the arm. "You just made us all look incredibly stupid."

"Ow! I was just being friendly."

"Can we please hurry up?" Emily asked. She was mortified and couldn't wait to get out of the spotlight. As they approached the school entrance, a tall kid with a skull and crossbones on his jacket kicked over a trash can right in front of them. Will didn't even bother making eye contact. The others followed him as he stepped politely over the trash and went inside. They made their way through the crowd of students and found the administration office just as first bell rang.

The school officials were sympathetic and bent over backward to welcome them because they were survivors of the tragedy at Harrisburg. They were assigned lockers and given new student welcome packets. Natalie was thrilled that she and Will were put in the same world history class for first period. Emily was mortified that she and Rudy would be sharing first period chemistry.

"Come on, I'll walk you," Rudy offered.

"I really wish you wouldn't. Let's see, how can I say this delicately? Um, how about this: I don't want to be seen with you!" Emily rushed off down the hallway, leaving Rudy scratching his head as he set off after her.

Will and Natalie walked the long length of a hallway. Natalie did her best to stay as close to Will as possible as they passed a few stragglers. A couple of girls saw Will and smiled openly at him. Natalie took Will's hand and shot them territorial looks. *Back off, this one's mine.* But Will pulled his hand away. She wanted to protest but swallowed the words. She could feel his coldness. They reached the door to their history class. Will paused.

"Listen, there's no good way for me to say this, so I'm just going to come out with it. I think it's better if we aren't . . . together, you know?"

Natalie's heart thudded and she flushed with panic. "You mean . . . here at school?" she said.

"Yeah."

Will turned his eyes away from her. Why was he doing this?

"Will, look at me." She knew she sounded demanding, but she didn't care. He couldn't just say something like that and not explain it to her. Will returned his gaze to her. "Do you mind telling me why?" she asked.

"I don't want people to connect the two of us. I don't want . . . *them* to use you to get to me."

"I don't care. I'm not afraid."

"It's not about you being afraid, it's about not giving them an opening. Do you see what I'm saying?"

She didn't like it, but she did see what he was saying. She just wished he'd said something sooner, instead of springing it on her in the middle of the school hallway. "All right. I get it." She could pretend.

But first . . . She looked around. The coast was clear. She grabbed him and kissed him on the cheek. He blushed, then scanned the hallway.

"Wait for a second before coming in," he said.

He opened the door and walked in ahead of her. She hung back for a beat, then walked in, not even bothering to look at him. Fine and dandy. She would play the part of a distant friend; she would play any role Will asked her to. But there was one thing she could never do, even if he demanded it. She could never stop loving him with every beat of her heart.

. . .

At lunchtime Natalie and Emily found one another and went through the hot food line together, getting soup and sandwiches. Emily kept her head down, trying to blend in. All she wanted was to have one boring, normal school day. Rudy was already regressing back to his old Harrisburg self, his spine bent, his eyes downcast. He'd reached out to make friends, but after being rejected a half-dozen times, he'd retreated back into his shell. He stood meekly as others cut in front of him in the pizza line. When he finally got his double pepperoni pizza and coke, he looked around the lunchroom, spotted Natalie and Emily, smiled, and began walking their way. Emily wasn't pleased.

"Is it seriously gonna be like this? Do I have to hang with him at school, too?"

"Don't be such a meanie. He's been through a lot, Em, you could cut him some slack, you know?" said Natalie.

"I know I *could*. But I'm not going to. I didn't like him before, and I like him even less now. I don't trust him."

As Rudy was passing a table crowded with black-clad goths, a fat glam rocker wearing white sunglasses stuck out his foot and Rudy went sprawling, much to the delight of those watching. Laughter echoed through the lunchroom. Rudy stayed down too long. Natalie wondered if he was hurt and was about to get up and go help him when he stood, his spine now straight. He looked like a different person. The laughter stopped because suddenly everyone sensed that this kid, though skinny and short, was not someone to be messed with. Everyone, that is, but the glam rocker, who stood up, proudly displaying his pierced belly button. He glared at Rudy.

"What are you looking at?"

"I'm not exactly sure, but I'm thinkin' a brainless doofus," said Rudy calmly.

"Boys' room. Second floor. After lunch," spit the kid. "I wanna have a little *talk* with you, weasel face!"

"Wouldn't miss it for the world," said Rudy.

Will was just entering the lunchroom carrying his tray, and he caught the tail end of the confrontation. After a quick scan located Natalie and Emily and assured him they were okay, he joined Rudy as he sat down at a far table.

"Do you think you can manage to stay out of trouble on the first day, at least?"

"There's no trouble, no trouble at all," Rudy said.

"Make sure it stays that way," said Will. He ate his burger as he scanned the lunchroom again, looking for Blue Streak or the other she-demons he'd tangled with . . . or the girl with the emerald eyes. He'd seen a girl with strawberry-blonde hair earlier that morning in the hallway, but it could have been anyone. There wasn't really any reason for him to believe the girl was a student here. He just had a feeling.

Maybe it was just wishful thinking, because he couldn't stop thinking about her. She'd known what the shedemons were; he was sure of it. And she'd known how to drive them off. She had information he could use. But that wasn't the only reason she was foremost in his thoughts. He couldn't explain it, but he knew he needed to see her again.

Natalie was staring at Will from across the lunchroom and her heart was beginning to grow heavy. She knew why he'd put a wall between them. She'd even *agreed* to it. But that didn't make it any easier. In history class, as Mr. Wheeler had droned on about the Roman Empire, Natalie must have looked over at Will about a thousand times, and never once did he meet her gaze. When the class ended, Will was out the door and off to his next class without so much as a parting glance. Negative thoughts began to gnaw at her. One part of her knew, just *knew* that Will loved her as much as she loved him. But another part whispered that she was wrong, that she wasn't good enough for him. She just needed for him to look over at her once, to reassure her she hadn't imagined the way he felt about her.

"What's going on with you and Will?" asked Emily.

Natalie felt like her sister had just dribbled cold water down her back.

"What are you talking about? Nothing's going on," she said.

She knew she sounded defensive. She wasn't surprised Emily didn't buy it.

"Then why is he ignoring you? And why are you feeling so sad and afraid?"

"He's not. And I'm fine."

"Hey, don't pull that with me. We're in synch, remember? I can feel what you feel sometimes, especially when it's heavy, like right now. So how about sharing, huh?"

Natalie put her head in her hands and let down her guard. Why was she even trying to fool Emily? They always picked up on *everything* the other one was feeling. It was how Natalie had known Emily wasn't really dead back in Harrisburg.

"Oh God, okay. I'm sorry. Will said—this morning he told me we should pretend we weren't together, because *they* could use me to get to him. And he's right, but I hate it. It sucks. I know it's just pretend, but it feels like he's trying to force a wedge between us."

"Nat, you worry too much. Anyone can see that he's crazy about you."

Emily's words helped. Natalie took a deep breath. "You sure? I mean, you really think so?"

"I *know* so."

For the moment Natalie was reassured, and the girls went back to their lunches, chewing slowly. A group of boys walked by, strutting their stuff, but the twins ignored them.

A poster outside the second-floor boys' room featured a Fightin' Falcon screeching the words "BEAT ROOSEVELT!" Rudy walked by it

and entered the boys' room. The blubber-belly glam rocker was leaning against a stall smoking a cigarette, which he shared with his two
friends, who were both also on the flabby side and sporting plenty
of tats.

"Well, look who actually showed up," Fat Glam said, and wasted
no time before lunging at Rudy. Rudy sidestepped him with ease
and kicked him in the back, a move that sent the hefty boy sprawling into the urinals, his nose hitting with a sickening crunch.

He turned and blinked as he felt the blood gushing from his
nose.

"What the hell?!"

His comrades decided this would be a good time to jump in,
and one of them took a swing. Rudy ducked it and punched the guy
in the gut. The kid doubled over and heaved his lunch up all over
the tile floor. While he continued to retch, the other dude grabbed
Rudy from behind, but Rudy wasn't about to be held. He stomped
on the guy's metatarsals, breaking one of them. Howling in pain,
the kid immediately let go of Rudy and fell to the floor, clutching
his foot.

"Son of a bitch, man!"

Rudy stood his ground, folding his arms.

"So, did you have something you wanted to share with me?" he
asked Fat Glam.

All three of the bullies shook their heads. Rudy walked to the
urinal to relieve himself, and the three chunky guys took the opportunity to exit swiftly.

Will was approaching the boys' room as the trio stumbled out, one
limping, another smelling of vomit, the third with blood still trick-
ling from his nose. Natalie and Emily had followed Will when he
left the lunchroom, and they, too, saw the walking wounded. Then
Rudy casually strolled out and smiled.

"Hey. What's up?"

Will shook his head. There was no question about it. Rudy still had a little bit of demon in him. Maybe a lot.

"You need to listen to me," Will said. "We had an agreement."

"Hey, a dude's gotta defend himself. Truth?"

"Truth," said Will. And part of him was glad that Rudy wasn't just letting himself get picked on, for once. "I take it by the outcome that they weren't . . ."

"Infected? No. Just jerks. My guess is this school's full of them."

"I've yet to see a high school that isn't." The fourth period bell rang. "Come on," said Will, "let's get to class."

Natalie and Emily watched as Will and Rudy walked away. Natalie had tried to make eye contact with Will, but it was a no go. He was still pretending she didn't exist. Watching Rudy walk away, Emily's eyes narrowed. She wanted to say *I told you so*, wanted to crow about Rudy being a little beast. But she was actually kind of impressed that he'd stood up for himself, even if it meant he was a little wicked. She shook her head at her own feelings. Go figure.

Between fourth and fifth periods, the hallways were rivers of kids flowing to and fro, and Will stood in the middle of one, watching. Girls seemed to find him particularly interesting, as was always the case when he showed up as the New Kid. They found him dangerously handsome and would point and whisper. Some smiled, and some did their best to show him how thoroughly they were ignoring him. He was used to this kind of attention and let it all roll right on past as he scoped out the student body. He saw the usual assortment of gangsta wannabes with their pants hung low, goths with their purple hair and studded chokers, geeks and nerds and jocks and everyone in between. He thought he might have spotted a couple of demonteens, but he couldn't be sure. Everyone was giving him a pretty wide berth, and so far none of the Alpha males had come around to mark their territory by picking a fight with him. If he wanted to smoke out the demonteens at this school he'd have to rattle some cages, and he wasn't up for any overt confrontations just yet.

The hallways were clearing out, locker doors slamming and kids jostling and disappearing into classrooms as the fifth period bell rang. Will was going to be late. He started off toward his class, and as he rounded a corner, at the far end of the longest hallway in the school—the one that ended in a T at the trophy case—he saw something that made his pulse quicken: a flash of strawberry-blonde hair. He looked around to make sure no one was watching and then bent time as he ran the length of the hallway in two seconds. He should have been right behind her, but, amazingly, she was already at the end of another hallway and turning another corner. Again Will fairly flew down the hallway after her—and again she was ahead of him, darting into a classroom.

Will approached the door. It was an art class. He might catch hell from the principal, but he didn't want to lose the girl so he slipped inside. A flamboyant middle-aged teacher circled the room as the students set up in front of their easels and went about sketching the objects of the day: a gnarled piece of driftwood and an old Japanese blue glass float. The teacher, resplendent in her flowing African panoply, was doing her best to put out a "free spirit" vibe. She was playing New Age music from speakers hooked to her iPod, and she swept around the room making encouraging, nurturing sounds, the plethora of beads around her neck and wrists jangling. Will moved in counterpoint to her, playing cat and mouse, taking care to always keep an easel between them to keep himself out of her view. He continued this game as he scanned the room, hoping to find the girl before being discovered by Ms. Flamboyant. There were plenty of girls in the class, but he couldn't find *her*. He wondered if she had somehow passed right through the classroom on her way to who knows where else. He glanced around for exit doors but saw none. Maybe he hadn't seen her after all. Maybe he was following a ghost.

"Excuse me?" said the teacher, having finally discovered Will. "What have we here?" she asked playfully. "Are we lost?"

"Um, I'm new . . . I think I'm registered in this class."

The woman looked at Will knowingly. She'd heard it before.

"And your name is . . . ?"

"Will. Will Hunter."

"Well, Mr. Hunter . . . Will . . ." she held out her hand, smirking. "Let's have a look at your schedule." She stretched out the last word. *Shed-you-ul.*

Will patted his pockets.

"I think I lost it."

"Well then, let's not waste this opportunity. You have a striking profile. Come. Stand here." She pulled Will into the center of the room.

"Let's shift gears," said the teacher, "from the inanimate, to the intimate!"

She whirled and changed the music on her iPod, and the students in the room began sketching Will as he stood silent and still. Only his eyes moved. Even from his new, better vantage point he could not find the girl with the emerald eyes and was beginning to wonder if she even existed. Perhaps she had been a hallucination in the aftermath of the shedemons' attack.

"Thank you, Mr. Hunter," the teacher said after ten minutes of fruitless searching for the girl while the rest of the class used him as a model. "You can step down and find an easel for the rest of class."

But as he stepped away from the center of the classroom his eyes caught a reflection in the window, not of a student, but of one of the easels. His heart skipped a beat. He blinked, trying to bring the image into focus. Because the window was streaked, he couldn't tell if the image was what he feared it was. Maybe his mind was playing tricks on him. He turned his head, trying to figure out where the reflection was coming from. There, right in front of him. He walked slowly around the easel and there she was; the girl with the strawberry-blonde hair and piercing emerald eyes. And right now her eyes were staring, trance-like, at what she'd just sketched. It was a haunting rendition of Will's dream, the one featuring the Dark Lord's body lying on the marble altar.

"How did you . . ." Will barely got the words out before the girl snapped out of her trance and snatched her drawing, crumpling it up. She knocked over her easel as she bolted from the room. The other students gaped as Will ran after her. Moments later, he caught up to her in the hallway.

"Get away from me!" she said, looking around.

"That drawing. How did you see it? What you drew, I mean—"

His eyes were demanding. She met them fiercely.

"I told you to forget you ever met me."

He shook his head. "And I told you I don't shy away from trouble."

She kept looking around as though they were going to be swarmed at any second.

"Listen, I took pity on you because you were hurt. I shouldn't have; you took it totally the wrong way. Now it's time for you to back off."

"Hey!" shouted Will as she shoved him backward—with surprising strength—and moved swiftly down the hallway. She slowed down as a janitor came out of the teachers' lounge, pushing a trash can on wheels. When he'd gone past, Will zoomed down the hall and caught up with her again.

"I asked you a question about that drawing. I want an answer."

The girl looked up and down the hallway frantically, as though she knew something was about to go down. Her eyes narrowed in anger and she hissed at him.

"You have no idea what you're getting yourself into. Leave. Just leave LBJ High!"

If she'd known anything about him, she'd have realized that he wasn't the kind of boy who would cut and run when faced with mystery or danger. No, he was exactly the opposite. He would dig and dig until he found what he was looking for.

She spoke again, ominously. "There's nothing for you here."

"*You're* here," said Will. The two words stopped them both cold. He hadn't meant it to sound in any way flirtatious, but somehow it came out that way. He *was* drawn to her, but not like that. And he needed her for information. Unfortunately, he could tell by the suspicion in her eyes that he was going to have to work for it.

"What's your name?" he asked, trying to make his voice casual.

"My name is none of your business," snapped the girl.

Then a voice echoed through the hallway. "I'd like both of you to come with me, please." A woman was striding toward them. She looked formidable in her tall black boots, tweed skirt, and crisp blouse, and she carried a ticket book like a traffic cop.

Must be the school heat, thought Will. Indeed, it was the vice principal, Gloria Haynes, who had a reputation for policing the hallways with an unnerving vigilance. Her eyes narrowed at Will.

"You're one of the newly registered students, aren't you?"

"Yes," he said, staring guiltily at the floor and slipping into "embarrassed teen boy" mode, his best defense in situations like this.

"Not exactly off to an auspicious start, are we?"

"I guess not."

"And Loreli, the next time you have to depart a classroom, be advised that you will need to ask permission."

"Okay," said Loreli, her eyes also downcast.

Loreli, thought Will. *So she* does *have a name.*

After school Will did as his "behavioral infraction" write-up instructed and reported to detention. As soon as he entered he saw that Loreli was there, too, along with a goofy, small-boned kid in a faux-hawk who wasn't wearing any shoes and kept wiggling his toes nervously. Loreli was sitting all the way in the back on the left side. Will began to walk toward her, intending to plant himself right next to her. But the detention monitor, Coach Wasserman, a tall skinny guy with a big head and a gray crew cut, threw a wrench in that plan.

"Not gonna happen, pal. Other corner."

Will did as he was told and walked toward the corner desk all the way to the right. The desks were made of Formica and metal, and they were the kind that were so strong you could throw one across the room without breaking it. The room was painted a faint orange that was cracking in spots. One of the fluorescent lights overhead buzzed. Will sat down and opened his backpack. He took out some books and pretended to do his homework, but the only thing he was studying was Loreli. She was killer gorgeous, the kind of beauty that could suck the breath right out of your chest. She was doing an impressive job of ignoring him, but she could feel his eyes on her and glanced up angrily a few times, affording him a good long look at her amazing piercing green eyes.

There was definitely something portentous about this girl. Anyone could see that she was dazzling, but there was something else about her, too, something Will picked up on with his seventh sense. Loreli's green eyes were spewing tons of information, even if she wasn't aware of it. Will found himself inexorably drawn toward her. It wasn't like he'd forgotten about Natalie; he loved Natalie, even if they were doomed. But this girl . . . she was exuding a kind of irresistible charisma. Will worried he might be powerless against it. He remembered standing next to her earlier that afternoon, breathing in her scent, and how eerily familiar it had been.

She looked at him with those piercing eyes and slowly moved her lips. There was no mistaking what she was saying. *Go away.* But the more blatantly she rejected him, the stronger he was drawn to her. He knew that, one way or another, he had to get to know this mysterious girl. His gut told him it wasn't an option, it was a necessity, maybe even for his very survival. He had to know why she had been able to sketch his dream. What was her connection to him? His mind twisted in upon itself as he thought about it.

Out in the quad, Natalie, Emily, and Rudy were hanging out, waiting for Will to do his time. The four of them had come to school together, and they'd all leave together. Will had ordered Rudy to stay with the girls, and he more or less did, though he chatted up whoever would listen to him, and made frequent trips to the junk food and soda vending machines, wolfing down corn nuts like a ravenous beast and washing them down with root beer. When a Latino kid dropped his calculator and bent over to pick it up, Rudy gave in to temptation and lifted the guy's wallet. He couldn't help himself. Even though Will had given them all enough cash for whatever they wanted, he still liked the feeling of stealing it. Okay, so he wasn't perfect. He discreetly slipped the cash out of the guy's wallet, dropped it on the ground, and then, acting surprised, picked it up.

"Hey, you dropped this," he said. Mr. Polite.

The kid's hand went instinctively to his butt and he felt his wallet gone.

"Thanks," he said, taking it from Rudy.

He waited a moment before checking the contents. *Ripped off.* He stared at Rudy, and Rudy kind of hoped the kid would challenge him about it. But something in Rudy's demeanor made him decide to just get up and walk off. He left half a bag of Mini MoonPies on the table when he did, and Rudy proceeded to gobble them up. Emily was doing her best to study, but Rudy's mere presence riled her so much that she kept reading the same page over and over. Natalie was on edge, too, ever since she'd learned that Will had been sent to detention because he'd been caught in the hallway during class with some mystery girl. Who was she? Natalie had to know, and she wasn't keen on just sitting around and waiting to find out. Detention was in room 101, which was right around the corner. She told herself it wouldn't hurt to do a little recon.

"I'm gonna stretch my legs," she said as she got up.

She meandered over to the vending machines and pretended to be terribly interested in a Twix bar, then sauntered around the corner. She was able to lurk just behind a boxwood shrub and had a clear view of the detention room. There was Will, and his eyes were glued to a girl sitting across the room. Natalie's blood quickened in her veins. *Crap!* Why did the girl have to be so absolutely stunning? And why was Will staring at her like she was the last female in the universe? Natalie wanted to scream, to burst right into the room and confront him.

No wonder Will had been so distant all day. He must have seen this girl earlier and now had his eye on her. Even from a distance Natalie could tell her body was amazing, and her hair was gorgeous. Her lips, too, were sheer perfection. And the lip-gloss she was wearing was some amazing color Natalie had never seen before, a powerful, alluring shade of scarlet with a hint of orange. Natalie licked her own lips, at once envious and angry. She wanted to drag the girl out and kick her ass—even though she wasn't even looking Will's way.

Natalie told herself to stop, to back up or duck down before Will caught her snooping, but she couldn't tear herself away. And then Rudy came dancing up behind her holding a root beer, and Will's eyes flashed to the window, and their eyes locked. Natalie could tell immediately that he was angry—and why shouldn't he be? She was spying on him like a junior high dweeb.

"Thanks a lot, Rudy," she said, backing up and heading for the quad.

"What'd I do?" Rudy waved at Will, and then dug some bills out of his pocket to hit the vending machines again.

Loreli was released from detention first, and when Will got up and tried to follow, the coach held up a hand and read Will's detention slip.

"Not just yet, cowboy. Sit down. From what I read here, you were . . . 'clashing' with this young lady. So you can sit tight until she's good and gone."

Will sat down. The barefoot kid was writing something on a piece of paper. Then he crumpled it up and tossed it at Will, who caught it. It was a note. *I can help you hook up with her*, it read.

Fifteen minutes later in the hallway, barefoot faux-hawk boy was holding out his hand to Will.

"Twenty bucks. And you *know* she's worth it."

The guy was sniffling and running his hands over his stupid faux-hawk. It seemed like his snot was what was making it stick up. Will took out a twenty. The kid snatched it and stuffed it in his pocket, then got all conspiratorial, looking around as if the Feds were closing in on them.

"My name's Hawk. You're one of the new kids, right?"

"Your note said you could help me with Loreli?"

Hawk looked around again for enemies. The coast was clear. He smiled as if he was sharing the world's biggest secret.

"Straight up, dude, this is gold."

"I'm waiting."

"She's all over Rocco."

"Rocco?"

Hawk looked like someone had just slapped him with a fish.

"Man, what *solar system* do you call home? I know it's your first day, but you should have scoped out the pecking order, dude. Rocco Manelli is this school's über-Alpha male, and Loreli's got him in her sights. Whenever he has one of his secret rage parties, she tries to hook up with him. So far she's struck out. But she's the Energizer Bunny—*boom boom boom*—she just keeps on trying."

"And this helps me because . . . ?" asked Will.

"Because Rocco's having one of his super-secret ragers tonight, and the Hawk Man just happens to know where it's going down."

Hawk rubbed his thumb and middle finger together: money. Will took out a fifty.

"Rock and roll! I like you," said Hawk. "You speak my language. Tonight at the J & M. This is premium intel, bro."

"You got an address?"

"It's in Pioneer Square. Helen Keller couldn't miss it. Good luck." Hawk started walking away, then stopped and turned around.

"Oh, you don't know me and we never had this conversation."

Will stared at the kid until he got over himself and left.

Waiting out front, Natalie was nervous. Will came out and he nodded to her, but the way he didn't really look at her said it all. He clearly didn't appreciate being spied on. They zoomed home in the Beemer in silence, save for Rudy's off-key singing as he listened to tunes on the iPod he'd borrowed from Will, bobbing his head and alternately popping Red Hots and potato chips into his mouth. Emily stared out the window watching the world whiz by, attuned to the feelings of jealousy that were running rampant through her sister's brain. Natalie had told her about the girl with the green eyes, and how Will had been staring at her with such intensity. When the mystery girl had left detention and walked by them to the parking lot, they'd checked her out, sizing her up, looking for flaws. But she was exquisite, exuding a potent vibe—in the way she walked, even the way her hair bounced—that was a perfect mixture of purity and naughtiness. She was fire and ice, heaven and hell, angel and devil. *This chick totally knows what she's doing*, they thought. *Ouch.* Emily now looked over at Will, who seemed to be off in his own world. He was driving hard and fast, the tires squealing.

After a few minutes, Natalie couldn't take the silence any longer.

"How was detention?" she asked

Will just kept driving, looking straight ahead.

"Hello?" she tried again. "You okay?"

"Yeah. Sure. Just got a lot on my mind," said Will.

I'll bet, thought Natalie, but she bit her tongue. She wanted to tell him she was sorry for spying. If they could just talk, she thought, everything would be okay. But Will's body language was clear. He was in no mood to talk to anyone just now, even her. Maybe especially her.

Pulling the car into the mansion's garage, Will got out and went immediately into his lab. The surveillance cameras showed that everything with April was status quo: no better, but no worse. He spent the next hour assembling weaponry.

At dinnertime a McComb's BBQ truck pulled up and delivered chicken, fries, slaw, and apple pie. They all sat at the big table in the dining room and chowed down. Emily was studying Rudy as he demolished a chicken wing.

"*Eeewww*. Was that a crunch? Are you eating the *bones*?" she exclaimed.

"Not all of them," said Rudy.

"Well, don't let me stop you. Eat it. Crunch the bones. Tell me, this chicken, does it taste like human?"

Rudy acted like he was thinking about it.

"Kinda . . ."

Emily made a face and nibbled at her apple pie.

Natalie noticed that Will had changed clothes and was wearing new jeans, a fresh T-shirt, and a new leather jacket. She tried to act like she hadn't noticed, but her eyes danced around nervously.

No wonder Natalie's freaking, Emily thought. Will looked hot. Any girl worth her Victoria's Secrets would throw herself at him with all she had.

Though she'd intended to play it cool and not pry, Natalie couldn't stop herself from blurting out, "What's with the new clothes?"

Will looked down at his clothes as though he was seeing them for the first time. "They're just clothes."

Emily nodded. *Riiiiight.*

Natalie tried on a smile. It didn't fit.

Will stood up. "I'm going out."

Natalie couldn't help but ask him, even though she already knew the answer, "Where to?"

"It's better if you don't know." He held up his cell phone. "Text me if anything comes up."

"Come on, man, tell us," said Rudy. "What's happening? Going someplace good?"

"You wouldn't like it. Stay in the house, Rudy, got it?"

"Yeah, sure, I got it," Rudy answered glumly. "I can while away the time playing *Demon Hunter*!" He laughed hysterically.

Emily rolled her eyes. What a dork.

Will jetted to his lab and armed himself. He was heading for the garage when he ran into Natalie. She was standing in the open garage doorway, waiting for him.

"Time out, Will. Lay it out for me. What's going on?"

Will just looked at her.

"It's that girl, isn't it?" said Natalie.

"Yeah," said Will. He glanced at his watch, impatient.

"I thought so," said Natalie, doing a lousy job of hiding her disappointment and anger.

"Natalie, it's not like that," said Will. "There's something about her. I've got to chase this down. I saw her the night I was tracking Rudy. And she drew something at school. I don't have time to explain it to you, but I think she knows something. And even if she doesn't, the place she's supposed to be tonight, I've got to get out there and poke around, stir things up. That's what I do. You know that."

Natalie was getting the idea that she just couldn't play the jealousy card with Will, ever. She had to take the high road. Be secure. Be strong. Even if she didn't feel that way. So she mustered a supportive smile. "Yeah, I know. No problem. Just . . . be safe."

He leaned toward her, then stopped himself. Instead of hugging or kissing her, he squeezed her hand. He turned to go.

"Will?"

He stopped.

"You'll text me, right? Let us know what's going on?"

"Sure. No problem."

She watched as he went into the garage and shut the door behind him. She stood and listened as he started up the Suzuki, heard the garage door opening, the powerful bike taking off down the driveway. She hated this, hated being the wimpy, jealous girlfriend. She knew she needed to back off. She had what she wanted for the time being: a text, a promised lifeline. But had she just gotten a *handshake* from the boy she loved more than life itself? Lifeline or no lifeline, suddenly she was confused and upset all over again. She worried that Will Hunter, the love of her life, was slipping away from her.

Chapter Thirteen: Dirty Martinis

Will pulled his Suzuki to the curb in front of the old Pioneer Building and parked. The rain was coming down in a fine mist, typical of Seattle. He got off the bike and glanced around. Though it was drizzling, the streets were still busy, people coming and going, the hoods on their REI parkas pulled up, hands dug into their pockets for warmth. Will walked down the sidewalk until he came to the J & M Hotel. It looked like any other brick building in Seattle, an old one built in 1889. The hotel was closed down now, as was the adjacent J & M Café. There were lights on in the café, but the front door was chain-locked and the neon signs were off.

Will could hear music thumping, so he moved around the corner to the alley. A couple of guys well over six feet tall stood sentry by the back door, and Will knew he'd found the entry to Rocco's party. He kept walking and then doubled back, watching as two groups of teens scooted into the alley and were granted entrance to the J & M by the goons. Will knew he could take the big fellas out in about two seconds, but he didn't want to cause a scene just yet. So he walked to the adjacent building, scaled the fire escape, and climbed to the rooftop. Then he made the jump over the alley and landed on the roof of the J & M. He moved over to the lone skylight.

Peering down into the J & M, he saw a hundred or so teens hanging out, drinking, smoking, flirting, dancing, trying to be cool. He saw that one of the corners of the old café was dark. Finding the corresponding corner on the roof, he took out a Flareblade, powered it up to high, and cut a hole in the tarpaper roof. The diameter of the hole was just wide enough to allow him to slip through. He sank a line into an exposed beam and silently lowered himself into the café. Take *that*, Spider-Man.

The music was a thumping death metal song by Correl Shames, the kind of stuff that made Will grind his teeth. He scanned the room and quickly zeroed in on his target: Loreli. She was wearing a short black leather skirt and black tights with some kick-ass steel-toed boots that looked like she'd got them off a telephone lineman. She was orbiting a table where a tall, muscular kid with spiked bleach-blonde hair and close-set eyes was holding court. The way everyone around him was deferring to him, Will knew this had to be Rocco Manelli. Girls would approach him and preen and strut. If he liked what he saw, he grabbed their wrists and stamped them. Loreli looked frustrated as, after she'd made her play, one of Rocco's buffers shook his head and escorted her to the bar, where she sat, defeated, on a stool. Will saw that the girls who had been stamped made their way through a door to another room.

Will looked again at Loreli and again he felt an incredible, magnetic pull unlike anything he'd ever felt before. It was like what he felt for Natalie, but it was somehow even more powerful, primal, and intense. He walked toward her and began to sweat. He didn't get it; he was always, *always* cool under pressure. Why was this so different?

He took the stool next to her. She swiveled and gave him a dirty look.

"What are *you* doing here?" *You*, like a dirty word, like he was a piece of trash.

"I want to talk."

"Talk all you want. Just don't expect me to listen." She started to slide off the stool, but Will grabbed her wrist. Her emerald eyes flashed angrily.

"Leave me alone."

"Tell me about the drawing."

She yanked her wrist way. Again Will was surprised at how strong she was. She shook her head and continued to stare at him.

"Are you always this freakin' rude?" she asked.

"Only when I need to be. How did you see it? What you drew?"

She sighed, then went limp and hung her head, letting her hair fall over her face. Will touched her wrist, gently this time.

"I'm sorry if I hurt you. I didn't mean to."

After a beat, she slowly raised her head and looked up at him with cold hard eyes. "You couldn't hurt me on your best day. Now do us both a favor and vamoose. Beat it. Scram."

"No way."

He could almost see the wheels turning in her head. How could she get rid of him? But what she said next was a surprise.

"Okay then. Buy me a drink." It wasn't a request.

Wary, Will signaled to the girl in black on roller skates behind the bar. She had aqua hair and a barbed-wire choker tattoo. Will set a Benjamin on the bar. The girl didn't blanch at the bill, just looked at Loreli.

"Two martinis, dirty," Loreli said.

While the roller-skate girl was building the martinis, Loreli swayed on her stool to the music. Will could smell her, and again he was drawn to her in a way that he didn't yet understand but was doing his best to process. Sure she was awesome-looking and had eyes you could leap right into, and she was fit and sensual and all that. But it was something more, *much* more. Something deeper. A real and potent connection. He longed to know what the source of his attraction to this girl was, and he was determined to find out.

The drinks came and Loreli reached over and grabbed one, lifting it to her lips and drinking it down in one long, protracted sip as she held Will's gaze. When she finished, she ate the olive and kept the toothpick in her mouth. Then she reached for the other drink and picked it up too.

"Oh, did you want one?" she asked.

"Not particularly," said Will.

"I think you do," she said, moving the glass to Will's lips. "Come on, don't make me drink alone. I'm not gonna tell you what you want to know if you're so rude you won't even drink with me."

To placate her, Will drank the martini. His phone vibrated while he was drinking and he slipped it out and glanced at it. It was Natalie. He put the phone back in his pocket and then turned to Loreli.

"Now tell me about the drawing."

She leaned close to whisper in his ear. Anyone watching would have thought she was flirting with him. But her voice was cold, harsh, and unambiguous.

"If you keep playing with fire, you're gonna get burned. *Hasta la vista*, baby." She slid off the stool and moved to the dance floor just as the song changed. The new song was crazy fast, and the singer, who sounded like she was being flayed, spewed out unintelligible yelps and grunts. The song drove Loreli wild and she undulated fluidly, her movements syncopated and alluring. She danced with an unbelievable style and intensity, and a few teens stopped and watched in unabashed admiration.

Will was mesmerized. What was it about this girl that pulled at him so strongly? Whenever he looked at her, he grew warm inside. Something about her was so right it scared him. He began to move closer to her when the martini hit him. It wasn't just dirty, he realized, it was spiked with some kind of drug. Will's head exploded in a kaleidoscope of images. It was raining rainbows, the colors splashing on his brain. His knees grew weak. He leaned against a column for support. He wiped his forehead. He was sweating profusely, sweat running into his eyes, stinging them.

Loreli danced on. Will looked down and the floor came rushing up at him. His cheek was on fire. He slowly realized that he'd fallen. He got up and stood on uncertain legs. Rocco Manelli got up from his table and left. Loreli followed.

Will had difficulty walking—his legs were like bags of sand—but he was in pursuit. He couldn't lose track of her now. As he awkwardly jostled his way across the dance floor, kids shoved him back and forth. He fell twice, and the second time he went down someone kicked him in the neck. Angry, he rose up to find the culprit, but the room was spinning. He had to keep moving. Though his vision was blurry, he finally made his way to the door Loreli had disappeared through. He pushed it open and was immediately set upon by two large boys wearing red face-paint and black scrubs.

"Well, what do we have here?" one of them said.

"I'm not sure, Doctor," said the other. "Anyone comes through this door and doesn't know the password, we're supposed to operate."

"So, butt wipe . . . what's the password?"

"Whatever you think you're going to do, I would seriously rethink it," said Will, standing his ground. But he was woozy, and the scrubs boys saw it.

"Sorry, wrong answer. Now we're gonna have to operate."

And operate they did. They took out tape-wrapped pipes and went at him. Will tried a defensive move, dropping down and attempting to kick their legs out from under them. But he was seriously impaired—his legs just wouldn't cooperate—and the "doctors" used the pipes to hammer him from the back and front. One of them hit his cell phone, and Will heard it crunch, dead. Whatever drug had been in the martini was so powerful that it rendered Will helpless. If he didn't do something, and fast, these two were going to crack open his skull and pound his brains out. With great effort, he yanked out a couple of Cloakers and flung them wildly. He got lucky. The Cloakers wrapped around the attackers and tightened, cinching them up like trussed turkeys. They toppled over, impotent and screaming in pain.

Will got up and lurched into the nearest bathroom—the women's room, as it turned out—and took out a nasal spray from one of his jacket pockets and administered it as fast as he could, spraying twice into each of his nostrils. Then he turned on the hot water full blast and sucked at least a gallon from the faucet as a girl in a wolf shirt just coming out of a stall stared at him incredulously. As she left in a huff, Will was still drinking. He guzzled down another gallon of hot water, then moved into a stall and relieved himself. From both ends. It was a world-class purge triggered by the nasal spray, and it flushed the toxic hallucinogen from Will's body in under a minute.

When he came out of the bathroom he picked up the pipes the "doctors" had used against him. He was angry and hurting badly, but he didn't have time to waste. They were still trussed up, so he knocked them out with two precise blows to their heads, and then released the Cloakers. Then he looked around. *There.* A hallway leading to a door. He was down it quickly. If Rocco's goons decided to put the hurt on Loreli, it wasn't going to be pretty. Will hoped he wasn't already too late. The door was locked. He unzipped a flap on his jacket and removed a Blaster Key, which he inserted into the lock. He ducked as the lock blew, then kicked open the door and was hit with a gust of cold air.

He didn't want to start pulling out weapons just yet, so he kept his Megashocker strapped to his calf. The hallway was dark, and he used the light from his watch to see. It was, of course, no ordinary watch, and the light it emitted could be considerable when he needed it. In addition to the light, the watch housed an ultra-thin, retractable, two-foot steel cable for choking and/or garroting, and it was loaded with three Phosphor-Shots, blasts tiny but strong enough to create a distraction—especially to demons, whose eyes were sensitive to bright lights.

Using the glow from his watch light, Will went down a wooden stairway, the old boards creaking under his weight. The handrails were worn smooth from years of use, and Will's brain was still foggy enough that he had to use one of the rails to steady himself. The air grew progressively more damp as he went down one story after another. *Descent.* A rat skittered past his feet. *Descent.* He heard voices echoing from below and kept moving. The voices grew louder. *Descent.* He heard a slap, and then another. Someone was getting smacked around and he had a pretty good idea who. At the bottom of the stairs he found himself in a brick tunnel. Time to get moving. He hurried toward the sound of voices. Was Loreli's voice one of them? He couldn't be sure. Whoever the girl behind one of the voices was, she was in great distress. He rushed forward, then switched his watch light to low as he approached another tunnel forking off to the right. Taking light footsteps, he approached the corner and reached down to unstrap his Megashocker.

The shedemons were up on First Avenue in a black Mercedes van that was rocking to the doom metal sounds of Dead Man's Throne. It was a custom van, trimmed with red leather and fitted with a mini-bar and a table for four, upon which sat a cache of crystal meth in boxes. Each dose of the drug was in a mini-baggie with a red falcon stamped on it. Every dealer had their own "brand," and this band of four shedemons called theirs Satan Dust. The shedemons were sparked, their eyes glazed, brains simmering in the toxic swamp that crank created when smoked. Two were texting on their phones, one was counting money, and the other would venture out onto the street to complete a delivery whenever an order was called in. The shedemons never worried about getting busted and weren't particularly motivated by the money they raked in. They were doing *his* work, distributing evil in the form of what they laughingly called "crankenstein."

They loaded the pipe with more white chunks, fired it up with a mini-blowtorch, and passed it around, sucking the smoke into their lungs. Their brains took off like jets. Sure, demons on sky rocks got the meth mouth and the face sores—because when you were jonesing you felt like things were crawling on your face and you had to claw at them—and the sallow skin and sunken eyes, just like humans. But sometimes the shedemons could make all those symptoms go away by calling upon *his* evil power, and they'd look normal or, even better, beautiful. It was so awesome to serve him. He was their everything. They had pledged their everlasting lives to him.

When they got the signal from below, the shedemons closed up shop, locked the van, and flew into an alley, where they stopped and popped a manhole cover, one of them lifting it out with a finger and flinging it aside like a paper plate. Smiling, eager for the hunt, and amped up for any action that came their way—and there was bound to be plenty of that—they dropped down into the darkness.

Rounding the corner, Will surprised a squat, muscular demonteen who was built like a fire hydrant and looked about as smart. He was standing in front of a huge old wooden door, blocking it. He had Loreli by the throat and was slapping her face.

"Rocco don't wanna see you! You don't got the mark! How many times I hafta slap your stupid face before you hear me?" he yelled. "You don't got the mark, you don't get in!"

Loreli was showing amazing cool in this situation. Even though she was being slapped, she showed no fear. She was surprised to see Will, surprised that he had recovered so swiftly and thoroughly from the drug. That wasn't supposed to happen.

The chunky kid saw that she was staring at something behind him, read her eyes, and whirled and dropped into an immediate crouch. He didn't even try to hide the fact that he was a full-blown demon, and he sprouted a stumpy tail as his claws extended. Growling like a rabid dog, he leapt. Will was still feeling the aftereffects of the drug, and though he tried to sidestep the beast, he wound up with the kid's massive jaw clamped into his shoulder.

"Ahhhhh!" Will screamed in pain. And he dropped the Megashocker. The beast relaxed his jaw like he was yawning, and Will rolled onto his side against the wall, bleeding.

"I hope you're ready to die," said the demon. As he said the words, his jaw grew massive, muscular, and his teeth became longer and sharper. He was in super-kill mode and was already doing his victory dance. He flexed and leapt again.

This time Will was able to move more quickly, and he jacked a Flareblade into the creep's neck. The beast howled with pain, but he wasn't going down yet, not by a long shot.

Will stood up as the creature rolled into the corner and yanked out the burning Flareblade. Will dove for his Megashocker but was caught off guard as the demon spit a stream of toxic puke, hitting Will on his temple. Will felt his flesh sizzling. The beast jumped on top of Will like a monstrous hound and was about to tear his head off when the tip of the Megashocker came crashing right through his skull. The demonteen froze in morbid realization of his fate, then dropped to the floor of the tunnel and shook, finally exploding into fiery demon dust.

Loreli stood over Will holding the Megashocker. She'd just killed the beast and looked surprisingly composed after the experience. Will got up and took the weapon from her.

"I think you just saved my life," he said. "Thanks."

"Don't mention it," said Loreli.

"Of course, it was the least you could do after spiking my martini."

"You were bothering me."

Will stared at her for a second, then turned to examine the huge door. "This door. Where does it lead and why do you want to go there so bad?" he asked.

"Again, none of your business."

But Will was just as relentless as she was. "It *is* my business. Look, that guy just morphed into a full-blown demon and you didn't even flinch. So I've got a hunch that you know a lot. I want answers. Like about that drawing. And I'm not going to stop asking. Get it? I'm not going away."

"You're going away sooner than you think," she said. Her eyes narrowed into mean slits as the tunnel filled with a cacophony of shrieks.

"They're coming," she said.

"Who?" asked Will.

"*Them*," she said. "I think you met them before. In Gas Works Park? When they almost killed you?"

Will turned toward the sound, which was growing louder.

Will held the Megashocker in one hand and jacked a Flareblade into the other. "I'm not afraid."

"Well, Braveheart, this is a lousy place to make a stand. It's too confined, for one thing, and it's their turf. Who knows how many more will join the party?"

"I told you, I'm not afraid," said Will.

"It's not about *fear*, you idiot, it's about having a tactical advantage. Now come on." Loreli reached into her purse and pulled out a small porcelain ball that she threw to the ground. The tunnel erupted with a blinding flash, then filled with an orange gas as Loreli grabbed Will and yanked him down a long brick corridor and into a room. With shrieks and howls and coughing echoing behind them, Will and Loreli climbed a series of iron rungs until they reached the top, where Will shouldered open a heavy iron hatch. They climbed up through it and slammed it shut behind them. They stood up. They were in an alley. Loreli looked around.

"Where's your ride?" she asked. "We have got to get out of here, like, now."

Will wanted to stay and fight, but he was dying to know more about Loreli. He figured he'd learn more by going along with whatever she had in mind than by hunkering down and engaging in a splatterfest with the shedemons. But he was still wary.

"You're asking a lot, for me to trust you after you poisoned me."

She shrugged. "You wouldn't leave me alone. And anyway, you seem to be fine now. So is your ride nearby or not?"

Do-or-die time. Will made up his mind.

"This way," he said.

They ran down the alley, across the street, and in ten more seconds they were on his Suzuki. Loreli held on tight as Will throttled the bike through Pioneer Square.

"Up King Street!" she yelled.

Will complied, and the Suzuki blasted through the night like a bullet on wheels. Loreli clung to Will as the wind and rain whipped her hair.

"Where are we going?" he shouted.

"My place," she yelled back, her breath hot at his ear. Her body was jammed up against his and Will was puzzled by what he felt. She was muscular and had some heavy-duty core strength. He flashed on the thought that she might actually be a demon. If she was, he could be dead in two seconds. All she'd have to do was drive a fist through his back and claw out his heart. *Oh well*, thought Will, *so much for enjoying the ride.*

They shot onto the freeway and headed north, exiting on 45th Street and cruising up to 35th, where Loreli told Will to take a left. They drove for several more blocks until she told him to pull over. They were right in front of the entrance to the Calvary Cemetery. It had a nice view of Mount Rainier on a clear day, but the night was anything but clear as thick fog from Puget Sound continued to roll in, crawling over the high walls that surrounded the burial grounds.

"You live in a cemetery?" Will asked, turning with raised eyebrows. "Why am I not surprised?"

"Not *in* it, next to it. Right over there," she said, pointing to a modest, three-bedroom, drab brick house. "But I know this place well. And if we're going to fight, which is likely to happen any second now, I want it to be on *my* turf."

"You think they followed us?"

"No 'think' about it," she said.

"Then go inside your house and lock the doors. It's not going to be safe for you out here."

"I've got news for you, buddy," Loreli said, rolling her eyes. "It's *never* safe for me, no matter where I am. Feel free to take off."

"I'm not leaving," Will said.

"Well, if I can't get rid of you, then come on, we're gonna have to throw down pretty soon," she said, getting off the bike and slipping through a hedge.

"Wait!" called Will, but she didn't turn around, and he had no choice but to hop off his bike and follow her. Ducking down, he slid through the hedge, and then through the narrow opening in the wall she'd passed through. Once inside, his eyes swept over the cemetery, and he saw, through the thickening fog, the jagged, uneven phalanx of headstones, box tombs, hatchments, spires, and crosses. Some were jutting out at odd angles, others leaning from time. Most were marble, but some were made of concrete or sandstone. Loreli was nowhere to be seen. Will read a nearby headstone.

Behold and see as you pass by
As you are now, so once was I
As I am now, you soon must be
Prepare to die and follow me.

Not terribly comforting, thought Will. *And I don't intend to follow you just yet.* He called out for Loreli. "Where are you?"

"Here," came her voice, from a few feet away.

He spotted her and walked over to a large ornate tomb where she was kneeling. The tomb was a ghastly thing, replete with gargoyles, in "honor" of the Maggeti family. Loreli was on her knees in the tomb, removing objects from beneath a slab of marble she'd displaced.

"Planning on exhuming someone?" asked Will.

"Don't worry, I'm not a grave robber or anything," she said, arranging the objects on a scarf. Will looked down at what she'd retrieved: a collection of vials of liquid and a half-dozen small porcelain balls. They were beautiful, like Christmas ornaments.

"What are you, some kind of Wiccan?" asked Will.

"A witch? Don't be insulting. I am much, much more than some ordinary witch."

"Okay, then what are you?"

Loreli's lips formed a tight smile, and she was about to answer—until the night's silence was abruptly cleaved by a shrill keening. "Here we go," she said. "Party time."

Will grabbed her by the shoulders. He'd seen her go up against them before, but if these were her weapons, his chances—now that the drug had finished passing out of his system—were much better than hers. "Do what I said and go into your house. I'll take care of them. That's what I do."

"Good to know you have such a high opinion of yourself. It's going to come in handy, because these bitches are *nasty*. We'll have a better chance if we split up. If they happen to cut you open and rip your heart out, well, it was nice knowing you."

With that, she scooped up her accouterments and took off behind the tomb.

The shedemons, led by Blue Streak, had just arrived in their van. After smoking crystal meth for half the night, their hearts were banging like Formula One pistons and they were jacked up and ready to kill. They leapt over the cemetery wall and landed soundlessly on the damp grass, the whites of their eyes glowing. Just as they had in Gas Works Park, they spread out, moving like ghosts as they slipped in and out of the thickening fog, ducking behind tombstones as they crept ever closer to Will and Loreli. Blue Streak whistled and chirped orders, hanging back and watching like a general overseeing the battle.

Since he didn't want to be sliced and diced like he had during his first encounter with these merciless creatures, Will had taken the precaution of wearing his protective composite under armor, which he'd designed himself. It was a metal-like fabric, a composite of Nomex, Kevlar, and microscopic threads of titanium. He would be much harder to cut tonight. Maybe if he got lucky, one of them would break a nail and have a terminal hissy fit.

Two of the shedemons came swooping down out of the trees overhead, their talon-like nails extended. *Fightin' Falcons, indeed*, thought Will as he tucked and rolled under a marble bench, a defensive move that caused the shedemons to shriek and hover above him, slashing uselessly at the marble. Rolling onto his back, Will used his all his leg strength to kick the stone top, propelling it up so that it slammed into the duo, knocking them backward and out of the air. They landed on their backs on the ground a few feet away.

Will jumped up, and with one smooth motion threw four Series 301 Taser Darts—two with each hand—at the shedemons, who were just springing back up. One ducked, completely eluding the 301s, then bounded back up into the trees. But the other took a dart right in her forehead. As the taser did its work, she shimmied like a freaky Halloween prop, her whole body convulsing as her eyes rolled back in her head and her howls of agony filled the night. When she toppled over, Will rushed to her body. He wanted her alive: he had questions, *lots* of questions. The shedemon knew this, and when her eyes opened she tried to spit a toxic stream at Will, but he was expecting it, and ducked. Then he quickly zipped the tiny steel wire from his watch and wrapped it around the creature's neck, ready to behead her.

"The Dark Lord," he demanded. "Where is he? Tell me and I might let you live."

She was gagging and her voice was raspy as she screeched her response. "I don't *want* to live!"

The shedemon spit at him again; he caught a bit on his scalp and it burned. The pain angered him, and he allowed the red rage to flood through his body. It amped up his strength, and his muscles expanded and became more powerful. He tightened the wire around the shedemon's neck.

Will didn't see the next move coming. With her last bit of strength she pulled out a shiv and stabbed it into her own heart! Blood spurted from her chest. Will let her go and stood up, watching as she chanted a demon death mantra—some gibberish about being with *him* now—and then disintegrated in a shower of sparks.

Will heard a scream and whipped around. *Loreli.* Visibility was terrible; the fog was like a dull gray blanket draped over the cemetery. But he could make out Loreli's form forty yards to the west, moving from headstone to headstone, ducking down as shedemons lunged at her. One used a lance axe to rake at Loreli, but she was fast on her feet. Even so, she just barely avoided getting her head lopped off. The other threw a pipe chain, which hit its mark, wrapping around Loreli's neck. She went down hard. A third had a Bowie knife out and was advancing, clearly planning to behead her. Will's red rage flared up and he bent time and ran toward them, traversing the forty yards in two seconds, arriving just in time to whip out his Megashocker and drill Knife Girl in the ear. She went down shrieking in pain.

Loreli shot a quick look at Will, acknowledging that he'd just saved her. Then she uncapped one of her vials and slung the contents at the other attackers. The liquid seared their flesh with a sickening sizzling sound. Screaming loud enough to raise the dead, they lurched into backward airborne somersaults and, like wounded birds, took refuge in a towering Douglas fir tree. One of them was so badly wounded that she was unable to retain her balance and toppled out of the tree, landing head-first on a spire and impaling her brain. She shuddered and spewed blood until her body glowed yellow and then crumbled into glass dust.

His pulse racing, Will knelt to help Loreli. The red rage was ruling him now. He knew he should be scanning the cemetery for his enemies, but he was succumbing to a vortex of anger. He wasn't sure he trusted Loreli, but he did know it filled him with fury to think of her getting hurt.

Loreli whipped the chain pipe from around her neck. Will helped her to her feet.

"Are you okay?" he asked.

"Don't worry about me! Just focus on—"

Loreli didn't get a chance to finish her sentence. The other she-demon swooped down from above holding a headstone, which she flung at Will. He ducked, but the corner of the stone clipped the side of his head, tearing a nasty gash in his ear. He fell to the ground, his head exploding in stars. Two shedemons attacked immediately, and Will rolled over in time to see Loreli battling both of them in hand-to-hand combat. She was wielding a double-headed dagger and was awesomely fast. Will's brain swirled with confusion. He wondered again if Loreli was a demon herself and this skirmish was some kind of internecine battle.

The two shedemons managed to disarm Loreli and pounced on her like cats, their crimson fingernail talons extended. Clearing his mind, Will jumped up and grabbed one of them by her hair and yanked as hard as he could. The shedemon was strong but couldn't have weighed more than a hundred pounds. She went flying backward and her head slammed into a tree. Knocked senseless, she dropped lifelessly to the ground.

The other monster was swiping at Loreli, who was deflecting the blows expertly. But the shedemon was fueled by meth, her brain buzzing with madness, and, snarling, she used her jagged incisors to bite into Loreli's forearm. Loreli screamed. Will swung at the she-demon but she ducked, turned, and kicked him backward. He flew against a headstone. It knocked the wind out of him.

Sucking air, Will watched as Loreli regrouped, exploding one of the porcelain balls on the ground at the feet of her attacker, who was instantly engulfed in a cloud of blue smoke. Loreli grabbed the she-demon's throat as her eyes bulged out. With four swift kicks, Loreli brought the shedemon to her knees.

Will was in awe. Who *was* this girl? *She* must *be a demon*, he thought. *She has to be!* It's not like he'd never seen demons fighting each other before. They did it for sport. But then why hadn't Loreli attacked him? He watched as Loreli used her dagger to gore the shedemon in the eyes. The creature brayed in disbelief and pain before toppling sideways and exploding into tiny fragments of light.

Loreli looked at Will, eyes blazing with fury and the dagger held in a throwing position. She must have realized he'd found her out. She was wicked fast, and he knew she could sling the deadly blade at him in a millisecond. So he whipped out a Taser Dart and threw it sidearm at her, nailing the dagger, knocking it from her hand. She glared at him.

"Not a good move, Will!" she shouted, then broke a wrought-iron spire off a tomb and hefted it like a javelin. She had a crazy look in her eyes now, like she was looking not at him, but right through him. He knew she was going to throw the spire.

"No!" he shouted. But she flung the spire at him with all her might. It whistled as it cut through the air. With time-bending speed, he dropped flat on the ground as the spire rocketed past him, coming so close it sliced his right cheek.

The red rage swept through him and he leapt to his feet and flew at Loreli, knocking her backward and pinning her on the ground as he yanked out a Flareblade.

"You're one of them! You tricked me! You lured me here to kill me! But it didn't work out so well for you, did it?"

She was astonishingly, disarmingly calm.

"Will . . . look behind you."

Will looked back and saw the remaining shedemon impaled on a tree, writhing in death. She must have snuck up behind him armed with a chop sword and been about to behead him when Loreli had thrown the spire.

It was clear that Loreli's throw hadn't been meant for him after all. But he'd seen the malice in her eyes, seen her move insanely fast. He knew she wasn't human.

Will saw movement to his left. Blue Streak was jumping the wall, fleeing the scene. He heard the van start up and peel out.

He turned to Loreli. "This proves nothing!" said Will. "So you sacrificed one of your own. I know your kind. Your cruelty is sickening. Tell me where the Dark Lord is, and I promise I'll kill you quickly."

"You don't want to kill me, Will Hunter."

"Oh really?" said Will, moving the Flareblade to within an inch of the soft flesh of her neck. "And why not?"

Loreli smiled. "Because I'm your sister."

Chapter Fourteen:
Sibling Rivalry

On the top floor of the mansion, Natalie paced, nervous as a cat on ice. She peered longingly out the window, replaying the conversation she'd had with Will earlier.

It's that girl, isn't it?

Yeah.

I thought so.

It's not like that.

Natalie had run a gamut of emotions with Will Hunter in the time she'd known him; she'd practically been to Hell and back with him. But this was different. *That girl* made Natalie want to scream. Just the thought of her green eyes made Natalie's brain feel like it was wrapped in rubber bands that were growing tighter with every tick of the clock. Her nerves were so jangled she was ready to hit something. When Emily approached her from behind, she jumped.

"Emily, you scared me! Why are you sneaking up on me?"

"I'm not. Nat, what's wrong?"

Biting a fingernail, Natalie said, "Will's out looking for that girl, from detention. But he said he would text me. And it's been hours!"

She looked out the window for the thousandth time, her eyes hungry for the sight of Will. But all she saw was darkness and rain. This was torture.

"If he said he'll text you, he will. Don't worry," said Emily.

Don't worry. Natalie had repeated those very words to herself over and over, trying to hammer them into her brain. But they just wouldn't take. She would try to calm herself with her inner voice— *He'll be fine; he's strong and he knows what he's doing*—but in her brain she saw devastating images. Like on a movie screen she saw Will with Miss Green Eyes, touching her, holding her. Then she saw him surrounded by demons, fighting for his life—and losing. The fear was strong and it was in control. There was nothing that Natalie could do *except* worry.

"It's going to be okay, Nat," said Emily.

"How do you *know* that? How do you know *anything*?" Her fear was making her crazy.

Emily winced and her eyes filled with tears. Natalie immediately regretted her words.

"Oh, crap. I'm sorry, Em. I'm just . . . not myself. I hate waiting. This is just not like him." But Natalie knew this wasn't true; it was *exactly* like him. He'd always been mysterious and often seemed to be distancing himself from her both physically and emotionally. And who could blame him? He had the future of the world on his shoulders.

She needed to stop thinking so much; she needed to clear her head. But fear prodded her again, the worry like a rash on her skin. What if something had happened to him? What if he wasn't texting her because he was hurt, because he couldn't move, because he was near death? She couldn't pace back and forth in front of this window any longer. She wasn't the kind of person who could just sit back and let life deal her the cards she'd have to play. She dealt her own damn cards. She had to do *something*. She pushed past Emily and walked into Will's room.

"Where are you going?" Emily asked.

The keys to the BMW were on his dresser. Natalie picked them up.

"I'm going for a drive. You coming?"

Emily bit her lower lip. As much as she feared cruising around the city in the middle of the night without Will, the notion of sending Natalie out there alone was worse.

"I'll get my coat."

Will was still in shock, still trying to process what had just happened, as Loreli unlocked the front door of her mother's house and led him inside.

"I think you've got some explaining to do," he said.

"Food first. You want something to eat?" she asked.

"No, I'm fine," he said, looking around. The place was depressingly ordinary, and somewhat unkempt, another unremarkable middle-class house with drab furniture and dull walls. All the slat blinds were closed and the house had a faint chemical smell about it. The sound of a TV played lightly from somewhere, but other than that the house felt unoccupied.

Will followed her into the kitchen and was pleasantly surprised to find that, unlike the rest of the house, it was sparkling clean and brimming with life, the counters jammed with appliances—coffee maker, food processor, toaster—and bowls of fruit and jars of nuts. Loreli reached into the refrigerator.

"Suit yourself, but I'm famished. A little kick-ass like that always makes me hungry." She pulled out half a pan of cake, cut a generous piece for herself, and took a huge bite. Will's stomach growled. He eyed the cake.

"What is that?"

"Apple pudding cake. Old family recipe."

Will could smell the cinnamon. "On second thought, maybe I'll have a bite."

They polished off the cake and drank a quart of ice-cold milk. Then Loreli grabbed a can of V8 from the fridge and left the kitchen. Will followed. They made their way down a hallway and into the TV room, where a middle-aged woman was curled in a papasan chair and covered with an afghan. *Family Feud* was on TV. The woman's eyes were closed and she was snoring raggedly. On the small table next to her were two empty 750ml bottles of Stoli and an ashtray overflowing with butts. The woman stirred as Loreli took the bottles and set the can of V8 down in their place, then emptied the ashtray. Opening her eyes, the woman looked blankly up at Will. She opened her mouth to speak, but no words found their way out.

"Mom, this is Will, a . . . friend from school. Will, this is my mom, Tanya."

"Nice to meet you," said Will. Tanya said nothing, but shifted in the chair and reached for a bottle. When she saw that she'd grabbed a V8, a complaint bubbled up inside her. But then her stomach told her she needed something other than alcohol, so she drank the juice. Then she lit a cigarette. When she spoke, it was nearly a whisper.

"Thanks, honey."

"No prob, Mom. We're gonna go do some homework." Tanya was obviously too out of it to realize it was so late at night.

Loreli signaled to Will and he followed her out. She led him down a flight of wooden stairs into a musty basement filled with books, cardboard boxes, paint cans, garden tools, and other junk. She moved to an antique wooden armoire with an oval mirror on the front. She swung open the doors, pushed aside some hanging clothes, and stepped inside.

"You coming or not?" she asked Will as she disappeared.

He followed her into the armoire. The back had been cut out, so the armoire was actually a doorway to another, secret room. Loreli's lair.

Will stepped in and was immediately taken aback by the size of the room, which was considerable, perhaps fifty feet square. Clearly she'd had some construction done to the original floorplan of the house. The walls were lined with shelves, stacked with canisters and bottles and beakers filled with a bounty of colorful powders, liquids, and herbs. A central workbench held microscopes and Bunsen burners, scales, and myriad other chemist's tools. A bank of computers hummed, and Will's game, *Demon Hunter*, was alive on one of the monitors. He stepped over to the station and touched the keyboard. An avatar he recognized—the green fox—popped up, and his spine tingled.

"You're Jade16." He shook his head slowly with the realization.

"The one and only," said Loreli proudly.

"You've been kicking ass. You're amazing at it. Off-the-charts good."

"What do you expect? I told you, I'm your sister."

Will's eyes continued to explore the room. There were crystals and feathers in abundance, and aquariums stocked with exotic-looking fish, and terrariums full of snakes, frogs, salamanders, and lizards. There were also cages holding mice and one that was home to a black-footed ferret. The ferret padded back and forth in his cage, his suspicious eyes never leaving Will.

"Hey, Sebastian, how's it goin'?" Loreli smiled at the ferret, then opened the cage and pulled him out. The little guy immediately ran up her arm and perched on her shoulder. It barked a tiny, high-pitched bark at Will.

"He's okay, Sebastian. You don't have to claw his eyes out. At least not right now."

"Thanks for the vote of confidence," said Will.

"You're welcome. Just don't mess with him. He can be mean if he wants to be."

"You mean if *you* want him to be." Will eyed Sebastian warily. Not exactly a demon-level threat, but Will wasn't exactly keen to get into a tussle with a feisty little carnivorous mammal.

"He sleeps eighteen hours a day," she said. "But when he's awake he's kinda perky. He loves to play. Hey Sebastian, you wanna play hidey-seek?"

Sebastian's head bobbed up and down and he chattered loudly. Then he hopped off Loreli's arm right at Will, landing on his shoulder and using it as a launching pad to spring onto an overhead pipe. He scrambled down the length of the pipe and then jumped down behind some wooden barrels, then darted around on the floor, looking for the optimum hiding place. Will heard him skittering around but couldn't see him.

"He's not going to leap out and claw me, is he?" asked Will.

"Not unless you make a threatening move toward me."

Will saw a dish of small white balls on the lab counter and picked one up.

"Um, unless you want to see spots for the rest of the night, that puppy is something you will want to set down verrrry carefully," said Loreli.

Will thought following her advice would be prudent, so he set the small white sphere down gently.

"It's a simple flash orb," said Loreli. "Here, put these on." She handed him some dark goggles and put on a pair herself.

Will put the goggles on, then Loreli picked up one of the orbs and tossed it hard onto the concrete floor, where it detonated, causing a powerful blast of white-hot light that filled the room for a full five seconds. Even though he was wearing the goggles, Will had to close his eyes, and even then he had spots floating.

"Very nice," he said. "And you use these to . . . ?"

"Incapacitate demons, of course," she said. "Sometimes you need a little time to maneuver, you know?"

"Yeah, I know. But the question is, how do *you* know? And exactly why is it that you think you're my . . . sister?"

Loreli picked up a pinch of blue powder and tossed it above a candle. A little blue cloud formed, and within it, he could see tiny bolts of lightning.

"It's not complicated, Will. I'm just like you. The Dark Lord is my father, too."

Bang. There it was. And she said it so casually, when he still had trouble even thinking it.

Will thought back to watching her move around. He knew that she was different. But he also knew that she could be a demon pulling some elaborate ruse. Narrowing his eyes, he laid a couple of moves on her, attempting some half-speed hand chops that a normal human being would never be able to block—but a demon, or half-demon, would. Loreli blocked his chops easily.

"I see you don't believe me. You want to test me. Okay."

Loreli did a standing backflip, grabbed an overhead pipe, and kicked Will across the room.

He flew through the air and *wham!*—slammed into the far wall, breaking the plaster. Sebastian yelped and zipped out from behind a chair.

But Will wasn't finished. He leapt up and, time-bending, sprang across the room and flew at Loreli, tackling her. She squirmed out of his grasp quickly, rolled to her left, and kicked him in the back. When he hit the wall it knocked a beaker from a shelf. The beaker hit the floor and shattered, spilling yellow liquid on some ants, which started to grow larger and glow and pulsate.

"Oooookay! Now look what you've done," said Loreli. She swept the glowing ants into a bottle, sealed it, and then turned to Will. "Do you mind if we take this outside?"

The backyard was dominated by four towering pines, their graceful tops swaying in the wind. One of the trees had a couple of swings hanging from a branch. A light rain had begun to fall. Coming out through the back door, Loreli turned and issued a simple challenge: "See if you can catch me, brother."

In a flash she was up the tree, climbing like a leopard. Will jumped after her, and the chase was on. She moved like lightning, and as Will clawed his way to the top he saw that she'd already leapt to another, taller tree. As he turned, she sprang down and kicked his shoulders, knocking him backward. He fell to the ground and felt a sharp pain as the air huffed out of his lungs. He gasped for a moment, watching in awe as up above Loreli jumped from tree to tree, swinging. Her speed and agility were astonishing. Catching his breath, Will jumped up and scrambled up the tree. He gave her a bit of her own medicine as he anticipated her next jump and vaulted ahead of her. They fought hand to hand, not with lethal blows, just showing off their moves. *She's good*, thought Will. Then *wham!* He took one in the face. *Okay, she's better than good*, he thought. *She's great.*

Will was flummoxed. She was quite possibly his sister, and most definitely a girl, so he wasn't quite sure just how to treat her in a fight like this. While he was considering this, she kicked him off the top of the tree, and as he fell he hit four branches, cracking through two and bouncing off the others, finally righting himself just as she landed next to him after swooping down like Batgirl or something. She seemed to love sparring with him and fought with a wry smile on her face, like a fierce ninja with wild green eyes.

He was staring at her when she caught him with a lightning-fast kick to the side of his head. It was a hard enough hit that he felt the red anger surging inside him. He dove at her, but she'd anticipated his move and leapt straight up onto the next branch.

"Getting a little pissed off?" she taunted.

She broke off the branch next to her and swung down, and as Will ducked she dropped past him and did a mid-air twist, kicking him again before landing on the branch below.

He kneecap was throbbing. Still seeing red, he jumped down after her, swinging twice. She ducked both, and his fists slammed into the trunk of the tree. She made a clucking sound and laughed, and the skirmish continued. Will's red curtain lifted, and he finally began to get the best of her, feinting left and high, then punching her low and kicking her off a branch. She fell backward and he time-bent to the max and swooped down and caught her. As he put her down, she exhaled.

"Thanks for catching me, bro. You saved me a world of pain. I'd like to return the favor, but—" She faked a punch and he fell for it, and she caught him on the chin with her elbow, laying him out. He blinked up at her and she extended a helping hand.

"Okay, I get it," he said, accepting it. "You're amazing."

"You threw down some pretty cool moves yourself. But you're a hothead. You let your anger take over sometimes."

That struck a chord with Will, but he didn't want to acknowledge it so he stared off into the distance.

"Did I hit a nerve?" Loreli asked.

When Will didn't answer, she pressed him.

"Do you ever wonder about stuff? Like . . . since you're half human and half . . . *him*, which half is really running the show?"

Will didn't want to admit that that very question had been tormenting him for weeks, ever since the battle in Mount St. Emory. When he was younger, he knew he had an amazing capacity for violent rage but he had no idea where it came from. After he found out he was the son of the Dark Lord, it all made sense. But knowing where it came from didn't solve his problems. Every time he felt that red curtain or rage descend over his mind, he worried that someday it might take over entirely.

"Why are you trying to make me talk about this?" he said. He was angry now, and it showed.

"Oh, I don't know," she said. "Maybe because I'm your sister and I haven't had anybody to talk to about this stuff before?"

She suddenly looked vulnerable, like she had feelings, too. Will softened.

"Okay, I get it. Yeah, I wonder about my dark side. How about you?"

She didn't hesitate, but just let it right out. "Not a day goes by that I don't think about who I am and what I am and where I really belong."

They stood in contemplative silence for a few moments, and then Loreli went in to get some ice packs and drinks. Will sat on one of the swings. A moment later she was back with the packs and cokes, and they drank sitting on the swings while they iced their bruises. The trees provided a thick canopy so they were out of the rain. Will noticed a nasty scrape on her neck and pulled out a small healing patch.

"Try this," he said.

"What is it?" she said, pulling back.

"Just a healing patch." When she just eyed it warily, he said, "Fine. Bleed, scar, maybe get an infection, see if I care."

She accepted the patch.

"So, after that little game in the trees, I think we've safely established that you're not your average female homo sapien," Will said while she was putting it on her neck.

"I'll take that as a compliment," she said.

Loreli finished her coke and crumpled the can in her fist, crushing it like an NFL linebacker. Then she looked at him for a minute. "You wanted to know about the drawing?"

"Uh-huh."

"Okay. I was there, in art class, in front of the easel, and my hand just . . . started moving. I sort of blacked out standing there. The next thing I knew, you were standing right beside me, freaking out."

"That's because that image, that *exact same image*, the one you drew, with him lying on that altar . . . it was in a dream I had. It looked like he was dead."

"I had the same dream. He was just lying there, not moving."

They thought about this for a moment. Then Loreli spoke. "But he's not dead, is he?"

"No." Will felt the pain welling up inside him. "My mother's in a coma," he told her. "His . . . spirit came and took her. Not her body, but what's left of her mind, her consciousness. I'm going to find him and I'm going to kill him and bring back my mother."

"Finding and killing the Dark Lord isn't going to be easy."

Will's eyes flashed with anger. "Nothing in my life has been *easy*." He took a deep breath, calming himself. "Just like nothing in yours has been, probably. Look, if you really are my sister, meaning you have . . . *him* as your father, then you gotta tell me . . . how did it happen?"

"Pushy," she said, but she was smiling a little bit.

"I'm going to get more than pushy if you don't start laying it out for me."

"I'll tell you on two conditions," she said. "First, you must swear on your blood never to reveal my secret to anyone. And that means *anyone*. Best friends, girlfriends, parents, whatever. What I tell you—and what I've already told you—remains a *secret*, guaranteed. I want a lock on this."

"You're in no position to make demands," said Will.

"I'm in the perfect position to make demands," she said. "I can reach into my pocket and pull out an orb and blow you up any time I want to. Plus, I'm the one with the information you want to know."

Will shook his head. "Okay, fine, relax. Secrecy guaranteed."

"Swear on your blood?"

"I swear on my blood. It's a lock."

"Good. Now for the second condition. You gotta go first. You have to tell me about how it happened with *you*."

Will thought for a long time, but couldn't come up with any downside to being honest with her. And so he told Loreli all about how, at the ripe old age of eight, he'd had a rite of passage like no other: how his father Edward had shown him an ancient book and instructed him not to open it until he turned thirteen. And how that same fateful night the Dark Lord had arrived in a violent storm and kidnapped his father and burned his house down. He told her how, when he turned thirteen, he decoded the ancient book and learned that it was his fate to be a Demon Hunter, and how he'd spent years tracking the Dark Lord from school to school, only to finally be led into the beast's trap for a fateful ceremony in the bowels of Mount

St. Emory. It was there, in the demon world's sacred underground cathedral, that he'd learned that the Dark Lord was his father and that he intended for Will to rule the underworld by his side.

Loreli listened as he told the whole story, nodding occasionally in sympathy. He'd had an amazing and painful life. When he was finished, she spoke softly, reverently.

"I'm sorry he killed your dad, Will. I mean, your adoptive dad. But what you did down in that cavern is already a legend. I mean, that's how I found out about you. When you put the squeeze on them, demons sometimes talk. And every demon on Earth and beyond knows how you turned the Dark Lord down, how his own son not only shunned him, but defeated him in battle. I didn't really believe it until I heard you tell the story just now. What you did down there . . . it was amazing."

"It was my only choice."

"Don't be modest. It wasn't your only choice. You could have gone over to the dark side and ruled a kingdom. It was a difficult choice. But I would have made the same one."

A few minutes of silence passed as they watched the misty rain drifting down out of the sky and listened to it pattering as it hit the clogged gutters. Loreli sighed, then pushed off with her feet and swung.

"At least you *had* a father, even though he wasn't your blood. Me, I never had anything like that. All I've ever had is my mom, and, as you saw, she didn't fare too well from going through what she went through and having me. She turned to the bottle a long time ago, and I can't say that I blame her. She needs to be medicated, one way or another."

"How did she . . ." Will's voice trailed off. But Loreli knew what he was asking.

"Her mom, my grandma, grew up poor as dirt in the hills of Mississippi. The men were moonshiners, and when Grandpa got killed in a feud, there just wasn't any way out of those hills except for one. When my mom came of age, Grandma took her down to New Orleans and shopped her around. She took her from brothel to brothel, and then sold her to the highest bidder. That was all they knew; there wasn't any other way. At least, that's the way the family used to tell it when they were alive. So my mom worked as a 'lady of pleasure'—that's the polite way of saying it—and sent money home whenever she could. Grandma cried every night, but the family had food.

"While the other 'working' girls spent their earnings on clothes and jewelry and Southern Comfort, my mom saved all of hers. She was going to quit, run away back home. In fact, the dark deed happened the very night that she was going to give up the life."

Will looked at Loreli, and for a moment he didn't see the kick-ass femme warrior but a young Southern girl who'd suffered a world of hurt. She continued.

"That night, the Prince of Darkness came to the house of ill repute near Bourbon Street, looked over every single girl, and chose Mom. Bought and paid for her for the entire evening, and then did what he wanted to do. Mom knew he wasn't an ordinary man, and afterward she was sick inside—not just in her stomach, but in her soul. When she found out she was pregnant, she went for an abortion, but the Dark Lord showed up at the clinic in the form of a mad bomber. As the building burst into flames, Mom took it as a sign that she should reconsider the procedure. She went home to the hills and Grandma, and suffered through a long and painful pregnancy. Finally, on Halloween night, she gave birth to me. The Dark Lord must have been watching, and I guess he wanted a boy, because the skies opened like crazy that night and the rain washed our entire hillside clean away. It was a miracle that we walked away with our lives."

"I'm sorry," Will said

"Sorry?"

"It's a hell of a life, if you'll pardon the pun."

"It's better than no life."

Will nodded thoughtfully. He was inclined to agree with her, except for the fact that being half demon and having pledged his life to destroying evil and exacting revenge on his biological father—who just happened to be the Devil—kind of put a damper on the whole "happiness" thing. It was a fact that had been hitting him harder and harder lately, between what happened to his mother and knowing he had to send Natalie away. Happiness? That wasn't part of Will Hunter's destiny. There was only one moment when he could picture himself happy: the moment when he was driving a stake through the Dark Lord's heart.

He asked Loreli, "All the chemistry stuff you do—"

"Alchemy," she said.

". . . how did you learn it?"

"I guess I was just born with it. When other little girls were playing with Barbies and Beanie Babies, I was mixing stuff up in the basement. I once made a bomb out of Dr Pepper and blew a hole in Mindy Carpetta's leg. She was my best friend. Well, she *was*, until that little incident."

A tiny smile crept onto Will's face but didn't linger.

Loreli continued. "Anyway, I'm kind of a prodigious reader, and I just have this unreal capacity for retention, for learning stuff. When I was eight, some brainless zombie—a demon wannabe, you know—somehow found out about my lineage and started harassing me. He'd crawl out of his grave every night at midnight and come looking for me. He'd claw his way up the cottonwood tree next to our house and stare in at me through my window and whisper his stupid curses, thinking he was cool because he was one of the undead. Any other eight-year-old girl would have screamed her lungs out, but me? I was never afraid of stuff like ghosts and zombies and monsters under the bed and all that. I guess being half demon helps.

"Anyway, I got tired of his nocturnal visits, so one night I slipped out and followed him back to his grave just before sunrise. Once I knew where he was buried, I built these little bombs made out of bleach and gasoline and some other stuff. Then I went into the cemetery one night—this wasn't here, this was when we lived in Callahan County in Texas—and when he woke up and started crawling out of his grave, I let him have it. That zombie lit up like a roman candle and screeched like a skinned cat, and as I watched him, I felt such a powerful sense of purpose, such satisfaction, knowing I'd ridden the earth of an evil being. It was a rush, let me tell you, and right there and then I knew I'd found my calling. I've spent most of my life since learning my . . . trade."

"From what I've seen, you've learned it well."

"Thanks. One of these days my skills are going to help me fulfill my ultimate quest."

"And what's your ultimate quest?" asked Will.

Loreli's eyes flashed with anger. "To kill the beast who raped my mom, rejected me, and then left us both to die. I'm going to kill the Dark Lord."

Will nodded. "Well, just in case you don't already have enough motivation, there is one other thing," he said.

"What's that?"

"He might have a sword."

"So? That's no big deal."

"Yeah, well . . . it might not be just some ordinary sword. It might be the Sword of Armageddon."

"That doesn't sound good."

"Yeah, I didn't think so either."

They kept talking through the night, exchanging stories of their bizarre childhoods and troubling teenage years. They were outcasts, kids who'd missed out on so many simple joys because they'd been chosen by the gods of fate to lead different lives and embrace extraordinary destinies. Like Will, Loreli had been a loner. After Mindy, she'd never had another best friend. She'd never had a boyfriend, never been to a school dance. She'd once belonged to a science club, but because of her phenomenal abilities she was envied and shunned by her peers. So hers had been a lonely existence, living with a shell of a mother. She hadn't had the benefit of an ancient book to guide her, but she'd evolved into something of a demon hunter herself, and had spent the better part of her life searching for the Prince of Darkness. She had to admit that much of her life had been down-right painful and lonely. But she was determined.

Will, too, shared his pain of being a perpetual outsider, and how many nights he'd lain awake scheming of revenge on the black crea-ture who had taken his father. And now that same creature had his mother's consciousness held captive. He was going to defeat him. He didn't yet know how, but he had some ideas. When they were done talking, Will gazed at his half-sister, and their eyes held for a long, long time. He could see the pain behind her eyes, the years of suffer-ing. He decided that their meeting was no accident, that it must be part of a larger plan, part of the universe unfolding. Will reached out his hand. Loreli took it and squeezed.

And then the reality finally sank in. He had a sister. He wasn't alone anymore.

Chapter Fifteen:
Fears Realized

It had been a long night. It was just before sunrise now, and they both knew they weren't going to get any sleep. So they took Will's Suzuki and cruised into the U District to Java Jungle, a pre-Starbucks relic of a coffee shop favored by old hippies and other fringe dwellers who preferred the funky vibe and mismatched furniture to the sheen and gleam of the franchise shops. This morning it was quiet and almost empty. They both had straight coffee served in thick, chipped old porcelain mugs.

"Tell me about the shedemons," Will said as he drank.

"Is that what you're calling them?"

"It's as good a name as any."

Loreli nodded and took a sip of her coffee, then added more sugar. "They serve him unquestioningly. Their allegiance is total."

"Like every other demon," said Will.

"Yeah, except their dedication is a little more intense. They not only *will* die for him, they *want* to die for him. It's like it's a . . . privilege or something. So they can be reborn bigger and better from the demon dead someday when the Dark Lord opens the portal. They're kind of like the Satanic version of nuns. They're totally celibate, 'married' only to the Dark Lord."

"Where did they come from? I've seen demons all over the country, but never any like them. It's like they're . . . supersized or something."

"It's the methamphetamine. When they're high on it, they're crazy out of control. Rocco Manelli, he's the big dog at our school, the Alpha demonteen. He recruits them, runs the whole drug ring. I was trying to infiltrate his pack when you showed up at the party. He hangs out down below."

"In the Under City," said Will.

"Yeah. How do you know about it?" asked Loreli.

"I have a . . . friend, who had an encounter with the shedemons. They took him to the Under City. He said he saw the Dark Lord's body."

"Just like in our dreams, and in my drawing."

"Yeah."

Will had a surge of hope. From what Loreli had said about Rocco, that door in the club would lead Will to the Under City. If he could get through it, he could go and finish the beast off for good.

"I'm going down there," he said, almost to himself. "I'm going to find the Dark Lord's body and blow it to smithereens."

"Too messy," said Loreli in disagreement. "Acid. I'd use acid. There's a special batch I made that can eat through hardened steel."

They drank their coffee.

Lorelai mused, "Killing the Dark Lord . . . our father. We've certainly got our work cut out for us."

Will stiffened. He should have realized this was where their conversation was leading.

"Listen, Loreli, I know you're more than able to take care of yourself. And your flash bombs and everything are awesome. But I work solo. There's no 'us' here."

Loreli's cheeks flushed with anger.

"Excuse me, but you're not going to play me like that. You can take your solo act and shove it. There *is* an 'us,' whether you like it or not. And if you're planning to make him pay, you're gonna have to find him first. I know the area, and the people. You don't. You need my help."

Will opened his wallet and pulled out a few twenties, and put them on the table in front of Loreli. "Look, I think you'd better let me take care of it. Those are for a taxi. I'll let you know when it's done."

He stood up and started moving toward his bike. He made it all the way out the door before Loreli raced around lightning fast and stood in his path.

"You're crazy if you think you can just ditch me like this," she said, clamping her hand on his arm.

"I need to go do this alone."

"I never wanted a partner either. But when you saved my life tonight it made me think. It made me think that this was all *meant* to happen this way. You and me. Together."

Will shook his head, but Loreli grabbed his wrist tighter.

"Will, there's a *reason* why we found each other."

Will wavered. His whole life he'd been a lone wolf. But then again, back in Harrisburg, Natalie had pulled his ass from the fire, and that was without any training or super-human abilities. He couldn't totally discount the value of having an ally, especially one as skilled as Loreli. But he'd just met her, and she was used to working alone, too. Could he really trust her in a fight like the one they'd be walking into?

"My whole life I've been in this thing alone," Loreli said. "And then you come along. It's *got* to mean something."

Loreli couldn't hold back any longer, and she moved closer to Will and wrapped her arms around him, hugging him. She held him tightly and whispered in his ear: "We're in this together. We're family."

She had tears in her eyes. And so, Will realized, did he.

Natalie had been driving the BMW around Seattle for hours. She refused to go back to the house until she was sure Will was okay, and he still wasn't answering her texts. If he was hurt somewhere and she didn't find him, she'd never forgive herself. But she needed caffeine.

Turning the corner to a coffee shop Will had taken them to when they first arrived in Seattle, Natalie saw Will first—she'd recognize his big strong back anywhere—and she felt relief wash through her. *He's alive, he's okay!* But then her heart stopped as Will shifted, revealing a scene that punched Natalie in the gut. Not only was he with *her*, they were hugging. The image burned like acid. Natalie saw Loreli's face, saw her arms around Will, saw her perfect lips gently brushing his cheek, saw her whispering in his ear. Natalie's world seesawed back and forth and she lost control of the car. She swerved, slamming on the brakes, tires screaming, and the BMW skidded into the parking lot, punching into Will's Suzuki, totally mangling it.

Emily, who had been dozing in the passenger seat, let out a shriek. "I knew this was a bad idea! Geez, Nat, what *happened*?"

"Dammit!" said Natalie, slamming her fist into the steering wheel.

"Well, this is messed up," said Rudy from the backseat, surrounded by Dick's Drive-In cheeseburger wrappers from their 2 A.M. stop.

"Gee, ya think, Einstein?" Emily snapped. She looked like she was ready to slug him.

Natalie's anger ebbed and she shrank into the seat as Will stormed toward the BMW, Loreli a few steps behind him. When he opened the door, she thought he was about to yank her out and shake her but he just spoke to her evenly.

"Are you all right?" he said.

Natalie nodded slowly. She felt like a fool and wanted to tell him so. But her eyes had found Loreli and were locked in on her. She couldn't pull them away. Loreli was unreadable, her expression a perfectly blank canvas as she took everything in. *Watching as the pathetic jealous girlfriend makes a self-indulgent scene*, Natalie thought. It was a nightmare.

Will looked at Emily and Rudy. "You guys okay?"

"I'm okay, Will," said Emily.

"I'm fine, dude, but your bike . . ." said Rudy. Will didn't even bother looking at the Suzuki.

"What are you *doing* out here?" Will asked Natalie.

"We were just . . . you said you'd text me, and . . ." Natalie's voice trailed off. "I was worried," she said lamely. She still couldn't stop looking at Loreli, who was smiling now. Probably laughing at Natalie.

"My cell phone is broken," Will said tiredly. "You didn't have to panic." He shook his head and glared at Rudy. "And Rudy, I told you to stay put."

"I know, man, but Dick's . . . their cheeseburgers, they just call out a siren song to me, you know?"

Will thought over his options. The best course of action right now was to calm down and get off the streets.

"Get in the back, I'm driving," he said to Natalie.

"What about your bike?" she asked.

"Forget about it," said Will. He could buy ten more just like it and throw them all off a cliff and not care. He opened the back door and firmly guided Natalie into the car. Then he turned to Loreli.

"Get in, I'll give you a lift home." He held the door open for her. She hesitated, looking at Natalie.

"Are you sure?"

"Just get in."

Loreli offered Natalie a friendly smile as she climbed in next to her, but Natalie had trouble returning it. They were only a few miles from Loreli's house, and Will drove frighteningly fast. But the ride seemed to last forever. Loreli and Natalie sat side by side. Natalie shuddered—she didn't want to be touching *her*, but she couldn't help it because Rudy was a seat hog. Loreli broke the silence.

"So . . . you guys are all new at LBJ, right?"

Natalie stiffened. Even her voice was beautiful, like a seraph's. This girl, this *creature* who'd had her arms around Will, was a nightmare.

"Yeah. I'm Rudy," said Rudy, "and that's Emily up front, and this is Natalie," he said, hooking a thumb toward her. "They're twins," he added.

Loreli laughed. "Gee, I hadn't noticed. Listen, it's great to meet you guys."

"The pleasure's all ours," said Rudy.

An icy silence followed. Natalie leaned her head back against the backseat. She could smell Loreli's musky perfume.

"Listen, I know how hard it is being new and all, and well, if any of you need anything, feel free to give me a shout, okay?" said Loreli.

Rudy smiled like he'd won the lottery. "Oh yeah! Tiiiiight!"

Natalie clenched and unclenched her fists. The perfume was making her feel nauseous. Up in the front seat, Emily turned on the radio. Loud. In another moment, they arrived at Loreli's house and she got out.

"It was really nice meeting you guys. Any friends of Will are friends of mine."

Natalie closed her eyes. Emily sighed.

Loreli then spoke to Will in a low tone. "Walk me to my front door?"

Will shut off the Beemer and escorted Loreli to her front door. Rudy was bouncing in his seat to the music and staring at Loreli.

"Man, are you kidding me? She is *smokin'* hot!"

Natalie and Emily both turned and stared daggers at him. He wilted.

"Well, excuse me. But she *is* . . ." he muttered.

At her front door, Loreli touched Will on the arm.

"I'm going down there tomorrow night. I mean, tonight." She looked up into the sky, at the sun just coming up and the sky turning from a dark purple to a dull gray. "I want you to come with me. Meet me at First and Yesler at 10:30. Okay?"

Will sighed. "Let me think about it."

She shrugged. "Suit yourself. I'm going with or without you. But I can *help* you, Will. It makes sense for us to do this thing together."

"I'll see you at school," he said. Then he turned and walked back to the BMW.

"Thanks for the ride," she called after him.

The BMW drove away and Loreli whispered to the gray morning, "Brother . . ."

On the drive home, Will kept checking the rearview mirror, but Natalie wouldn't return his gaze; she'd only stare out the window and watch the raindrops smear the city as it went by. He'd ignored her before, and two could play that game. She was trying to let her anger give her strength. But the truth was that she didn't know how to handle this. She'd always been so certain of her relationship with Will. *Relationship.* That's what they had, wasn't it? Right now she wasn't convinced. In fact, it felt like her world was crumbling around her. She touched something on the seat beside her. It was a tube of lip-gloss. It must have fallen out of Loreli's pocket. Natalie's fingers wrapped around the tube and she squeezed it angrily. She reached over to power down her window and was about to toss it out—she pictured it landing in the gutter, pictured *Loreli* landing in the gutter, rolling like a corpse— but at the last second she changed her mind and slipped it into her pocket instead.

Once at home, Will led everyone inside.

"It's been a long night. Try to get a couple of hours of sleep," he said. "We'll go into school late."

Exhausted, Rudy and Emily trudged upstairs. But Natalie waited, and when Will tried to walk past she stopped him.

"I have a question, and I'm only going to ask it once," she said.

She was acting tough, but her eyes were red with pain. They spoke to him in their familiar way; they were pleading with him. Will wanted to take her in his arms, wanted to tell her everything about Loreli so she wouldn't worry, wouldn't suffer needlessly. But he'd sworn on his blood not to betray Loreli, swore he wouldn't reveal her secret to anyone. And he would keep his word.

Maybe this was a good thing. He knew he couldn't have a future with Natalie, and that he had to convince her to let him go, for her sake. Maybe letting her believe something was going on with Loreli was the only way to do that, no matter how great her present pain. The last thing he wanted to do was hurt her. But what if hurting her meant saving her? What if hurting her made it so that she would get over him and go on to live a regular life, even find love with some guy whose blood wasn't polluted? He straightened his spine, hardened his heart, and spoke without emotion.

"I'm listening," he said.

She faltered. His eyes were vacant and the tone of his voice was foreign and almost cruel—he was like some guy she'd never even known, let alone the boy she'd fallen head over heels in love with—and it stabbed like a knife. But she made herself go on, so hurt and angry she was shaking.

"What's going on with her, Will? Who is she to you?"

Will looked away. "That's not something you and I are going to discuss. Go upstairs and get some sleep."

He turned and headed into the lab, leaving Natalie staring after him. She felt like she'd just fallen off the planet and was tumbling through space. She climbed the spiral staircase in a daze. Once in her room, she locked the door behind her and closed the drapes. She sat down in front of her vanity, staring at herself in the mirror. How had this happened? Even if Will had fallen out of love with her, how could he treat her that way, like her questions weren't even worth answering? His dead eyes had wounded her in ways she never knew existed. *I will not cry*, she told herself. And in that moment, she did not. She was in too much shock; the pain was too great. Her hands shook. Her insides churned. If she cried now, she was afraid the tears would never stop.

She told herself that whatever was happening, she *would* handle it. She'd battled demons, for God's sake! Maybe he was just tired. He'd been out all night, too (*with her*). And taking the BMW out to look for him had been a mistake. He was probably angry. She just needed to put it in the past. Loreli was new, but Natalie and Will had a history. Natalie had to keep her wits about her and not let jealousy take over her brain, and she'd be fine. They'd be fine.

She took her jacket off and the tube of Loreli's lip-gloss fell onto the floor. Natalie stared at it a long time, as if it were the only thing in the room, before she picked it up. It felt hot to the touch. She unscrewed the cap and pulled out the applicator. The liquid gloss shined brightly, even in the dim light of the room. Her hand trembling, she touched the wand to her lips, gently applying the purloined gloss. When she was done, she looked in the mirror. Her lips weren't just beautiful, they were intoxicating. She couldn't take her eyes off them. They felt hot, and the heat spread from her lips to her mouth to her cheeks, her throat, her brain. Her body flushed with the heat. It felt good. She imagined Will looking at her lips with longing. In her mind, he was standing behind her now and put a gentle hand on her shoulder, then tilted her chin up. Her head was spinning, her mind churning, her brain tumbling. She melted into his arms. Her vision blurred. Dizzy, she held on to the side of the vanity, then toppled over, collapsing onto the plush carpeting.

In his lab, Will worked on some of his high-tech weapons and then inputted the day and night's exploits into his *Demon Hunter* game while the others napped. He included the fight in the J & M basement as well as the skirmish in the cemetery, but omitted his scrap with Loreli. He saw that Jade16 had logged on and was racking up kills and points. He would have to speak to Loreli about that. It

wasn't good for business to have one player totally outclassing everyone else. The closer the front-runners were to the rest of the pack,
the better the sales, and sales were what kept Will's bank account
full.

He thought about whether he should go down to the Under City
with Loreli. He believed that she wanted the Dark Lord dead just as
much as he did, but that was the problem: they might get in each
other's way. He made his decision. He would tell her at school that
he'd go with her that night, but it would be a lie. Instead, he'd go
right away. That would give him a head start, and he would go down
on his own. Maybe he could even kill the Dark Lord before school
got out. He did an inventory of his arsenal and decided which weapons he would take. When he had his cache assembled, he sat down
in a lotus position on a mat on the floor and meditated.

Natalie was lying flat on her back on the carpet. She opened her
eyes and looked up. Above her, the ceiling was a swirling galaxy of
sparkling stars. Her brain thrummed with thoughts and emotions
and imagery, her heart pumping furiously, her temperature rising.
Stumbling into the bathroom, she threw up. *Was she getting the flu?*
She half-wondered if it was her jealousy that was causing her sudden sickness. She drank some water and that seemed to help, but
her world was still tilting as she made her way back into the bedroom. Feeling like her skin was on fire, she peeled off her clothes
and crawled into bed, tossing off everything except one sheet, which
she pulled up to her neck. She closed her eyes.

And then the terrible dreams came rushing in.

*Will and Loreli together at school, laughing, walking down the hall-
way. Natalie follows them, her feet sinking into the floor as though it's
made of sand. She opens her mouth to yell at Will, to somehow stop him
from this madness, but no words spring forth; she is mute. Will walks
Loreli to her locker. Enlarging into a demon beast, muscles bulging, he
rips the locker door off its hinges for her. She's impressed; it turns her*

on. She touches his face. Her tongue emerges. It's at least six inches long. Sinking down into the quicksand floor, Natalie gazes at the locker. It is a portal to darkness. Will, now back to normal, steps inside with Loreli as Natalie cries out. Don't go with her! Help me! I'm dying! *He hears her. He turns and looks. His eyes are carbon black.*

The dream changes. Natalie is in a forest, adorned in black from head to toe, wearing thigh-high leather boots, her lips glistening with the feral red gloss, her hair windswept. She is beyond beautiful; she is transcendent. She carries one of the fighting sticks, which morphs into a snake with scarlet eyes, hissing, angry tongue flicking. Shadows emerge from the foliage and surround her. The shadows are Loreli, cloned and repeated, a hundred copies now lunging at her. Natalie, black Natalie, dressed-in-black Natalie, clenches her hand tightly around the snake, which turns into a white-hot staff, and with that staff she cuts down the advancing Lorelis like they're so many stalks of wheat. The setting sun bleeds into the sky and Natalie surveys her victory, the carnage at her feet. She hears Will and turns as he approaches her. He is smiling proudly, extending his hand, pulling her into his arms. They kiss deeply, passionately. The moment is breathless, magnificent, and Natalie is overflowing with joy. They break apart and open their eyes. Their eyes are liquid black.

Variations of the dreams flowed like a river through Natalie's brain until Emily woke her a few hours later.

Will ceased his meditation. His mind was clear, his purpose strong. He showered and shaved and got dressed. He had a plan. It was time to rally the troops and head off to school.

Rudy and Emily were in the kitchen. Emily picked daintily at some fruit and yogurt while Rudy built a leaning tower of pancakes and spread copious amounts of butter and jam on his creation, then smothered it in syrup. When he started to eat, Emily picked up her bowl and moved to the far end of the table. She put her headphones on and tuned in to her laptop in an effort to block Rudy out. She was disgusted as he double-forked his pancake masterpiece, devouring it with a vengeance. When Emily looked up at him, he opened his mouth mid-chew.

She shook her head. "Freak."

He motioned for her to take out her ear buds. She did.

"I know you want some of these," he said, through another mouthful.

"Thanks but no thanks," she said. The truth was, she *did* want pancakes, but she was too proud to admit it.

Rudy went and got a plate, piled on six pancakes, fresh strawberries, whipped cream, and syrup, and set the plate down next to Emily.

"If you think I'm eating that, you're crazy."

"I never claimed to be sane."

Rudy went back to his leaning tower of pancakes and dug in. He closed his eyes and groaned with delight.

Finally, Emily broke down and dug into her stack with her fork. They tasted heavenly.

Rudy snuck a peek at her. "Not bad, huh?"

"I've had better," she lied, but then she felt bad dissing Rudy's efforts. "Okay, they're great. Fantastic, really." And then she ate some more as Rudy beamed.

Will came into the kitchen.

"Where's Natalie?"

"Up in her room," Emily said. "Won't come out. She didn't sleep well this morning. Neither did I."

She gave him a disapproving look. She wasn't keen that she'd had to share Natalie's nightmares about him and Loreli.

Will frowned, and went upstairs and knocked lightly on Natalie's door. "Natalie, it's time for school."

He heard her up and moving inside and tried the door. Locked.

"Natalie?"

He could have easily picked the lock, or kicked it open for that matter, but he knew their conversation the night before had been rough. The least he could do was respect her space.

"Nat? At least let me know you're alive in there."

Natalie stood in front of the door but didn't open it. She was wearing a T-shirt and boxers and was nowhere near ready for school. Her head was still fuzzy and she was having trouble shaking off the residue of her nightmares. The harder she fought them, the more the bad thoughts lingered. She couldn't face the world. Couldn't face school. Couldn't face Will.

"I'm not going," she said.

"Why not?"

"I think I've got the flu. Don't worry, I'll live."

"Let me see you."

"Geez, Will, I said I'm okay." Her words sounded harsher than she'd meant them to. But she needed him to leave her alone until she could get her head back together.

Will wasn't sure what to do. Was she really sick, or just unwilling to face him? Given his plan of action for the day, he decided it might be best to let her stay home.

"Okay. I'll call you later. I'll have some chicken soup delivered."

He waited, hoping for some morsel of acknowledgment. He wasn't sure what he wanted her to say, but he wanted her to say something, anything. Silence. He frowned.

"Okay, I'm gonna go now," he said, and turned to go.

As soon as she heard him hit the steps, she slid to the floor. He was headed off to school, where Loreli was, while she was here at home, alone. Suddenly she wanted to change her mind, to make them wait for her to get dressed so she could go with them, so at least she could keep an eye on Loreli and Will. But when she pictured seeing them together, she knew she wouldn't be able to handle it. What was wrong with her brain? Why was she so angry, confused, and paranoid? She felt like she'd followed Alice down the rabbit hole.

She heard the garage door open, and went back to bed.

DEER PARK, IDAHO

In the small Idaho town of Deer Park, it was another quiet evening. Jackson Computers had closed for the day, along with Wally's Tire Center and the Discount Mart. The all-hours FoodMart stayed open, and Pete's Dragon, the local watering hole, was just starting to show some signs of life. On Main Street, Maria Wells was walking her dog, Toto. She still carried the guilt of stealing Toto from his owner's car over in Spokane. The car had been hot, she told herself; she was doing a good thing, saving a little life. But she'd kept Toto's original collar and today she'd made up her mind. It was time to finally do the right thing, the moral thing. She was going to call the owner, 'fess up to her crime, and return the dog.

Also on Main Street, Jerry Browing was jogging, listening to Rihanna on his iPod and thinking about his best friend's sister, Judy. She was young and impressionable, and Jerry had taken advantage of her. Sometimes he felt so bad about it, he lay awake at night rehearsing apology speeches: to her, and to her brother. Jerry jogged past an old man, Max Magar, coming out of Patton's Pharmacy. Max had his prescription for Viagra and was planning on having a sensual evening at home surfing for porn on the Internet while his wife was out at her book club. Max had stopping having romantic feelings for his wife years ago. He told himself what he was doing wasn't wrong. But then his heart spoke to him and he wondered if maybe there was some way he could rekindle his affection for his wife. Maybe it was time to start being a good husband again.

At exactly the same moment, all three denizens of Deer Park— basically good souls who had just now, in this fateful moment, decided to do the right thing—paused and looked up. The sky quickened, the clouds above growing thick and swarthy and dark. The day had been a windy one, but now the air was thin and cool and the whole of Deer Park was eerily quiet. No dogs barked. No birds chirped. Not even the crickets dared break the silence.

Max squinted as thunderclaps rattled the pharmacy windows and the skies opened up. At first he thought it was snowing, as the sky was filled with white. But it wasn't snow. It was hail. *It doesn't seem nearly cold enough for hail*, thought Max. The hail came down harder. Jerry kept on jogging, smiling at the sensation of the hail pellets showering him. Maria didn't like the hail one bit, but there was no building to take refuge in so she found comfort under the branches of a sprawling Western hemlock by the park.

People in the FoodMart were startled at the sound of the hail hitting the roofs of parked cars. A couple of teenagers ventured out to dance as the white pellets hammered down in a staccato drumbeat. The teens waved to Max as he shuffled quickly to his car. He looked up into the sky one final time. His last thought was disbelief—he was about to be hit by a hailstone the size of a microwave oven. All hundred pounds of the giant hailstone struck Max Magar on the head, crushing his skull, breaking his neck, and shattering his spine. And then he was dead.

Jerry Browing had just decided to get out of the hail and was running fast toward the FoodMart when he was crushed by a similarly huge stone. Maria saw the massive hailstones hitting the ground around her and reached down to pull little Toto up into her arms. Fortunately for Toto, she did not succeed as she, too, was crushed. She lived just long enough to gaze up into the sky, where she saw the face of the Devil. Toto yelped, tugged his broken leash away from Maria's death grip, and then pattered down the street, stopping to sniff at the body of an unfortunate teenager that lay mangled under another massive hailstone.

The hailstorm that hit Deer Park, Idaho, was brief but deadly, lasting exactly one minute and six point six seconds, and killing seven people.

Chapter Sixteen:
The Under City

Will, Rudy, and Emily arrived at LBJ High just in time for the class change between third and fourth periods, and Will took advantage of the opportunity to prowl the hallways, looking into faces, trying to read eyes. Since he carried his own smoldering intensity, most kids shifted their gaze away the moment he made eye contact. Just like every school Will had ever attended, LBJ High had its share of jocks and hippies and punks and bikers. Everybody wanted to wear a uniform. The problem was, you could never tell what kind of uniform a demonteen would wear. The clean-cut glee club guys in pastel polo shirts, the lumbering, leather-clad tattooed skinheads, the tie-dyed group in their bell-bottoms—any of them could be infected. The old saying, "You can't judge a book by its cover," was true for demonteens too. Even with everything he knew about them, Will was coming up empty; the demonteens were pretty deep undercover. But they were here. He could feel them. He would just have to keep looking in between classes.

Back home, Natalie was starting to feel better. The chicken soup that Will had promised to have delivered arrived, and the fact he remembered made her wonder if she'd overreacted that morning. She opened her drapes and windows, and mentally pushed last night's horrific dreams outside. *Go away!* She went into the bath-room, washed her face and brushed her hair, and drank a glass of water. She stared at the tube of lip-gloss, and decided not to bother with it. Then she got dressed, snagged her backpack, went down-stairs, and grabbed an apple on her way out. She caught a bus head-ing toward school. She'd talk to Will again, and this time she'd be strong and secure and reasonable. He hadn't answered her question about Loreli, but that didn't necessarily mean anything was going on. She'd seen them hug, but she hugged Rudy sometimes. No big deal. She would find Will at school and get a ride home with him afterward. She promised herself she'd be calm and cordial, to prove that she was strong and that she trusted him, trusted *in* him. She was feeling *good*. Even though the skies were gray, nothing was going to rain on her parade. Not today. Today was a rebirth.

Will sat in the lunchroom finishing his turkey sandwich as he watched red projectiles zinging back and forth. It was the same in every school. Food fights always broke out more frequently when cherry tomatoes—or "cherry bombs"—were served. He ducked out without getting hit. As he was passing the woodworking classroom, he heard a muted cry and decided to investigate. Inside he found a couple of juniors, Rita Winston and her friend Cindy Becker, tor-menting a freshman girl. Rita had the girl up on the workbench with her ankle in the vise and was slowly tightening it while Cindy tore through the girl's purse, taking her cash and what looked like a bag-gie of pot. Will smiled at his good fortune. His whole plan for tonight hinged on finding a shedemon and tagging her with a subcutaneous tracking chip so she could lead him to the Under City, and it looked like he'd just found some.

But when he entered the room, ready to fight, instead of offering resistance Rita and Cindy crumpled in fear.

"Hey, sorry, we messed up," said Rita, immediately releasing the frosh from the vise.

"You want this?" asked Cindy, holding up the cash and dope. "It's yours!" She tossed it at Will as she and Rita ran for the door. Will grabbed them by their wrists. They didn't act like shedemons, but he had to check, just in case. He did Cindy first, thumbing her temples.

"Ow!" she shrieked.

She was clean. Same for Rita. He let them go.

The freshman girl smiled at him. *My hero!* Will turned and left. The girl was disappointed. She'd already run the movie through her mind of Will falling in love with her and the two of them getting married. At least she'd gotten her stuff back. She picked up her cash and the dope, stuffed them in her purse, and rubbed her ankle.

Out in the crowded hallway, Will spotted Loreli coming at him. He hadn't gotten a chance to talk to her yet, so when she grabbed his elbow and herded him around the corner to her locker, he complied.

"About tonight," he started, but then she threw her arms around him and started giggling and shaking her amazing hair. Will was confused. Had she somehow lost her mind in the last few hours? She was acting like a girlfriend, not a sister, and it was creeping him out.

Then he saw something out of the corner of his eye. It was Rocco Manelli, striding all King Shit down the hallway with his posse. *So this is for his benefit*, thought Will. When Loreli grabbed his face in her hands and kissed him, he kept his mouth closed like she did, but she made it look good, getting all breathless and flushed. Then she broke away and tossed a scathing look in Rocco's direction, as if to say, *Take that, Alpha dude.* Rocco took the bait. He was next to them in a flash, his buddies not far behind, and pounded his fist into Loreli's locker, denting it.

"Having fun, kids?" Rocco growled.

"Like you can't even imagine," said Loreli.

Rocco glared at Will. "Who are you?"

"Nobody," said Will. Best not to antagonize him here in the hall-way where other people could get hurt. And maybe he could use Rocco. Will had wanted a shedemon, but he figured Rocco would do. He started planning how he was going to tag him.

"You got that right," said Rocco with a sneer. "A nobody. Come over here, Loreli."

Rocco grabbed her by the wrist and yanked her across the hall. Will started to follow but let Rocco's goon squad hold him back. *That's right, I'm just a regular guy, a nobody.* With his back to Will, Rocco pulled something out of his jacket and did something to Loreli's wrist. Then he looked at Will and put one of his huge paws behind Loreli's neck. Then he pulled her face into his, lick-ing her from jaw to hairline, his eyes never leaving Will's. *Take that, nobody.* Then Rocco released Loreli, his goons let go of Will, and they marched off, another victory under their belts.

Loreli rejoined Will.

"What was that all about?" he asked.

Loreli was smiling. She held out her hand, and then turned it over.

"He *double*-marked me." She had two small blue symbols stamped on the inside of her wrist. They were five-pointed goats' heads. *Typical lame Satan crap*, thought Will.

"What does that mean?" he asked.

"It means we're in. I don't have to crash the party tonight, I can walk right in."

"What about me?"

"He thinks he's going to turn me into one of *them*. So he double-stamped me, which means I can bring a guest. It's the typical ini-tiation. He gets a girl down there with her boyfriend, best friend, whatever, then infects her with the help of you know who, and then she's ordered to kill her 'guest.' Nice, huh? My guess is he can't wait to see me morph into a shedemon and waste you."

"Charming."

"Come on, bro, I *told* you we met for a reason. This is all going down like it's supposed to. We're both going to get what we want," she said, hugging him.

Will thought about it. This changed everything, and he began to alter his plans accordingly. He wouldn't have to find a shedemon or figure out how to tag Rocco. Loreli's way was faster. He let her hug him.

At the other end of the hallway, Natalie stood frozen, grief clutching her heart. She'd seen everything, and her interpretation of the events—the males clashing over Loreli, the close, hushed conversations, the *kiss*—all added up to one thing: There was *definitely* something going on between Will and Loreli. *He's practically* glued *to her*, thought Natalie. The bell rang. Trembling, she stood waiting for Will to turn and see that she knew—*one* one thousand, *two* one thousand, she waited—and then, deciding she couldn't bear to look at him right now, she walked away. She felt like she'd been punched in the gut.

Will turned around and looked in her direction. But all he saw was an empty hallway.

When Emily came home from school and Natalie wasn't there, she began to worry. She waited, doing homework, avoiding Rudy as best she could. He always seemed to find a way to wander over to wherever she happened to be. He was seriously getting on her nerves. Not just because he was an ex-demon, or former demon, or part demon, or whatever, but because as much as she wanted to dislike him, she was starting to get used to him. In fact, she was finding little things about him that were even kind of . . . cute.

Twenty minutes later, she was agitated. Where *was* Natalie? In the old days, Emily and her sister used to strap on their iPods and run together in the afternoons. Emily was the one in better shape, because she swam, too. But since they'd arrived in Seattle, the only exercise she'd gotten was stick fighting with Natalie. She wondered if maybe Natalie had felt better during the day and had gone out for a jog. It was worth a shot. Except . . . Emily didn't feel like running alone. So, reluctantly, she went looking for Rudy.

They ran down Galer Street to First Avenue West and logged a mile. Emily was listening to some Beatles tunes on her iPod, which always cheered her up and chased nasty thoughts away. Early on Rudy had dropped back to jog behind her, letting her lead, his eyes magnets, her body like steel. She hated that she felt more flattered than creeped out. Emily ran where she thought Natalie would have run, but though she looked up and down every street, there was no sign of her sister. They passed a religious nut wearing sandals, a monk's robe, and an Oregon Ducks baseball cap. He was spouting his ideology and handing out pamphlets. They ran past him, and when they backtracked fifteen minutes later, he was gone. But his pamphlets were blowing everywhere, and one flew up into Emily's face. She grabbed it and was going to drop it, but she didn't want to litter so she stuffed it in the pocket of her running shorts.

After an hour, she gave up and jogged back to the mansion, Rudy still at her heels. Emily looked upstairs and downstairs, but no Natalie. She tried Natalie's phone again, but there was still no answer. She wanted to ask Will if he'd seen her, but he was down in his lab and as far she could tell he hadn't left it since they had come home from school. Natalie was probably avoiding him, anyway.

She took the pamphlet out of her pocket, and was about to crumple it and toss it, but the image on the front caught her eye and she started reading it instead. It was about the story of Moses, when poisonous snakes beset his people and they were living in terror—something Emily knew plenty about—and the Lord told Moses,"*Make a snake and put it up on a pole; anyone who is bitten can look at it and live.*" The lesson was about fear and how to conquer it. Moses was being told that he should present to the people the very thing that they feared the most, and that by learning to face it directly and not shy away, they could turn that thing from an object of terror into something they could live with. That which you fear is the thing that can also *cure* you of your fears.

The lesson was not lost on Emily as she watched Rudy dance around the kitchen, making a post-run snack. She knew she had to face her fear of demons head on. Learning to defend herself was one way to do that. But so was spending time with Rudy. She looked at Rudy. Strangely, he had become, in his own goofy way, her staff. Just by being there, and making her remember, he had become the key to her recovery.

Natalie showed up after dinner, in the middle of a game of cards Rudy had talked Emily into playing to try to distract her from worrying. When Emily tried to talk to her and find out where she'd been, Natalie just shook her head and went upstairs. And when Will went to check on her before he left that evening, she wouldn't answer the door. Emily wanted to ask Will if he knew what had happened, but it felt disloyal to her sister. Emily could feel Natalie's despair, even stronger than it had been that morning, but this time she could tell that pushing wouldn't get her answers any sooner. She'd just have to wait until Natalie was ready to talk. Emily just wished there was something she could do to help.

At 10:30 that night, Will parked his Mitsubishi EVO downtown and met Loreli at the intersection of First and Yesler. She was wearing a long leather duster coat, which Will figured was where she stashed her alchemistic weapons. For his part, Will was traveling on the light side, with a small backpack containing two Variable Flamer Pistols with backup loads and a dozen Power Choppers. About the size of a child's toy block, the Power Choppers were a particularly nasty and painful weapon, and Will loved using them on demons. He also carried his trusty Megashocker, though when he got to the Dark Lord's body—*This is the night it's going to happen*, he told himself, *this night I will get my vengeance*—he would call upon his Power Rod to do the deed.

As usual, Loreli looked amazing, almost surreal in her beauty. She was one potent chick. Will couldn't help but think that if they made it out of this Godforsaken mess alive, if they actually did the impossible and fulfilled their quest and were able to go on and live normal lives, Loreli was going to make some lucky guy incredibly happy.

He took a closer look at her duster as he approached. It was definitely loaded down. "You look like you're packing," he said.

She opened her coat just enough for him to see the plethora of stuffed pockets in the lining.

"You, too. What's in the backpack?" she said.

"A little of this, a little of that. In case we need help getting in."

"Getting *in* won't be a problem. Getting *out* might be another story."

They walked a few blocks down to the J & M Café but tonight it was silent. Rocco had moved his rave. They'd have to find another way to the Under City entrance. Loreli had an idea. They kept walking and came to a small storefront advertising Seattle Underground Tours. They entered, and the owner, Smiling Bob, was quick with a handshake. Once they'd bought their tickets and joined the rest of the group, he began his spiel, pouring the adults champagne and Will and Loreli some sparkling apple juice since this was the "Champagne on a Full Moon" tour, and regaling Will, Loreli, and the gaggle of tourists with tales of Seattle's sordid "underground" past. He talked playfully about speakeasies and hookers and blue movies, cracking little jokes as he went, keeping everything PG-13 so as not to offend. Then he led them all past a gallery of old photos of Seattle, dating all the way back to June 6, 1889, the date of the Great Seattle Fire. The fire was supposedly started by a glue pot that boiled over, caught fire, and ignited some nearby wood chips. Since nearly all of the buildings in the area at that time were built of wood, the fire spread quickly, eventually ravaging twenty-five entire city blocks. Miraculously, only one human life was reported lost, but it was calculated that one million rats had burned to death.

Will listened impatiently as Smiling Bob continued with his patter, leading the group through an arched doorway and down a long flight of concrete steps, into a basement that wasn't a basement at all, but was actually the original street level for the underground city. When the old city had burned down, since it was near sea level and frequently flooded, the city fathers had simply decided to build the new city one level up, literally on top of the old one.

Smiling Bob did his best to make the old underground Seattle seem spooky and intriguing, but it was mostly just a bunch of deserted rooms and passageways filled with dust and debris. Bob had dressed it up a bit, adding a few mannequins, and if you tried real hard you could imagine a city down here once upon a time. But there was nothing particularly scary about it. *If these tourists only knew about the* real *Under City*, thought Will, *they'd no doubt get their butts back on their cruise ships and never visit Seattle again.* Up ahead, the tour group had bunched up while listening to another of Smiling Bob's tall tales, so Will and Loreli stopped at an old decaying mirror and pretended to gaze into it.

When the tourist group moved on again, Loreli tugged on Will's arm and they stayed back, then quickly peeled off from the group entirely, stepping over a chain barrier and moving through an old barbershop. Loreli found a narrow passageway that led to another set of stairs.

Down they went, Loreli lighting the way with a Moon Stick she pulled out of her duster and held aloft. They talked quietly about their plan of action once they reached their destination. The walls were cool to the touch, and the bricks gave way to stone. The air surrounding them began to warm up. Will supposed that was only natural when you were going to Hell. They continued down and now heard faint music, the thundering bass beat of some industrial techno. They passed graffiti, much of it painted on the walls in blood. More Satanic stuff, symbols of goats' heads and pentagrams and crap like that. Will was so used to it he barely even saw it. Fighting demons for all these years, he'd seen it all. They walked down a long sloping embankment where human skulls had been impaled on stakes.

"I love what they've done with the place," said Loreli.

They climbed down another flight of stairs, stepping over a demonteen writhing in agony—going through crank withdrawal, no doubt—and rounded a corner and moved down a passageway that became broader with higher ceilings. Torches dotted the walls, tossing bizarre shadows around.

They approached a huge red door that at first looked to be built of wood, but, upon closer inspection, revealed itself to be fashioned out of some sort of ghastly membrane. *Probably the skin of prisoners*, thought Will. *Great. Gives us something to look forward to.* As they got close enough to touch the door, Loreli reached out a hand to knock and the door recoiled, making a bleating sound like a baby goat. Then it was opened from the other side, and a diminutive blonde girl with sunken, unblinking eyes stood in the doorway.

"Let's see your mark," she said.

Loreli held out her wrist. The little female demon inspected it, then waved them through. Will's skin crawled as they crossed the threshold. *No turning back now.* They went down more stairs, the music growing ear-bursting loud, industrial techno mixed with vintage Seattle grunge sounds: Nirvana, Alice in Chains, Soundgarden. At the bottom of the stairs, they found themselves in an immense cavern teeming with demons: demonteens, shedemons, and mature demons. The massive hall was a rogue's gallery of street thugs and runaways, scofflaws, pimps and hookers, addicts and killers—all fallen souls who had turned to the dark side and gone the demon way. This was the *real* Seattle Underground.

As was their custom, the demons were clad in a vast array of black leather outfits and showed plenty of tattooed skin. The place was rocking, and of course, being demons, everyone was engaging in some form of vile debauchery. Will and Loreli passed demonteens drinking beer and vodka, hammering down shots of tequila, smoking crack cocaine and crank, frying their brains. They passed unclean kids tattooing each other and piercing every body part imaginable. They saw them knife fighting and playing Russian roulette. As Will and Loreli passed, an unlucky demonteen boy blew his brains out. *What have you got to lose*, thought Will, *when you're already dead?* He saw demonteen boys beating a demonteen girl and his stomach turned. He *loathed* these creatures. In a way they were the spawn of the Dark Lord, just like he was. But he wasn't one of them. He would *never* be one of them. He would rather die.

Will and Loreli passed the kid from detention, the one with the freak hair who called himself Hawk. He wasn't barefoot now; he was wearing some kind of snakeskin boots and tight leather pants with slits in the thighs. His was so baked his eyes were glazed over, but he managed to recognize Will and Loreli through his druggy haze.

"Lookie who we got here. Ha! Rocco's down at Fire Lake," he said. Then he sidled up to a shedemon and put a move on her, whispering something in her ear. The shedemon wasn't impressed. She pulled out a knife and cut his chin. He yelped in pain but smiled, thinking in his twisted brain that this was a positive reaction. Will shuddered with revulsion. He had half a mind to call down his Power Rod and start hacking these odious creatures to bits right then and there. But he restrained himself. He had a bigger goal tonight.

They continued their descent and Will checked his watch, a modified altimeter that gave him readings not only on his altitude, but on how far beneath sea level he was. They were nearly six hundred feet down now. If Will's hunch about the Dark Lord's resting place was correct, they were getting close. Just a little further, and they'd be six hundred and sixty-six feet down.

They reached Fire Lake, which was an expansive lagoon of filthy sludge dotted with patches of burning oil and God knew what other flammable liquids. Demonteens were romping to death metal riffs, slamming into each other, throwing fists and elbows, gleefully drawing blood. Pain was *good*. Pain was *fun*. It was all part of the madness down here in the Under City. Evil fed upon evil. Will imagined a serpent devouring itself, eating its own tail.

Rocco was hanging out with his posse and some shedemons. They were having a knife-throwing contest. A beautiful shedemon was lashed to a slowly spinning wooden wheel, her limbs splayed. She was laughing and writhing erotically as Rocco threw knives that sank into the wood just inches from her limbs. Then Rocco decided to show off a bit and closed his eyes and threw hard. The knife whistled through the air and sank into the girl's thigh. Blood spurted and her shrieks of pain were ear-splitting. Rocco's posse laughed. The wounded shedemon yanked her wrists and ankles free, dropped to the ground, then pulled the knife out of her thigh. With eyes on fire, she hurled it back at Rocco, who ducked. The blade sank into the forehead of the demonteen behind him, who grabbed blindly at it before wailing and pitching over dead. Rocco and the others roared with laughter.

And then Rocco spotted Loreli. He motioned to the demonteen DJ, who, along with his equipment, was perched on a rocky ledge above the throng. He was wearing a headdress of painted antlers glued to a retro skateboard helmet. When he saw Rocco's signal, he amped up the music so loud the walls shook.

Rocco moved quickly over to Loreli and grabbed her. Will folded back into the crowd. Using the same classy technique he'd employed in the hallway, Rocco licked Loreli from neck to forehead, sliming her good. She endured it, but tensed up. Rocco didn't dig it and slapped her hard in the face. Will bristled, but continued to hang back.

Rocco began dancing, a crude pelvic thrust, preening for Loreli as he hip-bumped her over toward the wooden wheel.

"You want to play?" he asked, pointing at it.

"Whatever you want, Rocco," said Loreli. She was being docile, playing possum.

"Alrighty then, let's all play Wheel of Fortune!" shouted Rocco as the onlookers bellowed with laughter.

Will watched for a few more seconds as Loreli was lashed to the wheel. This was his chance to get to the Dark Lord alone, without Loreli. But he was worried about leaving her alone like this, strapped down and surrounded by demons. She'd gone up there voluntarily, though, so it must have been part of her plan. If Will was going to act, he had to do it now.

"Close your eyes!" said Rocco. Loreli complied.

Will took three steps backward and was swallowed up by shadows. He looked around and saw an archway cut into the stone to his left. It was flanked by two immense demons wielding battle pitchforks. Will moved toward them, walking quickly, careful to keep his eyes cast downward as Rocco continued with the ceremony, yelling now at Loreli.

"What do you hear, babe?" said Rocco, holding a hand to his ear. "Do you hear *him* calling your name? Do you hear the Dark Lord?"

Loreli threw herself into the ceremony, clenching her eyes shut, writhing and making it look as though she was straining to "hear."

The demonteens began a chant. A whisper at first: "Hear him!"

Then louder: "*Hear him!*"

Then even louder: "*HEAR HIM! HEAR HIM! HEAR HIM!*"

Will moved toward the sentries, closer, closer. The moment they began to react, he crossed his arms behind him and reached into the slits in his backpack. They stared at him dumbly as he whipped out his Variable Flamer Pistols. The demons were about to protest when he cauterized their eyeballs. As they screamed, so did Loreli, and Will seized the moment to garrote the sentries, shove their bodies aside, and race through the archway. Ten, twenty yards, bending time, down through the entry tunnel, and then he was in the vault.

There, there it was! The Dark Lord's body! He was lying on a raised marble altar, two massive battle-axes by his sides. There were dozens of urns of blood nearby, just like Rudy had described. The beast's feet were enormous, and his bulky arms, legs, and torso were charred and held fast with sinewy tendons that writhed like worms. Will was trembling. The body quivered; the beast was still alive. His chest rose and fell slowly, but everything else, from the top of the golden battle helmet he wore to the soles of his feet, remained still as stone.

There were seven shedemons, led by Blue Streak, guarding the Dark Lord. Seeing Will, they turned in unison, hissed, and bared their fangs. They were big, they were strong, and their eyes blazed with madness. Two of them fired crossbows. Will bent time and ducked, evading them.

A shedemon leapt across the room and slashed at him, leaving a nasty gash in his thigh. She clenched a hand around his neck and squeezed. Using his Megashocker, Will plunged an uppercut through her chin. Her brain fried and her comrades howled as she rolled off him and exploded, dead. Will knew the others would be on him soon, but this time he was heavily armed and better prepared. He grabbed a handful of Power Choppers from his backpack. He threw four Choppers, and two hit their marks. The small blocks hit the shedemons in their chests, then instantly opened and transformed into the monstrous killing machines that they were, blades whirring as they burrowed swiftly into the shedemons' chest cavities. One second, two seconds, *blam!* They exploded. The afflicted shedemons were blown to bits, their bodies liquefying, obliterated into mere fragments. It was a terrible mess.

Out on the wheel, Loreli very slowly opened her eyes, stared at Rocco, and nodded, indicating that she had heard the Dark Lord calling out to her in her mind, repeating her name three times. It was time for the second stage of infection: welcoming evil into your mind.

"Now think of some bad, bad things, babe," said Rocco.

Loreli closed her eyes again as the crowd began to whisper: "Bad things . . ."

And louder: "Bad things!"

Now shouting: "*BAD THINGS! BAD THINGS! BAD THINGS!*"

Loreli squirmed and tossed her head back and forth. Then she stiffened and grimaced, as though possessed by some unspeakable memory that brought her immense pain. Again she opened her eyes slowly and nodded at Rocco.

"Spin the wheel!" he shouted.

And Loreli began to spin.

Inside the vault, Will tried to dodge another lunging shedemon, but she managed to kick him in the head. His nose gushed blood. He went down. She had a dagger and was about to stab him in the heart when he hit her in the torso with a Power Chopper. It buried itself in her chest, churned, and exploded upward, blowing her head off.

On the altar, the Dark Lord's body trembled. The body appeared strong and powerful. Will wondered, *Why doesn't the beast rise and fight?*

The three remaining shedemons were fanning out, moving with blinding speed. Seeing the beast's body move brought a wave of painful memories into Will's brain. He fought them, trying to clear his head, *Gotta keep focused!* But his oldest friend, his reliable anger, surged up within him and distracted him.

Screeching a war cry, Blue Streak got to him and sliced him with her razor-sharp nails. Man, he hated these creatures! They were nothing but pain machines. Blue Streak continued her assault and got in some good licks before he managed a powerful kick to the side of her head. Her eyes went white. She was temporarily blind and swooped up into the darkness.

Will's neck was bleeding and his anger flared again. Shedemons came at him from the left and the right. If Will wasn't careful, his anger was going to bring him down. He breathed deeply, and was able to dial it down some. He flung a Taser Dart at one of his attackers, immobilizing her long enough to hack off her hands with his Megashocker. The other two attacked, and he took hits from them as they sliced and diced, but he was able to dodge and kick and punch his way out, finally blasting them with the last two loads from his Flare Pistols and his remaining Power Choppers. When the dust settled he was aching and bloody, but he was standing in a field of shedemon corpses. Blue Streak was not among them.

Will looked up into the darkness for her. He saw nothing. So he stepped over the corpses and approached the Dark Lord's body. He looked at the creature lying there, twitching. He stepped closer.

The crowd of demonteens watching Loreli was in a frenzy now, all eyes locked upon her as she rotated on the wooden wheel. Rocco threw a knife. *Thunk!* A cheer. *Thunk!* Another cheer. Rocco threw two knives at once, and when they missed he angrily threw a third, sidearm. This one connected, slicing the tip of Loreli's little finger. She cried out in pain, but did not open her eyes. Blood had been raised. The third stage.

"*BLOOD! BLOOD! BLOOD!*" cried the demons.

"Stop the wheel!" said Rocco.

Two of Rocco's goons stopped the wheel and cut Loreli loose. She stepped to the ground, her eyes still closed as she shook her hair and casually smoothed her duster.

"Open your eyes," said Rocco.

She did. They were still a shimmering green and radiated health. She wasn't infected! There was a moment of shocked silence. Then the demons roared in anger.

Loreli went to work, moving with inhuman speed. She reached into her duster and brought out handfuls of spheres and orbs, which she threw with agility and precision. She threw them high into the ceiling and low to the ground. Orbs exploding above formed clouds of sparkling heavy gasses that unleashed a toxic rain while the earth erupted in flames of emerald. Backlit by the pyrotechnic show she'd unleashed, Loreli cut a fearsome figure, a Valkyrie from Hell—or, in this case, thought the terrified demons, from Heaven. It was chaos on a grand scale.

Exploding one more sphere to mask her escape, Loreli vanished from view.

In the vault, Will was frozen with rage. Staring at the Dark Lord, he was reminded of all the pain this creature had visited upon him—how the monster had killed his father and even now tormented his mother.

"Return her to me!" said Will.

The Dark Lord said nothing. But his left hand slowly clenched into a fist—except for the middle finger, which remained stiff. Will was so angered by this gesture that he began to see red spots. At first they were like raindrops on a windshield, these tiny blotches of red, but then they spread, melding together and forming a film that covered his vision. The beast's voice spoke in his mind: *Bring me pain and I will visit upon you the wrath of a thousand hounds of Hell!*

"Then I will end it here and she will come of her own accord!" shouted Will. Still the Dark Lord remained silent. It was time to put an end to this beast once and for all.

"I'm going to enjoy this," Will said.

He reached up and tapped the code into the Power Rod retrieval patch on the back of his neck. As he waited—one second, two seconds—he visualized using his Power Rod to hack the Prince of Darkness into a hundred pieces, forever ending his reign. Three seconds . . . four . . . five. Where was his Power Rod? He tapped the code in again. Five more seconds passed. Ten. The Power Rod did not come.

Will reprimanded himself. He'd been so obsessed with finding and destroying the Dark Lord that he hadn't thought it through, hadn't done his due diligence. He should have deduced that at 666 feet beneath sea level, the retrieval patch's signal might be blocked.

It didn't matter. He still had his Megashocker. He could do the deed with that. His brain was thrumming with anger, his vision blurred with scarlet. He turned his Megashocker up to maximum power and envisioned how he was going to thrust it through the Dark Lord's eye sockets, obliterating his sinful, malevolent brain.

"Time to face your doom!" said Will.

Unnoticed, Loreli had entered behind him, moving silently between the unused urns of blood. And as Will began to remove the Dark Lord's helmet, Loreli raised her dagger. It was time to fulfill her destiny. That it would involve the death of her own flesh and blood was tragic but necessary. Will yanked the helmet off the Dark Lord. It lifted into his hand so easily—*too* easily!

There was nothing inside.

Will stood in shock. Loreli, too, was dazed and lowered her dagger. The two of them stared in disbelief. The Prince of Darkness had lost his head.

Chapter Seventeen: Inferno

Will was frozen. The sight of the Dark Lord's headless body filled him with fear and confusion. But the Dark Lord was *not* frozen. The headless beast's hands wrapped around the axe handles by his side, and then he sat up, ready to kill. Still Will stood transfixed. Loreli, too, had been rendered temporarily immobile by the horrific sight, but the gears in her brain turned swiftly as she formulated a revised plan.

Loreli grabbed Will's shoulder. "Will, come on! We have to get out of here."

The sound of her voice spurred Will to action, and he started backing away from the altar, holding the Megashocker in front of him.

The Dark Lord's corpse leapt awkwardly off the marble slab and, his back to Will and Loreli, began blindly swinging his mighty axes. They cut through the air with terrifying whooshing sounds. The headless ogre moved in fits and starts, twitchy and convulsive, but the Dark Lord's power was still there.

And Will saw red again. He'd failed. He'd been moments from his goal, and he'd failed. The Dark Lord still lived. As the Dark Lord's body reached them, Will dodged a swipe, then raked the

Megashocker across the beast's muscular back. Unable to scream since he had no head, the monster merely cringed in pain, then whirled and frantically hacked at the air again, one of his mighty axes crashing into a stone column, crumbling it.

Pulling away from Loreli, who was trying to tug him toward the doorway, Will attacked again and again with the Megashocker as the Dark Lord's headless body spastically fought on, swinging the massive axes, lashing out in every direction. Will had to block several of the Dark Lord's blows, and somehow his body—though bereft of head and thus of sight, and still moving awkwardly—was beginning to sense where its enemy was. Will took a step forward, fully prepared to duel to the death with the twitching, headless monster. The situation terrified Loreli.

"Will, no! We have to leave this place now!"

Will again slashed the Megashocker across the Dark Lord's scaly back. "I'm going to cut him to ribbons!"

Will lanced the monster's shoulder, the fiery Megashocker blade sinking deep into his flesh.

"It's futile!" Loreli yelled "You can cut him into a thousand pieces and they'll only gather them and the body will regenerate!"

Will continued to attack in a red rage, thinking *This is for you, Edward, my real father. This is for you!* Will struck at the beast mercilessly, slashing at him over and over with the Megashocker. A couple of times he thought he heard the sound of metal striking metal.

Loreli moved to stop him, to try one last time to talk some sense into him. It was an unwise decision, because out of sheer luck the Dark Lord blindly swung his axe and it cut Loreli's shoulder. She cried out in pain and dropped, her body swiftly going into shock.

"Loreli!" Will erupted with fury and put the Dark Lord down with a flying kick. But seeing Loreli injured was enough to break the rage's hold on him. The massive beast toppled sideways, and Will knelt down and scooped his sister into his arms. He ran, carrying her, down the length of the entry tunnel.

The main cavern was still reeling from Loreli's alchemy, but the smoke had begun to clear, and as Will came lurching out from under the archway he was spotted by Rocco and a phalanx of his minions.

"There! *Get them!*"

Will and Loreli were trapped. Led by Rocco, dozens of enraged demons rushed toward them, many of them bearing swords, maces, and lances.

Loreli was bleeding badly and losing consciousness. She knew she was passing out, and, kicking into self-preservation mode, she used her left hand—her right was totally useless now, due to the gaping wound on her shoulder—to open her duster.

"The Flame Sticks," she rasped. "In my coat. Take one!"

Will reached in and grabbed one.

"Break it in half . . . the lake . . ."

Will understood. He cracked the Flame Stick in half and then threw it. It burst forth with a flare as it flew into Fire Lake, which erupted like napalm. The roar was deafening. It was a deadly and beautiful diversion, because the lake not only caught fire but exploded like the surface of the sun, molten lava leaping out and splashing down, landing atop terrified demonteens, who shrieked as they burned to death.

Will bent time and ran like the wind, weaving his way through the confused and frightened hordes. Seeing the life draining out of Loreli spurred him on, so he ran even faster. As he passed Rocco, he leapt, twisted, and kicked, catching Rocco in the throat. As Rocco dropped to the ground, his eyes bulging, Will ran up a set of stone stairs with Loreli in his arms. Up and up they went, finally blasting out of the doorway in Smiling Bob's Underground Tours.

Will looked down at her. Her eyes were closed and she was unconscious. He felt her neck. Her pulse was weak.

He rushed her out the door, onto the street, up Yesler and into his parked EVO, where he put her in the passenger seat. He pulled a six-inch healing balm patch out of the glove compartment and placed it on her wound. Then he fired up the EVO. A woman in a gigantic Chevy SUV had pulled up and was blocking him. He laid on his horn. She was on the phone and waved him away dismissively. He got out and screamed at her.

"Move your car!"

Again she swatted at him like he was nothing more than a mosquito. Will reached a finger to the back of his neck and tapped in a code on the Power Rod retrieval patch. He could hear the rod screaming down through the sky and held out his palm. *Whap!* He activated it. With two swipes, he chopped the SUV down to the size of a Mini Cooper. The woman actually kept yammering on the phone for a few seconds before she realized what had just happened. Then she started screaming. But Will was already in his EVO and pulling out past her. He shot through the city streets.

In minutes he was at the mansion, carrying Loreli in through the garage. Rudy and Emily were squabbling in the kitchen over the last piece of Patty's Pizza when Will rushed through the door with Loreli in his arms.

"What happened?" said Rudy.

"Watch the street!" said Will.

Rudy moved to the window and stared outside, the whites of his eyes going huge.

"Are they gonna, like, attack or something?" he asked.

"I don't know, just keep an eye out!"

Rudy glanced at Emily and saw that she was trembling. He wasn't very good at talking to girls, and Emily made him especially nervous. But he figured it was time for him to say something that sounded brave.

"It's going to be okay," he told her.

She looked out the window, her eyes wild with fear. Rudy wanted to say more, but he couldn't think of anything. He felt like he'd failed her. But when he patted her ever so softly on her shoulder, she didn't flinch or turn away.

• • •

Will dashed down the hall and into the guest room. Loreli's lips were blue. He gently placed her in the bed and quickly changed the healing patch on her shoulder. He touched her face. It was cold. Again he felt for a pulse. Still there, but growing even weaker. She'd lost a lot of blood, and even with the healing patch, she needed fluids and she needed them fast. He set up an I.V., then slapped up a vein on her arm, pressed the needle into it, and taped the tubing to her forearm. The saline started to drip. Then he took her temperature. She was hot, 101 degrees. He wiped the perspiration off her forehead with a damp cloth.

"You're going to be okay, you're going to make it," he said. He wanted to sound reassuring, but his voice had the slightest tremor of falsity in it. He wasn't only trying to convince her, but himself as well. She *had* to be okay; anything else would be a disaster. The fact that she'd been wounded was his fault, and he felt the weight of responsibility bearing down on him. He checked under the new healing patch. The chemicals were doing their job, and already her deep wound was looking better, coagulating rapidly, the tissue repairing itself.

Pacing like a panther at the window, Rudy kept up a vigilant watch. But the mansion would not come under siege this night.

Hearing the commotion downstairs, Natalie rose from her bed. Her brain kept repeating the scene in the school hallway with Will and Loreli on a loop. It was like a knife in her gut seeing them touching, whispering, their lips meeting. She had skipped the rest of the school day, just walked right out like a zombie and wandered the streets. With each step she'd taken, she'd asked for answers and gotten none, even though she'd walked for miles. When she came home, she'd taken a long hot shower. Afterward she'd once again applied the purloined lip-gloss, and in minutes her mind was racing along the fringes of anger and despair. Every time she closed her eyes she was assaulted with painful images, her mind crowded with nightmarish visions of the boy she loved in the arms of the emerald-eyed vixen.

She wouldn't talk to Emily and she refused to answer her door when Will knocked on it before he went out. She didn't want to hear him say where he was going because she already knew. He was going out with *her*. Now Will had come back, there was noise downstairs, and Natalie felt like she was in some kind of weird limbo. Had he brought Loreli back there? Could Natalie possibly endure the pain of seeing Will acting out feelings for someone else? She doubted it. But she couldn't just hide up in her room. It felt weak. She opened her closet and stared at the clothes inside. She would get dressed, then go downstairs and face whatever she found there.

In the guest room Loreli opened her eyes to find Will sitting by her bed, watching her. Seeing that she'd regained consciousness, he smiled and made a peace sign.

"How many fingers?"

"Two."

"Very good. How are you feeling?"

Loreli shifted, rising up slightly on her pillow, and winced as pain shot through her shoulder. She could still feel the blade cutting into it. But she was strong, and she willed the pain away and conjured up a brave smile.

"Better. Thanks to you."

Will's face darkened with guilt. "It's thanks to *me* that you were almost killed in the first place."

Loreli nodded. She wasn't going to argue. Will's anger had overshadowed his judgment in a tight spot. He had been driven by it, ruled by it, forced to obey it.

It was as if Will were reading her mind. "I got mad," he said, "and the red rage came over me. I wasn't thinking as clearly as I should have been. The thing is, when I get mad, I get stronger, and if I'm stronger I feel like I can kick ass. But . . . it doesn't matter how strong you are if you're acting stupid."

"The mind is a far deadlier weapon than the fist," said Loreli.

"Yeah, I get that," said Will.

She reached up with a weak hand and touched his arm.

"I understand the feeling, Will. I really do. I used to feel the same way. I'd get so mad that I'd lose control. It's who we are; it's part of us. And it's because of him. His blood."

Will's interest was piqued. "Did you see red, too?"

"Yeah, and as it got more intense, sometimes things would just go . . . black. When I was in ninth grade, down in San Francisco, I was following some demons who'd been harassing this homeless family in the Tenderloin. They got the dad drunk and baited him into fighting another homeless guy for money. They gave both men baseball bats and made them go at it so they could videotape it. The guy's family, including his little girl, watched. She started crying. I couldn't take it, I just started shaking, and the red madness took over. I threw down some smoke and used the bats on the demon creeps who'd started it all. I totally lost control . . . just beat them right into the ground. I was so intent on putting them down, I didn't see another demon attacking the family. The little girl was killed. I can still see her eyes sometimes at night when I can't sleep. After that night, I knew I had to deal with it."

"What do you mean 'deal with it'?"

Loreli's eyes softened. "There's a way to make it go away."

Will felt a great yearning rise up within him. But his logical mind wrested control.

"That doesn't seem possible."

"I'd have thought that after all we've seen in this life, you and me, that you of all people would know that anything's possible."

"You're saying that you used to have the same anger . . . issue I do, but you did something and now you don't? Ever?"

"That's right."

"Tell me. What did you do?"

"It's the blood, Will. It's all about the blood."

"You mean *his* blood." The blood that made them . . . different. What made them stronger and faster and smarter than regular humans. "It runs through our veins, we can't change that."

"Maybe you're not as smart as you think," she said.

"Okay. So make me smarter," said Will.

"I found a way to purge myself of his blood. You're gonna laugh, but I call it 'demon dialysis.' I modified a dialysis machine and used it to filter his blood out of my body, so it's *me* running my life, *me* making my decisions, *me* staying cool, calm, and collected."

Will's eyes narrowed. If she was telling the truth, the consequences were far reaching. He was at once terrified and thrilled at the prospect of purging himself of the Dark Lord's blood. But being the son of the Prince of Darkness—while a terrible curse—*had* given him advantages over mere mortals, and helped him fight demons. He couldn't risk losing what powers he had, could he? But what about Loreli? She obviously had powers equal and in some cases surpassing his, so if she had indeed conceived a system of purifying her blood, she had done so without sacrificing the intellectual and physical abilities she'd inherited from their father.

"You want to think about it," said Loreli. "That's good. I'd expect you to. Just know that I can help you, Will. And consider, just *consider*, the idea that your life could be so much better. You wouldn't have to be afraid of yourself anymore."

"I wouldn't lose any of my powers?"

"I can't guarantee you anything. All I can tell you is that I didn't lose even a half a step. What I lost was his . . . his awful hold over me."

The thought of losing his sense of self, his abilities—even if they were inexorably bound to the Dark Lord—terrified Will. Loreli could see it in his eyes.

"Sometimes," said Loreli, "in order to get one thing you want you have to let go of another."

She reached up and slid her fingers around Will's neck, rubbing in what Will assumed was a gesture of comfort, but he was afraid she might touch his Power Rod retrieval patch, so he firmly removed her hand. It felt sweaty, and he wiped the perspiration from his skin. Loreli now appeared wan and spent, and like what she was: a girl who'd just been wounded by the Devil. She breathed in deeply and exhaled slowly.

"I'm tired . . . I think I need to sleep," she said. She closed her eyes and sank back into her pillow.

"I'm glad you're okay," said Will, softly.

Loreli appeared to already be asleep. Will rose and felt the exhaustion pulling at him, too. He was growing more tired by the second—as if there were weights on his eyelids—and he decided he'd better shut down for a couple of hours himself. Casting a parting glance at his sleeping sister, he went to the master control panel and armed the house. Rudy appeared beside him.

"Hey, you okay?" he asked.

"Yeah," said Will. "Just tired."

"Where were you? What happened? Did you smoke any demons?"

"A few. I'll bring you up to speed tomorrow."

"You still want me to keep a lookout?" Rudy looked behind him at the window. "Emily went to bed. I gave her the last piece of pizza." Rudy was disappointed about the pizza but hopeful about Emily.

"No. We're good. If they aren't here by now, they aren't coming. Get some sleep."

Will wearily climbed the stairs, so tired he wondered if he could even make it to his room. He did, and he closed and locked the door behind him. Rudy lingered on the first floor, peering into the guest room at Loreli. She was smokin' hot even just lying there. Rudy shook his head, dazzled, then went upstairs, too.

A few minutes passed. Loreli opened her eyes and waited. She'd watched Rudy through slitted eyes, and she knew what was coming next. Or rather, *who*. Another minute passed, the grandfather clock in the hallway ticking. When she saw a shadow in the hallway she closed her eyes again, and kept them closed as she felt someone approaching. It was Natalie creeping into the room. Loreli continued to lie very still. Natalie stared at her, her eyes slowly sweeping over every inch of her adversary, from her cascading hair and her perfect skin to her long eyelashes and the subtly beautiful medallion around her neck. She was flawless. It was easy to see what Will saw in her. Though Natalie was of course unarmed, in her mind's eye she saw herself bringing a swift death to this interloper, this love thief. *Bad thoughts. Bad thoughts.*

Loreli spoke, her lips moving, without opening her eyes. "Natalie . . ."

Natalie's skin prickled. Loreli's voice was disarming, so smooth and honey-sweet. Already Natalie felt on the defensive. She needed to hold it together, to take control. Was Loreli even awake?

Loreli's eyes finally opened. Natalie, who had never had the full force of those eyes turned on her before, almost gasped. These were not the eyes of a mere mortal, they were the eyes of a goddess. Frighteningly beautiful, and so alarmingly green they seemed to shimmer in the dull light. Loreli had some kind of intense mojo, an unearthly power not dissimilar to Will's. She tried to sit up and winced, and only then did Natalie notice she was injured.

"What happened to you?" said Natalie.

"Will and I ran into . . . some unpleasantness. But we're okay. We . . . protected one another."

Natalie clenched her jaw and balled her hands into fists. She tried to breathe deeply, but her lungs felt shallow and her eyes watered. With her uninjured arm, Loreli reached over and slid a tube from her coat, squeezed out some cream onto her fingers, and casually spread it over her face as she spoke, massaging it into her skin.

"Natalie . . . I see the way you look at me, I see the pain in your eyes."

"What makes you think . . ."

But Natalie couldn't even finish her denial. It was futile. She knew how her eyes belied her emotions, offering them up for all to see. Other people could read her like a billboard.

"I'm sorry for your pain," said Loreli. "But you must know that Will and I are . . . linked."

"*Linked?* You just met," said Natalie.

"I know. But it feels like we've known each other our whole lives."

Loreli looked at Natalie with pity. She fingered the medallion around her neck.

"Don't tell me he hasn't *told* you about us," said Loreli.

"No. He wouldn't . . ."

Her voice trailed off sadly, so Loreli finished the sentence for her. "He wouldn't tell you anything about me, would he."

Natalie's stony silence was her answer.

"Oh, dear. You love him very much, don't you," said Loreli. It sounded condescending. "I'm sure he'll talk to you. When he feels the time is right."

Natalie's muscles were tightening and her head felt like it had a metal band around it that was getting tighter by the second. She stared furiously at Loreli.

"I'm here, you're here, so why not just say what you're hinting at?" asked Natalie.

Loreli shook her head slowly from side to side. "I wish I could, I really do. But he's sworn me to secrecy. He won't let me talk to you about . . . us."

Us. The word was brutal, murderous.

"He might have kissed you, but Will is in love with *me*," said Natalie. But a voice inside told her, *It's over, done, finito, he's fallen for her.*

"Of course he is. But love can be ephemeral, and you're losing him," said Loreli.

"You don't know what you're talking about. You don't even know him!"

"You're wrong. I *do* know him. In a way, he and I are closer than the two of you could ever be. You know, he's different from normal boys. He has different needs."

"I know what he needs," said Natalie. She tried to be firm with her voice but was quickly losing control. She felt that at any minute the floor would become liquid and she would fall into it and drown. Loreli, with her stunningly beautiful face, just kept smiling that annoyingly condescending smile.

"You *used* to know. But things have changed."

"He still loves me." If she could just say it enough, it would be true, and Loreli would disappear.

"If he loves you, if he truly loves you as much as you believe he does, then ask yourself this question: Why won't he tell you about us?"

"He will. He would have. He's been . . . busy."

Loreli now looked stricken, as though holding in a painful secret. She forced a brave sad smile for Natalie.

"I'm really sorry. I don't want you to blame me, to hate me. None of this is my fault. Things just . . . happen. Come here. Come closer."

Natalie wanted to run away. But she moved closer, and when Loreli held out her hands, she took them.

"Your hands are dry. Here, try this."

Loreli extracted another tube from her coat and squeezed a dollop of hand cream into Natalie's palm. Numbly, Natalie rubbed the cream in, and it softened her hands instantly.

"That's better now, isn't it?"

Natalie didn't respond, just kept rubbing the lotion into her hands and her wrists. It heated on her skin, and the warmth spread quickly.

"Listen, Natalie. I don't think he'll talk to you about us, I think he'll just . . . stay silent. And keep shutting you out. But it's worth a try. Go to him. Go and see."

"I will," Natalie said, standing up. She turned and left the guest room.

Loreli listened to her light footsteps, silently counting off the seconds as Natalie climbed the staircase. At the top of the stairs, Natalie found Will's room and tried the door. It was locked.

He would tell her. He *would*. He had to. She tapped lightly. "Will?"

Loreli's words echoed. *He'll just . . . stay silent.*

She knocked again, harder and louder this time. "Will?"

Keep shutting you out.

"Will, I need to talk to you," said Natalie.

Silence.

"Please . . . ?"

She put her ear to the door. Silence. She took a breath to speak again, louder this time. *One last chance. Cross your fingers. This time he'll do the right thing. This time he'll come and open the door.*

"Will . . . I need you."

Count to five. One. He'll come. Two. He's probably walking to the door right now. Three. He'll open it and tell me everything. Four. He won't hide things from me, will he? Five. Tell me the truth, Will, just tell me the truth!

Silence. The door did not open. *Shutting you out. Shutting you out.*

In his room, Will was facedown on his bed, out like a light, sleeping dreamlessly, a small patch on the back of his ear inflamed from the dab of narcotic potion his sister had rubbed there. Out in the hallway, Natalie turned from Will's door, and on suddenly wobbly legs she made her way back to her room, closing her door with a click, shutting herself in, shutting the world out. She sat on her bed and gazed out the window, wringing her hands. She felt lightheaded as she watched the stars fall out of the sky.

Chapter Eighteen: Seeking Father

Will awakened tangled in his sheets. His head felt heavy. He had to look at the clock twice to make sure it was right. He'd actually slept for four hours straight, a heavy, narcotic sleep, which, judging by the condition of his bed, he'd had to claw his way out of. It was already nearly dawn. He decided that decompressing from the battle in the Under City, combined with the guilt of getting his sister wounded—not to mention inhaling lungfuls of smoke from the burning Fire Lake—had made a potent cocktail that had knocked him out. There were more important things to worry about—like finding and destroying the Dark Lord's head. He got up and quickly showered and brushed his teeth, then went downstairs to check on Loreli. The guest room was empty, the bed made with precise hospital corners. Obviously her shoulder had healed up just fine, which didn't surprise him.

In the kitchen a fresh pot of coffee had been brewed. He poured himself a cup.

"Loreli?' he called. There was no answer.

He moved downstairs and found her in his lab with her own cup of coffee, working on one of his computers.

No one touched his computers. *No one.* He was about to ask her just exactly what she thought she was doing when she cut him off with: "We have to find the head. You were still asleep and I didn't want to waste any time."

She moved out of the way and Will sat down, taking back control of his computer. First he checked the screen monitoring April. Nothing had changed.

Then he turned his attention to Loreli. "It must have been blown off his body in the blast," he said. His fingers flew over the keys as he brought up the files associated with his extensive searches of the blast area surrounding Mount St. Emory. "The demons have been over every square inch within the blast radius."

"How do you know?" asked Loreli.

"I had a little encounter with them, here," he said, pointing to the mountains above which he'd found his Power Rod.

"They must have found his body parts and pieced them together," said Loreli.

"But they didn't find the head."

"And if we can find it . . ."

"Then we can destroy it, and bring an end to this thing once and for all."

As Will began typing furiously, the monitors lit up around him, displaying graphs and maps and computations.

"Since it wasn't within the projected coordinates of the blast pattern, we'll have to look outside it," said Loreli.

"I've already done that," said Will. "I expanded the parameters for miles and searched everywhere."

"What if . . . somehow someone or something, an animal maybe, found the head and moved it? It could be someplace that's already been searched, or even someplace further away."

"That's what I'm thinking, too," said Will.

He continued typing and the U.S. military's version of Google Earth came up on the screens.

"Wherever the head is, it's still . . . conscious. I can still hear him in my head sometimes. He's still able to conjure up thoughts, emotions, still able to propagate evil."

"If you were him, and your followers couldn't find you, what would you do?" asked Loreli.

Will thought about it. What would he do if he were immobile and wanted to be found? "I'd send out a signal," he said. Just like in the Boy Scout handbook.

Will began typing again, searching, going from computer to computer, screen to screen.

"What kind of signal?" said Loreli.

"He's evil, he exudes evil. Look for acts of violence, crimes, whatever." Together Will and Loreli worked on the computers, and in an hour they had amassed a list of hate crimes, kidnappings, murders, suicides, and other horrific crimes that had occurred since the blast at Mount St. Emory. They studied them and narrowed the list down, focusing on only the most terrifying. But the crimes didn't follow any discernable pattern, and Will couldn't find what he was looking for. He *had* to find the Dark Lord's head soon. For his mother's sake, and for the sake of all those who would suffer should the Prince of Darkness find his way to wholeness again and swing the Sword of Armageddon. Frustration was setting in.

And then he got a break. He happened upon a blogger's rant about giant hailstones that had killed seven people in Deer Park. Further investigation led him to bizarre reports of four rafters finding a "river of blood" in Noxon, Montana. Sensing that he was on to something, Will shifted the search from crimes to freak occurrences and strange happenings, and came across the scorched adulterers in Davenport, the group of mourners struck blind en masse on the Thompson Falls Dam, and the purity pledge teens whose skin erupted in Potlatch, Idaho. Will suspected that all five events had something in common: the Dark Lord.

Five more minutes of research, and Will had part of the puzzle solved. The events loosely corresponded to five of the seven plagues listed in the Book of Revelation. Deer Park, Noxon, Davenport, Thompson Falls, and Potlatch. Five events. Five points. By connecting the points where the events had occurred, Will formed a five-pointed star. For Satanists, a potent symbol: the pentagram.

"This is it. This is him. It's his work," said Will.

"How do you know?"

"Call it a hunch, whatever, but it's him. No doubt about it."

Will used a graphics program to overlay the pentagram on the map. It was rough, but it fit. He calculated the center of the graph and came up with Coeur d'Alene, Idaho.

"The head's here. Coeur d'Alene. Let's find out what's happened in Coeur d'Alene . . . anytime after the Mount St. Emory eruption."

They both began searching, using four different computers.

Loreli was the one who found it. "Will, I think I have something."

She was pointing to a story about little eight-year-old Zachary Hastings, who had used a baseball bat—a gift from his grandfather—to brutally maim his family. When questioned, Zachary said he'd heard a voice telling him what to do, and that he believed the voice belonged to the Devil. Will's eyes lit up.

"Bingo. Good work. This is it. Gotta be. I'm gearing up."

Will was up and packing, loading weapons into his backpack. Loreli watched, amazed. In a matter of hours, Will Hunter had accomplished what a thousand demons had been unable to. He'd found the Black Prince's head.

"I'll call you when I . . ." he hesitated. "When I've destroyed it."

Loreli stood up.

"You can't think I'm letting you go after that thing alone. I'm going with you."

"You're injured."

"I *was* injured. I'm fine now, thanks to those healing patches of yours. So finish packing, and let's go."

Ditching her hadn't worked so well the last time. Will gave in and finished packing. Leaving Loreli in the kitchen, he went upstairs.

In his room, Will could not get Natalie out of his mind. He hated the idea that, if something happened and he never came back, the last conversation they'd ever have had happened through a closed door. And if Loreli was right—if there was a way he could purge himself of the Dark Lord once and for all—maybe there was a chance for the two of them to be together. Maybe he had been putting up a wall between them for nothing. There was no time now to talk to her now, but he couldn't just leave. So he dashed off a note.

> *My dearest Natalie. I know these past few days have been difficult for you, for us, and I want to you know that no matter what happens, that you are forever in my heart. You have to trust me now, trust that there is a good reason I have not been sharing everything I'm doing. I'll tell you everything as soon as I can. In the meantime, please believe that I have loved you since the first day I laid eyes on you and I will love you for eternity.*

Will folded the note four times, went out into the hallway, and slipped it into the crack of Natalie's door just above the doorknob. She couldn't miss it. Then he went downstairs and into the kitchen where Loreli was eating like a horse, polishing off her second bagel with cream cheese and strawberry jam, fueling up for their upcoming journey. Will opened a drawer and pulled out a handful of protein bars and stuffed them in his pockets, then filled his stainless steel travel mug with hot coffee.

"Let's hit it," he said.

"Gotta make a quick pit stop first," she said. "Two minutes."

Will didn't like having to wait any longer but he nodded. Loreli started for the downstairs bathroom, but as soon as she was out of eyeshot she changed her course, went upstairs, and found Will's room quickly. She went in and wasted no time messing up his bed even more than it already was, yanking up the sheets and twisting them. She whipped out a small bottle of perfume and sprayed the sheets, then took off her medallion and dropped it on the bed.

Out in the hallway she noticed the note stuck in Natalie's door. She took it, unfolded it, and quickly read it. This was a bonus. Smiling, she put the note in her pocket.

Will wheeled the BMW out through the big iron gates and away from the manor while from the passenger seat Loreli watched the early dawn's first attempts at remaking the world. They headed down the hill to Mercer Street where they caught the freeway, and headed south to I-90 East, starting the roughly 260-mile drive from Seattle to Coeur d'Alene. Will was in a foul mood, ready to kick some ass. The gray skies and blowing rain didn't help. He kept thinking about what the Dark Lord had done to him and how much it hurt, knowing his mother was in mortal danger.

He drove fast. More than once he saw headlights in his rearview mirror, someone on his tail, but they never stuck and so he couldn't be sure if they were being followed or not. He pushed the German machine far over the speed limits, hitting 175 and then 180. He'd never driven this fast with a passenger in the car, but if Loreli was frightened she didn't show it. He continued to push the BMW faster and faster. Time was not his ally. If the demons found the Dark Lord's head before he did, then they'd be able to resurrect him, and the beast would no doubt be in a nasty mood himself, having had his head blown off in a volcano. So Will needed to get to Coeur d'Alene fast. He drove harder even as the weather became more severe.

Twice more he scrutinized trailing headlights, but he sped away from them so easily he concluded he wasn't being followed. But that didn't mean he let his guard down. No way. He would be one step ahead of everyone this time.

The third time he saw headlights following them, he slammed on the brakes and went into a sideways drift, skidding to a halt. Then he got out and pulled out a couple of Flareblades and held them at the ready while Loreli stood on the other side of the car, prepared to offer backup if it was needed. The surprised carload of teens who'd been trying to keep up with him swerved, their mouths agape, and sped past, destined for some pretty nasty dreams about the lunatic in the middle of the highway wielding two burning knives. Will and Loreli got back in the car and pushed the pedal to the metal. They made it to Coeur d'Alene in two hours and seventeen minutes, only having to outrun the state police once.

Cruising into Coeur d'Alene, they searched for 11786 Bouldin Lane, where the "Hastings Possession"—as it was being referred to in the media—had occurred. They passed a police car and Will slowed. When the cops pulled a U-turn to bird-dog him, he knew he'd have to lay low for a few minutes—a high-speed chase through the streets of Coeur d'Alene was the last thing he needed right now—so he pulled into a Tastee-Freeze. The cops pulled over across the street and watched as Will got out and went to the order window, bought a couple of cheeseburgers and cokes, and brought them back to the BMW. If they had to stop anyway, they might as well take advantage of it.

While they ate and drank and waited out the cops, Loreli began to probe. "The girl, Natalie. Is she your girlfriend?"

Will chewed slowly before swallowing. "Do we really have to talk about this?" he asked.

"I guess there's my answer." She smiled.

Will clenched his jaw. Sometimes girls drove him nuts. He sighed. "I rescued her and her sister from Harrisburg. Their parents were killed, so I brought them with me. I wasn't going to just leave them there."

"It's okay to love someone, you know," she said.

"It's not exactly safe," said Will. "For them or for us."

Loreli neatly folded up her yellow cheeseburger wrapper.

"We're still half human," she said.

"Okay. Do you have a boyfriend?" Will asked.

"No. But . . . I could. For years I wouldn't even think about it. Every time I'd meet a guy, even see a guy I liked, I'd play the flash-forward game. You know the one? You imagine kissing the person, falling in love with them, hooking up, moving in, getting married or whatever . . . and then the little bundle of joy arrives."

Neither of them needed to mention that the little bundle of joy had a 50/50 chance of having scaly skin, horns, and a barbed tail.

"But things have been different since I figured out to get rid of *him*," she said, voicing the same hope he'd allowed himself that morning.

Will finished his cheeseburger and watched as the cops across the street started up their patrol car.

"Now if I met the right guy, I could actually have a relationship," said Loreli.

"I'm happy for you," said Will. It came out snarky, but he meant it, even though the bitter taste of his own unfulfilled love was on the tip of his tongue. He couldn't help but take a few seconds and fantasize about what his life would be like if he were able to fully love Natalie. The concept seemed inconceivably rich.

"If you wanted to give the whole dialysis thing a try, maybe you could, too. But you're a guy," said Loreli. "Guys are different, they don't sit around thinking about how cool it would be to be totally in love."

Will could have told her she was wrong, that he'd thought about it a thousand times. But what was the point? So he stayed silent.

A tricked-out Nissan Altima driven by a hot Asian chick screamed by. Across the street, the patrol car came to life, headlights switching on, blue and red flashers blasting to life and siren wailing, tires squealing as it pulled out in pursuit. Will looked over at Loreli. It was time for them to get moving.

"Let's go," he said, and backed the BMW out of the Tastee-Freeze lot and onto the highway. In two minutes they picked up Anders

Parkway and hung a left on Tanning Street, then a right on Bouldin Lane. Will drove slowly now, approaching cautiously. The house was a four-bedroom split-level affair set into a hillside on a good acre of land with old-growth pines. The lights in the house were out. It had the look of a home that had been abandoned. A Commander RV parked outside had a FOR SALE sign on it.

Will pulled into the driveway. The moment he saw the house, he knew it was a place of dark and ugly secrets. And the RV—something about it made Will's skin crawl. The thing sat there on its fat haunches like some giant beast, its grille a smug smile.

They got out. Will slipped on his backpack, Loreli her duster, and they walked to the front door of the house. Will closed his eyes and used his seventh sense to investigate his surroundings. The house was giving off some very malicious vibes, the kind found at the sites of mass murders and slaughterhouses. Will tapped on the door perfunctorily, though they both knew no one would answer. The Hastings were long gone, and who could blame them? Will took a step back, lifted a boot, and was ready to kick the door down.

"Wait a second, Superman, just hold on," Loreli said. Using a tiny spray bottle with a WD-40-style tip she spritzed the lock, which hissed and smoked. Then she turned the handle and the door opened easily.

"Maybe not as much fun, but less noisy," she said. Then she turned and stopped him with a hand before he crossed the threshold.

"Hey . . . if we get in a shitstorm, are you gonna stay cool this time?"

"Don't worry about me," he said. He wished she hadn't made the comment. He *would* stay cool this time. He felt rotten about how things came down last time and wasn't going to make the same mistake again. He was in control.

They entered the house. Will's skin crawled. He could sense the Dark Lord's presence. Or was it just wishful thinking? He *wanted* to be close; he wanted to find him and destroy him so badly he could taste it. They explored the downstairs. It was just like millions of other middle-class homes, with its bargain furnishings and cheap, framed art prints on the walls. They went into the kitchen and Loreli opened the refrigerator. For a moment Will pictured the Dark Lord's head sitting there on the shelf next to the milk and orange juice. It wasn't, of course. The refrigerator was well stocked, but the produce and milk had gone bad and smelled. Loreli shut the door and ventured elsewhere. Will noticed a calendar stuck on the front with a goofy "Got Fun?" trout magnet from Hector's Bait Shop. The trout was smiling. Will was staring at it quizzically when he heard Loreli.

"Oh God," she said.

She had left the kitchen and was now standing at the bottom of the stairs. Will joined her and they stared at the dark bloodstains on the deep-pile chestnut carpet. The night Zachary had been possessed, he'd caught his father totally by surprise outside the doorway to his sister's room, swinging hard and striking him in the kneecap, then in the face, breaking his nose. Face bleeding, head spinning with shock and confusion, Andrew Hastings had tumbled down the stairs, and hit the landing with a pronounced grunt as his head slammed into the wall and he slumped over and bled on the carpet. Twelve seconds later, the voice in Zachary's head commanded him to attack his mother, and he did so, striking her four times, twice in the knees and twice on the head, before she, too, tumbled down the stairs, landing on top of Andrew. Then Zachary went after his siblings. Fortunately for Megan, she'd hidden in the bottom of the clothes hamper, and Zachary, in his rage, hadn't been able to find her.

Will imagined the scene, saw it playing in the chambers of his brain, over and over. The parents at the bottom of the stairs in a heap, then, disbelieving, rising up—the blood flowing so very crimson—then patiently climbing back up on broken twisted limbs to hug Zachary to their loving bosoms, only to be bludgeoned again, to fall again, to suffer the same agonizing pain. The ghostly scene was in a loop, the phantoms sweeping up and down the stairs. No matter how many times they reached out to their son, he cleaved them, hurt them. And yet they came back for more, these masochists. Such is the stuff of parenthood; such is the stuff of love.

"I think he's here. I think his head is in this place," said Loreli.

"I think you're right," said Will.

"Can you sense where it is?" she asked.

"No. Not yet. Let's keep looking."

They looked in every room. Opened every door and cupboard. Checked under every bed and opened every drawer. They searched the entire house, floor to ceiling, but found nothing. Will was frustrated.

"It has to be here somewhere."

"But where?" asked Loreli. "If they picked it up somewhere and brought it in, where would they have put it?"

Then Will remembered something. The calendar on the refrigerator. He went to it. Martha Hastings had colored in the dates and made notes about their trip. *Fishing, camping, rafting!* One day, a Monday, had a frowning face. *Back home again.* Will remembered the reports about Zachary's possession. It had occurred early on a Tuesday morning.

"The kid . . . Zachary. He heard the voices the night they came home. That's when he was possessed. Maybe . . ."

Will moved to the front door. Loreli followed him.

"Maybe what?"

Will opened the door and looked out at the Commander RV parked outside.

"Maybe they picked the head up on vacation and brought it home with them."

Will walked quickly toward the Commander. It was unlocked. He checked inside while Loreli stood watching, hoping he would find the head. But the RV was empty. Will stepped out looking confused and angry.

"I can feel him. I know he's close."

Will could sense that the Dark Lord was close because in fact he was. His head—his filthy, feculent skull—was on top of the RV. It had been blasted out of Mount St. Emory like a cannonball and landed miles away in the stiff branches of a towering fir tree. Weeks had passed. Finally the Hastings family RV had backed into the tree, jostling it, and the Dark Lord's head had tumbled down and landed atop it. Then the interminable ride, the hours in the blazing sunlight. In all his thousands of years, the Dark Lord had never suffered such humiliation. Now he was finally close to being found and healed. His eyes opened. He knew he must remain silent with the boy so very close. He could hear help coming. In seconds, he would be on his way to freedom. In his mind he rose up 666 feet in the air, and he saw them coming. Two speeding vehicles carrying shedemons. His liberation was at hand! But, sensing danger, he dropped back down to earth quickly.

The boy was wily and was now climbing the side of the RV. He was going to look in one final place: the vehicle's roof. If the boy caught sight of him, it was all over. He would no doubt use one of his wicked weapons to destroy him. The Dark Lord had to think fast. The lips on the severed head smiled. He had an ace up his sleeve.

Will was climbing the side of the Commander because he had a mad hunch. If the head of the Dark Lord wasn't inside the RV, maybe it was on top of it. The head could have ended up on its roof, and then been transported out of the blast projection zone. That would explain why *his* followers had been unable to locate it. Will was about to lift himself up and peer onto the roof when he heard his mother scream.

"Will! Help me!"

The voice sounded like it was coming from inside the house. Will was stunned. *She was in the hospital this morning; I checked! Did the Dark Lord somehow break through my defenses? Did he kidnap her to set a trap for me here? I've got to save her!* Will leapt down and ran toward his mother's scream, fury quickly rising up within him. Loreli was confused. She hadn't heard the voice. It had only been in Will's head.

"What are you doing?" she shouted after him.

Will didn't answer. He reached back and tapped the retrieval patch on the back of his neck and, seconds later, the Power Rod screamed down out of the sky into his waiting hand as he ran inside.

"Mom!"

He heard another scream, from upstairs. He took the stairs two at a time, ready to kill now and ask questions later.

Now he could hear the sound of April crying! Will's pulse quickened. On the top landing, he kicked open the door to Zachary and Ben's room, stepped over the bloodstains on the carpet, and yanked open the closet door.

"Mom?"

Shirts hanging, toys and shoes on the closet floor. But no April. He heard her voice again.

"Will! Help me!"

He raced from the room and out into the hallway. Where was it coming from? He heard laughter now, the deep-throated, gravelly, mocking laughter of the Dark Lord.

"Come to save your mother, have you, son?" he bellowed. Will's head whipped around. Where was the monster? Was his head here, upstairs, and they had missed it? The voice had come out of the darkness.

"Show yourself!"

More laughter. And now, at the end of the hall, there it was: the Dark Lord's head. Floating. Translucent. Laughing that horrible, taunting laugh.

Everything Will saw now had a malevolent scarlet tint. Propelled by a tide of crimson hate, he blasted a series of fireballs at the Dark

Lord's head. But it vanished, and the fireballs hit the wall behind it instead, setting it aflame. Now the floating head was behind him.

"She's going to suffer, my son. Unless you bend to my will."

Will whipped around and fired again. He was hitting nothing, because the vision of the Dark Lord's head was just that: a vision. But Will was mad with rage. Dimly he registered Loreli watching from the top of the stairs, possibly even screaming, but Will couldn't hear her because the sound of a jet engine was roaring in his ears as he continued to attack the visage of the Dark Lord's head. *Slash, slash!* Nothing but air. The head moved about like a piece on a chess board. This was a game of the mind, and the Prince of Darkness was winning.

More laughter rang in Will's ears. And then he heard, again, the agonizing sound of his mother crying.

Will felt the rage pulsing through his entire body. He fought to remain calm but couldn't keep his blood from running hot. He hated the Dark Lord with such a passion that it blinded him to all else. Then, from the master bedroom, he heard a noise. He ran down the hallway and inside, where he saw his mother sitting on the floor, holding the Dark Lord's head in her lap. His dream. It was exactly like his dream.

"Mom . . ."

He walked cautiously toward her. The house was burning and filling with smoke.

"You can't help me now, Will."

As he stepped closer, he realized that his mother's lips weren't moving. The words—even though it was his mother's voice—were being uttered by the Black Prince.

"Your father is going to punish you now . . ."

"SHOW YOURSELF!" screamed Will.

The visage of April—and the Dark Lord's head on her lap—disappeared. The red rage had taken control. Will looked out the second-story window. Loreli had fled the burning house and was outside in the driveway surrounded by five shedemons. As they converged on her, she locked eyes with Will, a palpable pain coursing between them. Then she whipped on a pair of black eye guards and threw down a crystal orb. She was instantly cloaked in a cloud of white light that temporarily blinded the shedemons.

"Loreli!" Will shouted.

BOOM! A gas line in the house exploded and Will was thrown off his feet, his head slamming into the wall. Rising up, his vision blurry, he looked outside. Loreli was gone. He watched in horror as four shedemons, led by Blue Streak, landed on the roof of the Commander RV. Blue Streak knelt and picked up an object: the head of the Supreme Lord of the Underworld, the Devil himself. As Blue Steak carefully placed the head in an ornate container, the Dark Lord's eyes opened and stared at Will, mocking.

Will screamed, "*NO!*"

Blue Streak and the other shedemons sprouted fleshy wings and flew up into the night carrying the head of their Lord. Will turned to give chase, but a second explosion rocked the house, and the floor beneath him gave way. He plunged through it and landed downstairs. The first floor was thick with smoke and engulfed in flames. Will tried to breathe, tried to stand, but his lungs filled with smoke. His brain grew dizzy. He heard sirens in the distance.

His lungs burning with hot smoke, Will feared he was about to say goodbye to his life. With his last conscious effort, he flung his Power Rod toward the front picture window. It crashed through and sailed skyward. Then he clawed his way across the scorched carpet through the smoke-filled room toward the front door. He'd made it halfway there when a black veil fell across his universe. The burning grandfather clock struck twelve times and then collapsed.

Hours later, Will opened his eyes. He was in the field behind the Hastings house, lying in the middle of the corn patch in Martha's vegetable garden, unsure of how he'd gotten there. Every breath was torture. He sat up and got his bearings. His whole body hurt, but the pain of regret was even stronger. He'd failed and yet again fallen victim to his volcanic anger. Once again, he'd been unable to tame it. And his failure might have cost Loreli her life. It had almost cost him his.

Fire trucks had arrived and the house had been doused with flame retardant and water. No one had thought to look in the vegetable garden. Will got up and scanned the charred framework of the house, looking for Loreli. She was nowhere to be seen. The big Commander RV had burned, too, and was now just a smoking hunk of charred metal. Will began making his way to his BMW, which was where he'd left it.

A firefighter spotted him as he staggered to his car, and called out. "Hey! Stop! Are you all right?"

The guy approached Will.

"A girl. Did you find a girl?" asked Will.

"No. Nobody. No bodies, no one."

She must have gotten away. Unless the shedemons had managed to capture her. But no, Will had seen them leave. They'd only taken the head, hadn't they? He couldn't be sure.

Will got in the car.

"Wait! Let me call you an ambulance."

Will fired up the BMW, jammed it into gear, and took off down the highway. As he drove, he cursed himself for once again allowing himself to go to his dark place. Letting the red rage in was the prime ingredient in his recipe for failure. He had found the Dark Lord's head, had the beast's demise within reach, and he'd let it slip from his grasp.

He failed so many people: his mother. Loreli. Even Natalie. He'd been so distant, and hurt her so much, when that was the last thing on Earth he wanted. And she was still hurting. But she'd see the note he left her. She would be okay once she'd read his note. And when this was over he would go to her, and explain everything. Maybe there was even a chance for them to be together for real.

Because he knew now that, if he could find her, he had to take Loreli up on her offer to purge him of his father's blood. It was risky; even Loreli had said so. But the alternative—allowing the rage to take over again and cost him another opportunity to end the Dark Lord's life—wasn't an option.

Chapter Nineteen: Blood Betrayal

The Under City was rocking. The demonteens had recovered from the explosion in Fire Lake, and preparations were under way for a celebration. Kegs of beer were rolled in and cases of vodka and bourbon were opened up. A huge vat was filled with a concoction of wine, beer, hard liquor, and cat blood, a brew that only a demon could love. They drank deeply from skull cups for hours. The cave was lit with ten thousand candles and, fueled by their potent grog, the worshippers chanted a discordant song, waiting, waiting for their leader. And then all heads turned as the procession entered.

It was the shedemons, led by Blue Streak, clad in violently red robes, and they carried a golden hutch. Inside the hutch was the head of their master. His eyes were open and his anger was not hidden. He was furious at these morons; they'd been unable to read the signs and locate him. He'd deduced their failure and knew the boy would quickly figure out what they could not; the boy would come for him. He was fortunate the boy was headstrong and vulnerable; otherwise the Dark Lord's head might have been destroyed. So in his anger the Dark Lord spewed curses—animal sounds, really, not words at all—in every direction, shaming his followers, who cast their eyes downward lest they find themselves immolated.

Loreli, in a hood, stood in the shadows at the back of the crowd, observing in patient silence.

Into the vault the shedemons marched, these soldiers in the army from Hell, and Blue Streak carefully placed the Dark Lord's head upon the neck of the body. The sinewy worm-like organisms rapidly began their gruesome healing work. Outside in the main cavern the assembled worshippers beseeched fate to bring about the resurrection of their fallen hero.

"He will rise!" they chanted, a hundred times and a hundred times more.

In the vault the Dark Lord cursed as he rose up to a sitting position. His neck was still repairing itself, but he could lift a hand and gaze upon his bony fingers as he moved them, marveling at the miracle of his everlasting evil life. Shedemon yelped at shedemon and the news of the rising spread quickly out into the massive cavern. The Dark Lord's acolytes erupted in a chorus of cheers.

"He has risen again!"

They cheered and hooted and clapped and banged their skull cups and weapons on rocks, the great clattering noises mingling with the screams of glee now swelling into an ear-splitting cacophony. Pedestrians walking 666 feet above in Pioneer Square were convinced an earthquake had struck.

But the Dark Prince was not happy. For as he stood, he felt his strength, which had been growing steadily since the moment his head had been affixed, now begin to seep away. He toppled sideways ignobly, caught by three shedemons. He turned to them, his malevolent eyes boring into their damned souls.

"Fools! I cannot yet rise. More is needed. Tell them all to shut up!"

The command was passed down the line until it reached the great hall, and the assembled demons begrudgingly shut their yaps. The entire Under City went quiet. The Dark Lord lay down on the marble slab, closed his burning yellow eyes, and slept.

Out in the main cavern, Loreli's suspicions had been confirmed. The Dark Lord needed more to rise again. Hope surged within her. She slipped unnoticed out of the Under City.

Natalie awakened, her head foggy. Her hands were near her face. They still smelled of Loreli's lotion. The first thoughts that entered her mind were vague; she knew she was nursing a lingering pain, and as her head cleared she remembered the situation she was in. Will was, quite probably, in love with another girl. And not just any girl, but a seductive, dazzlingly beautiful girl. Natalie remembered how, after Loreli's challenge, she'd gone to Will's room and knocked on the door, trying again to talk to him, needing to be rid of the ache that pulled at her heart. But he had shunned her, and she had gone to her room shamed, like a dog with its tail between its legs, and crawled into bed. She'd prayed for the bed to swallow her up and suck her down into the darkness and keep her there. She wanted no part of conscious thought; her thoughts brought her nothing but painful feelings that gave birth to more miserable thoughts. She needed some sort of distraction. But first she had to get out of bed, and at the moment that seemed a monumental task. Her head felt like it weighed about a thousand pounds.

She sat up, and then made herself go to the bathroom. The mirror was not kind. She splashed water on her face, then decided a shower might help. She turned the water on full blast, good and hot. Maybe she could wash away all the bad parts of her life and emerge into a clean new world of optimism. At least it might clear her head. She stayed under the pulsing spray for a full fifteen minutes, then washed and conditioned her hair. She watched the bubbles sliding down her body for a long time, until the water went clear, and then shut the shower off.

Stepping out and toweling off, she met the damnable mirror again. *You are who you want to be*, she told herself. She was stronger than this. She finished drying off and then brushed her hair and put on makeup. She slipped on one of her favorite camisoles and pulled on jeans, then ventured out into the hallway. She saw that Will's bedroom door was open. She went in. Her eyes went immediately to his bed, and in that millisecond, in that horrible overpowering moment, all the starch went out of her.

The bed was a total mess, a battlefield. The sheets and blankets were twisted and crumpled, half the pillows on the floor. The room reeked of Loreli's potent, musky perfume. Natalie wanted to flee from the scent. But something in the bed caught her eye as it reflected the morning light, and she moved closer, drawn like a fly to a black widow's web.

The medallion. The stunning medallion—which just a few hours ago had been hanging around Loreli's neck—was lying in Will's bed. *Just as Loreli had been.* The medallion had no doubt come off during an act of passion that Natalie could not bear to imagine. But still the scenes played in her mind as she reached for the bewitching piece of jewelry. She would fling it into Lake Washington. Or perhaps she would find a hammer and smash it into tiny fragments. She lifted it in her fingers, its weight surprisingly heavy. She brought the bright piece closer to her eyes and saw that there were tiny air holes around the circumference, as if it housed some living thing. She smelled it. A kind of animal scent mixed with lavender. As acid tears fell, she squeezed it tightly in her hand and thought about how to destroy it. But then she changed her mind and boldly put the medallion on, thinking, wishing, that some of Loreli's magic might rub off on her, make *her* as irresistible and alluring.

She backed out of the room, her eyes welded to the bed as her imagination hurled her down a dangerous road. *Flash!* She saw Will and Loreli kissing. *Flash!* She saw them undressing. *Flash!* She saw them . . . it was too much. Her heart pounded and felt battered; she wondered if she'd been careless with it, if her love for Will (*I would die for you, I would!*) was somehow a mistake. She recoiled from the bed, away from the scene of the crime, the horror of it, the repulsiveness of it, then turned back to her room, shamed and hopeless. When Will said he was going to send her and Emily away, she had stood toe to toe with him and declared that they were in this together, that they would fight side by side—to the death, if need be. Now where was she? Who was she? It was devastatingly obvious Will no longer wanted or needed her. This was the last straw, the end of any hope she had for their love. A tiny voice inside her head whispered that her life was over.

A few minutes later, Emily knocked lightly on Natalie's door. Getting no answer, she knocked louder.

"Natalie? Nat?"

She pushed on the door. Locked. Worry rising quickly within her, she went downstairs and found Rudy in the kitchen (where else?) scarfing down bean burritos as he simultaneously built a skyscraper turkey, cheese, and everything-else-in-the-kitchen sandwich.

"Have you seen Natalie this morning?" she asked.

"Should I have?"

Emily made a disgusted noise.

Rudy rolled his eyes. He rarely had a clue what Emily was talking about and was even more clueless about why she always ragged on him so much.

"What do you want me to do?" he asked.

"Nothing. Just sit here and stuff your face. You're good at that."

Rudy looked stung and Emily regretted her words right away.

"Wait. I'm sorry. I'm just freaking out because something's wrong with Natalie. Something bad. I just know it."

Rudy stopped eating.

They went upstairs. Rudy banged on Natalie's door.

"Natalie? Come on. Open up!"

Emily looked at him helplessly. Rudy knew it was time for action, time to get ballsy. Halfway down the hallway was a heavy granite sculpture base. He lifted it up, carried it over, and in one powerful motion bashed open Natalie's door. Emily rushed in and he followed. Natalie's bed was empty. They checked the bathroom. Nothing. The closet—just in case. Nada. The door must have locked accidentally when Natalie had left the room.

"It's Saturday. Maybe she took off with Will or something," said Rudy.

Emily just closed her eyes. Rudy thought she looked like she was listening for some kind of voice that only she could hear. In fact she was; she was trying to "feel" her twin.

"Maybe," said Emily, wanting to believe it.

She opened her eyes. She felt empty, like half of her self was missing. But she didn't know what to do about it. Maybe Natalie really was with Will. Natalie had been so upset when she came home yesterday; maybe they were talking and it wasn't going well, and that's what Emily was picking up on. Even though it was warm in the mansion, Emily felt suddenly cold, and shivered. She turned and left the room.

Outside the bedroom window, just a few feet away, Natalie was standing barefoot on the frigid bricks of the ledge. She was looking down at an ornamental spire in the garden below and wondering what it would feel like to fall two stories and be impaled upon it. She clutched Loreli's medallion and inhaled its heady fragrance, and her head felt so light that she thought she might lift up into the clouds like a bird.

Down in the gaming room, Emily circled Rudy, wielding a bamboo staff. He had one, too, and regarded her warily. He felt bad about it because he knew Emily was still worried about Natalie, but he couldn't help noticing that she was looking especially foxy, with her wild eyes and her slightly mussed hair. She *was* wild, too; wild inside because she was tired of feeling scared all the time. She wanted to take control of her life somehow. She swung the bamboo staff hard at Rudy's head. His reflexes were keen and he ducked the blow, but then she surprised them both by catching him with an uppercut that glanced off his chin.

"Ow! That hurt!"

"It's supposed to hurt," said Emily.

Rudy blocked her next two blows and went on the offensive, but Emily was energized now, and moved fast; she was a natural, and she'd been practicing much longer than Rudy had. Rudy pumped his head up and down comically.

"Tell me again why you're playing whack-a-mole with my skull?"

Whack.

"I'm not going to be a victim," Emily said. "I need to practice. And you're here. So come on, give me something to work with!"

Smack! She whacked his knee and he jumped up and down.

"Ow! Hey, pain is not my friend, okay?"

Emily kept after him. "You're not even trying!"

"I don't want to hurt you."

"Don't make me laugh," said Emily. She faked a double up/down shot. He went for it, and she caught him on the side of the head.

"Come on, Rudy! If we get attacked by demons or zombies or God knows what else, I want to be able to defend myself."

Rudy rubbed the sore spot on his head, then his eyes narrowed.

"That's it! Boo-ya! You woke up the monster!" said Rudy, and he turned up the heat, going on the attack. Having a bit of the dark side still in him made him strong and fast, and he was a whirling dervish of blows; blows that Emily for the most part deflected as she taunted him.

"That's more like it, dork face. Much better."

"Dork face? I'll show you dork face!"

They sparred silently for a full minute, neither gaining an obvious advantage, an equal number of glancing blows landing. Then, being the bigger and stronger of the two, Rudy managed to bull her backward, cornering her.

"You're good," he said. "I wouldn't want to mess with you. Now do you give up? Can we go do something else for a while?"

Emily's shoulders sagged and she slumped down, appearing winded. Feeling sympathy for her, Rudy let his guard down for a half second. It was enough. Emily sprang up and clobbered him square on the chin.

"Ahhhhh!" He grabbed his chin, which was now bleeding. "You cheated!"

"I guess you haven't heard," said Emily. "There's no cheating in stick fighting."

Rudy dropped his staff and it clattered to the floor. He went to the mirror and checked his wound.

"You marked me!" Though he was tough, his pride was wounded and he looked about ready to faint as he examined the blood on his chin.

"Come here, you big baby," said Emily.

She was at the equipment bench and had the first aid kit out. She made Rudy sit and held his face as she dabbed the nick with rubbing alcohol. He cringed.

"Ow!"

"Sorry," she said.

"Oh, sure, *now* you're sorry."

She was close to him. Closer than she'd ever been. She could smell the lotion he'd used after shaving that morning, and the shampoo he'd used on his hair. She could hardly believe it, but she liked the smell of both. And his skin. He had great skin. Their eyes met in one of those frozen moments, the first sparks of attraction flying. It was Emily who, blushing, turned away. Her mind was twisted around a little, trying to figure out how in the world she could have momentarily been attracted to Rudy. Rudy! Not only was he a world-class dork, but he was a demon! Or an ex-demon, whatever. Not her type at all. What was she thinking? The only reasonable answer was that he'd hit her in the head while they were sparring and she'd gone temporarily insane. She again thought of Natalie. Where could she have gone? She turned back to Rudy.

"I'm gonna head down to the Seattle Center. Maybe Natalie's down there. She used to love it there when we'd come down and visit as kids." When he kept looking at her expectantly, she sighed. "You wanna come with me?"

Rudy smiled. "Sure."

This is getting good, he thought.

They went out and walked toward the city bus stop. While waiting, Rudy had the strongest urge to hold Emily's hand.

Emily could feel his eyes on her. It was not a bad feeling. She kept wondering how on earth it was possible that she now found herself attracted to the very thing that had given her so much misery, so much agony. *Maybe this is progress*, she thought. She let her hand dangle at her side. When Rudy took it gently into his own, she didn't complain. His hand felt strong. She liked that.

Will pulled up to Loreli's house and parked the BMW. He'd made a pit stop at a Shell station and cleaned himself up a bit, but he still had some minor scrapes and burns to attend to, which he did courtesy of some healing patches. He'd had the two-hour drive back from Coeur d'Alene to reconsider his decision to go ahead with Loreli's "demon dialysis," but he just kept coming to the same conclusion. His choice made sense in order for him to find and slay his adversary, and it made sense for his future with Natalie. But none of that mattered if Loreli wasn't here.

He'd driven around Coeur d'Alene looking for her but come up empty. He hoped she'd be here, back at home, safe. He looked at the house. All was quiet, but one never knew. He could easily be walking into a trap; the place might be packed with shedemons. *Well, so be it*, he thought. *If they're in there waiting for me, then they're going to learn the meaning of pain.* He checked his Megashocker, which was charged up, and he loaded a small, short-range Flayer Pistol for backup.

He got out and eschewed the front door for the back, entering without knocking. He heard a soap opera on the TV and, holding the Flayer Pistol in front of him just like a movie cop, he moved down the hallway. Loreli's mom Tanya was lying on the floor in front of the TV. He quickly knelt and checked for a pulse. She was alive and reeked of vodka. She hadn't been attacked; she'd just passed out. *Charming*, thought Will. He looked around the room. Some books and knick-knacks had been hastily tossed into moving boxes.

He rose up and moved down the hallway leading to the basement. He heard noises coming from beneath him. Loreli, he hoped. But was she alone? Will opened the door slowly and had begun to descend the stairs when an orange light exploded in front of his face and his feet were yanked out from under him. He tumbled down the steps and landed hard on the concrete floor. Loreli stood over him wearing her duster and holding the trip cord she'd just used to bring him crashing down.

"Oh, it's you," she said. Her voice was cold. "I thought for sure you were dead."

She turned and went back to work, packing up her menagerie of chemicals and herbs and beakers into boxes. Sebastian ran back and forth anxiously in his cage. Will got up, rubbing the back of his head. He'd hit it hard bouncing off a couple of stairs.

"Nice to see you, too, sis. I was afraid something happened to you back in Coeur d'Alene. I woke up in the field behind the house. What happened?"

"What happened is you blew a gasket and I had to get the heck out of there. I'm lucky to be alive."

"I'm sorry."

"At this point, I don't particularly care."

"Listen, Loreli . . ."

She stopped packing and glared at him. "You shouldn't be here," she said.

"Where are you going?"

"I'm leaving. They got the head. You blew it."

"I know," Will said. "You don't have to rub it in."

"I'm not rubbing it in, just stating the facts. You blew our mission and now the Dark Lord's back in business. I can't do this alone now, and clearly I can't count on you. The only way for me to have any chance at all to take him down is to get the hell out of here, start over, and try and take him by surprise some other time."

"Loreli." Will's eyes were imploring and intense as he spoke. "He's got my mother. I can't fail again. I can do this, I can take care of him, but I need your help."

"Are you not listening? I'm leaving," said Loreli.

He didn't blame her for being angry. "Do what you have to do. But before you go, do me a favor first."

"You almost got me killed and now you want a *favor*? Okay, brother, I'll bite. What *favor* do you want?"

"I want to deny his blood. Like you did. I want you to change me, with your machine."

Will spotted a device draped in plastic in the corner. He moved quickly to it and removed the covering.

"Is this it?"

"Yes."

Will was familiar with dialysis. He knew that it was done by using a special fluid called dialysate, a mixture of pure water and chemicals that was carefully controlled to pull waste out of one's blood without removing the substances the body needed. A semipermeable membrane (one with microscopic holes that allowed only certain types of particles to pass through) kept the blood apart from the dialysate. The membrane let the wastes and fluid in the blood flow through into the dialysate, but blood cells and larger molecules, like necessary proteins, could not fit through the holes.

Purging the evil—his father's influence—from his plasma, the white and red blood cells that comprised blood, was a physical impossibility. But he was intelligent enough to understand that when it came to the physical laws of the universe, there were many things that defied scientific analysis, things that did happen that shouldn't, things that were, quite simply, impossible. He was smart enough to know that sometimes hard science took a backseat to the unreal and implausible. Loreli was in possession of just such a thing.

Loreli turned slowly and looked at the machine, then back at Will.

"I don't have time," she said. And then she resumed packing.

Will grabbed her arm. "You don't have time not to," he said. "He's going to come back stronger than ever."

"Take. Your. Hand. Off. Me." Her eyes flared.

Will slowly removed his hand from her arm and spoke calmly. "You were right. The Dark Lord's blood pollutes me, twists me into knots so I can't think straight and I put the people I care about in danger. I have to defeat him, and I'm beginning to think that the only way I can do that is to perform this chemical . . . exorcism of yours. Loreli, please."

Loreli studied Will carefully, as though she were making up her mind. She went to a case, opened it, and extracted syringes, tubing, and plasma bags.

"There's no backing out," she said. "Once you're in, you're in."

"Let's not waste any more time," he said.

"Lie down."

She yanked a tarp off a padded folding table. Will took his shirt off and lay down. Loreli set up an I.V. and disinfected the insides of his arms with a pre-moistened alcohol towelette. He made fists and veins rose up in both his arms. She unwrapped a syringe and used it to get a glucose line going in his left arm. She was—not surprisingly—an expert with needles, and he barely felt the puncture. She turned the machine on and adjusted some levels on the front, pressing buttons. When she'd made all the adjustments she needed to, she unwrapped another syringe and pierced the vein in his right arm.

"You won't regret this," said Loreli. "It doesn't take very long. Just close your eyes and relax and . . ."

Will did not hear the end of Loreli's sentence. She had added propofol to his glucose line, and the drug pulled him quickly into a dreamy, semi-conscious state in which he could hear sounds but not make sense of them, and his brain was crowded by a thousand muddled images and sensations.

Loreli smiled at her half-brother lying before her helpless, vulnerable, and totally captive. She was proud of her accomplishment. Will Hunter was one of the most intelligent, resourceful, and cunning creatures on the planet, and she alone had been able to subjugate him. She had planted her seeds well, and they had grown.

Initially she had planned to lure him down to the Under City and mortally wound him right before her father's eyes, a heroic act that would no doubt have placed her firmly in the Dark Lord's good graces. But then she saw that her father, her Master, was headless, and therefore *had* no eyes with which to view her heroics. It was shocking, and painful, and it cut her to the bone. What had happened? Why hadn't the legions of demons, demonteens, and shedemons been able to find his head? The new plan came to her quickly, for she knew that Will Hunter could do what the armies of darkness could not. He would find it. He would find her father's head. And he did! He led her right to it. But the head was not enough. When she'd seen her father's headless body surrounded by so many urns full of blood, she'd deduced that more that just his head would be needed to restore him to full strength, and that she had an even greater duty to fulfill. That's why, when the house in Coeur d'Alene had burst into flames, she had dragged him out to safety. And after, in the Under City, her suspicions had been proven correct. The Prince of Darkness would need the blood of his first-born son to rise again.

There was, of course, no such thing as "demon dialysis." One could not remove the evil from one's blood. But she'd worked Will expertly; she'd totally played him. He'd wanted to believe so desperately. He was motivated to change his behavior, to cool down his hot streak. And she'd done such a masterful job of appearing calm in the face of all storms that he'd actually been inspired. He wanted to be like her. But *no one* was like her. She was unique; she was special. She was more than gifted. Surely now *he* would see that, too.

Loreli watched the blood as it was gradually pumped out of Will's body. She smiled again, knowing how easy it would be to simply suck him dry like a vampire, to keep the machine pumping until he died from loss of blood. But that was not what she had planned for her darling brother. No, she had a far more painful scenario in store. She would leave him alive—barely. He would wake up and have a nice playtime with Sebastian. And then he'd return home to Natalie.

Loreli had never experienced love. This fact haunted her, gripped her insides like a vise. And to assuage that pain, she had orchestrated a situation in which the most potent love she'd ever witnessed— the love between her brother and the pathetically ordinary Natalie— would twist in upon itself in a manner so ugly not even Romeo and Juliet's tragic end could compare.

Society was full of songs and books and movies and TV that proclaimed the power of love. And Loreli had spent her entire life looking for it. But it was not the call of romantic love that she heard; it was another kind of love that cried out to her.

As a very young girl she'd asked her mother about her father: who he was, the kind of man he was, and—most important of all— did he love her, did he really *truly* love her? At first her mother had said, *Yes, darling, of course your daddy loves you, he said so with his last breath when he flipped his pickup truck and lay dying out on the highway.* Years later, that twisted myth gave way to others, depending on how intoxicated her mother was. He died in the war. He ran off with a whore. He had leukemia. He's coming home any day now.

Eventually, Loreli locked her mother in the basement and sobered her up enough to drag the clawing, unvarnished truth to the surface. It was then that she learned who her biological father was and how he had shunned and abandoned her, even tried to kill her and her mother with a flood. As the months and years passed, her feelings had shifted from disbelief to revulsion, and then—even though she knew it was wrong, even though the creature had treated her badly, had tossed her aside like she was garbage—new thoughts began to stir within her young mind. *Why did he leave me? What's wrong with me? Why won't he love me?* Her initial hatred gave way to a fierce need for his approval: *I want my daddy to love me.*

For years she searched for *him*, finding and learning from demons, killing many in the process. She was rapacious, focused, intent; she needed to find him as much as she needed to breathe. When, in her sixteenth year, she heard his voice call her name three times, she succumbed with glee and became infected, crossing over to the dark side. She was, after all, the daughter of the Prince of Darkness. She'd reveled in her newfound status and rushed to him, thinking he would of course grant her audience. But, upon hearing of her intent to meet with him, he sent a lowly emissary to inform her that she was to keep her distance. She was outraged. Her heart stung. She would not be denied! She threw herself headlong into danger by defying his authority and disobeying his orders, battling her way into the bowels of Mount St. Emory, where she confronted him directly. She had seen the dual thrones and, claiming her birthright, demanded that *she*, not this Johnny-come-lately Will Hunter, be anointed to rule by her father's side.

The Dark Prince sat and listened quietly to his unwanted daughter's arguments. And then he stood. Her heart leapt as she imagined the next few moments. Her father would finally see her for the unique and precious person that she had become, and he would embrace her. It would be all that she'd ever dreamed of.

But the Dark Lord was nothing if not a dyed-in-the-wool male chauvinist. No woman—and certainly not this *mistake*, this bastard offspring—would ever rule by his side! The back of his hand came cold and swift, striking her face, hurling her backward, bruising her cheek and crushing her hope. She wept as he spit a curse and summarily banished her from his kingdom. Loreli was dragged from the cavern and shunted by demons from pack to pack, beaten, humiliated, and robbed of her dream.

When Mount St. Emory had erupted, she was lying unconscious in a Seattle hospital bed. Days later, after she'd captured a demonteen and learned the news—that the Dark Lord's plan for his son to rule by his side had failed—a fresh conspiracy took hold in her heart and mind. She would not be so easily dismissed! She would show her father his folly. Surely he would see now that it was she, Loreli, and not Will who was meant to rule at his side. She would emerge triumphant by defeating the object of her father's misplaced affection. With her alchemy, she would render Will Hunter useless, humiliate and destroy him, and bring unto him a slow and painful death.

And her father would be proud.

Chapter Twenty:
The Dark Side of Love

Natalie still stood on the ledge outside her bedroom window, feeling the cold leach up through her feet into her whole body. She'd watched as Emily and Rudy departed, leaving her alone in the big, silent house. Now the only thing she could hear was the wind, and the ringing in her ears. *Like he's calling you on the telephone*, she remembered Will saying, way back in Harrisburg, explaining how the Dark Lord's infection began. She thought she heard someone calling her name. It was a distant echo, warped and warbled. Was it real? Or just paranoia? No, there it was again: a voice. She shuddered, her body viscerally reacting to a memory. She had heard that voice before . . . at a rave in Harrisburg. Back then she'd blocked it out, combating the evil thoughts creeping into her brain with good thoughts, thoughts of her and Will together, in love. But now . . . could she summon the defense she needed?

She stumbled back to her bedroom window and climbed inside. Her head ached and she tried to think good thoughts. But the medallion around her neck emitted a powerful, intoxicating scent, a scent that swept her into a topsy-turvy world where she climbed high into the breezy void of her mind—and then came crashing down into darkness, down where mad monsters waited to ambush her, engulf her, punish her.

The battle for her soul had begun.

Loreli watched Will's skin color shift from a healthy blush to a sickly pallor as the machine continued to deplete his blood. She had siphoned off two pints . . . now three. Will's heart rate and breathing were both steady, but in his drugged dream state, he was clearly suffering. She could tell from his facial expressions. No doubt his subconscious was sensing that his life was being drained away and was fighting to survive.

Over the past few days, Loreli had come to love this unique sibling of hers. He was handsome, intelligent, strong, and compassionate. She admired his fighting skills and his dedication to his cause. He was a warrior through and through, fierce and lethal and capable of devastating brutality. She imagined that if things were different, she would want to have such a ferocious fighter at her side. It was almost a pity that he wouldn't be alive much longer. But she also hated him for having so effortlessly earned their father's love and then thrown it away. She was just as strong as he was, just as smart—smarter! Yet he was the one their father wanted, not her.

Still, a small part of her wished she didn't have to do this. *But it must be done,* she thought. It was her only chance for redemption. Her only chance to earn *his* respect and love. Down in the vault she had seen the urns of blood the shedemons had collected and realized that what her father needed was not just his head, but blood. At first she thought her own blood would suffice. What better sacrifice could a daughter make, than of her own blood? But her mother had contracted hepatitis B—a hazard of her former occupation—and passed the curse on to Loreli, which meant her blood would not be acceptable. Only Will Hunter's blood could heal their father.

She touched her brother's face, gently tracing the lines of his nose, his chiseled cheekbones, his strong chin. *What a waste,* she thought. He would have made a fine demon leader, an efficient sub-ordinate to her. But that could never be. To pave the path for her ascension, it was necessary to remove all obstacles. And the biggest obstacle of all lay right before her, his body weakening as the seconds ticked by.

She withdrew the needles from his arms and, swabbing at the puncture wounds, taped them over. There. Good as new. Except with a whole lot less gas in his tank. She had injected him with a delayed-release chemical, a brilliant drug of her own design that would, in a matter of hours, cause his brain to stop communicating with the rest of his body. Eventually, his body would fail and Will Hunter would surrender to the void, becoming a comatose meat puppet before finally meeting his death. Letting him live was too dangerous. She knew him well enough to know he'd come after her, and their father. She couldn't let that happen.

She took the units of blood, stored securely in thick plastic pouches, and packed them in a thermal valise. It was a beautiful thing, adorned with an upside-down cross dripping with blood. A nice touch, she thought. She was the cavalry coming to save the day, the princess in shining armor, the demon world's savior. As she continued to pack up, loading her duster with a variety of chemical attack bombs, she pictured herself smiling proudly as the demon masses knelt in supplication—oh, how wonderful the crowd's adoration would be, thrumming inside her! She imagined what she would say when they urged her to speak, how it would feel as she ascended the throne to rule next to her father. And who knew? Perhaps in her future she might yet find the love of a demon boy. He would be heart-stoppingly handsome, and they would feel such passion for each other!

She unlatched the door to Sebastian's cage and watched as her little friend pushed his way out and quickly climbed up her arm and curled around her neck. His body felt warm and he made a sound like a cat purring.

"I'll be back, Sebastian. Don't you worry about a thing. Soon I'll be royalty and we'll move into an absolutely ginormous castle. You will be adored, maybe even worshipped. But first I've got a little errand to run. Be good."

She unwrapped Sebastian from around her neck and placed him on top of his cage. Then she took one last look at her brother, Will Hunter, the mighty scourge of the demon race, the most feared demon hunter on earth. He looked almost . . . peaceful. But he would wake soon and discover the terrible truth: his reign was over. He would learn that things had changed in ways he could never have imagined: that his grand love wasn't so grand, and that he wasn't as clever as he thought. He was going to be in a world of pain.

Loreli got into her mother's 2004 Honda Accord and drove across town to Queen Anne Hill. She pulled up to the front gates of Will's London Mansion, which were closed and locked. Not a problem. She put on gloves and then retrieved a vial from a pocket in her duster. Uncapping the vial, she poured liquid on the gate's lock, which began to dissolve. Then she got back in the Honda and slowly nudged the gates open with the car's bumper until she could pass through. The front door to the mansion also presented very little challenge and she was able to breach it quickly. She entered the mansion and walked like a thief through the hallways and upstairs to Natalie's room. She tried the door. It was open. Just like her future.

"Natalie?" she called.

The room was dark. She reached for the light switch.

Wham! The base of a lamp came down hard on the back of her head, right on her occipital bone. She turned. *Wham!* It came down again on the top of her skull and she fell sideways onto the carpet. Natalie was standing over her holding the lamp, the base now wet with the blood from Loreli's scalp.

"Stay away from me . . ." hissed Natalie. She was crazed, her pupils enlarged, the drugs from the medallion having saturated her brain so that for every real thing she saw, her mind conjured a dozen hallucinogenic rivals. Hearing the Dark Lord's voice had sent her spinning out of control.

Loreli's head was throbbing. She reached up and touched her scalp, felt the heat of her own blood. She examined her fingers, marveling at the beautiful claret color blood turns when oxygenated.

"That wasn't very nice, Natalie," she said.

"How do you know my name?" said Natalie, her eyes wide and feral.

"It's me, Loreli," she said. "And I do wish you'd start treating me like a friend. Because that's what I am, you know."

Natalie was breathing heavily and had the glint of murder in her eyes. She was clearly not in the mood to befriend anyone, let alone her archrival for Will's affections.

"I should kill you right now . . ."

Loreli smiled a wicked smile. She saw that Natalie was wearing the medallion and knew that the chemicals within were doing their job.

"Would that give you pleasure?" she asked.

"You have no idea," said Natalie. And then she blinked, trying to clear her vision, because in her disconnected state Loreli's hair had morphed into a nest of squirming pin snakes. Natalie's hands trembled and she was sorely tempted to bring the lamp down again and again, hard enough to snuff out this malicious creature permanently.

"If you kill me, dear sweet Natalie, I won't be able to help you."

"Help me?" Natalie lowered the lamp.

"Yes, that's why I'm here."

Loreli stood up and the room whirled. She closed her eyes and clamped down hard on the pain rolling through her skull, and when she opened her eyes, the room was calm.

"I come bearing an olive branch. There are some things you should know."

Natalie remained wary and gripped the lamp in her hands, ready to swing at any moment. She was coursing with fear as again she heard the Dark Lord calling her name. Once . . . twice . . . three times. She forced herself to veer away from her loathing and guided her mind into calmer waters . . . a lake where she floated on top staring up at the clouds, and in the clouds was Will, smiling down at her.

"I know how much you love Will," said Loreli. "And I don't blame you. You and I, we've been cast into the ring in a fight for his heart. Fate brought the three of us together, and now fate has decided that you are the victor."

Natalie was stunned. Was she hearing right? It seemed like Loreli was ceding the fight. Was she really giving up?

"Will and I talked. Well, actually he did most of the talking. I gave it everything I've got, but apparently I'm just no match for you. Don't ask me why, but Will Hunter is utterly in love with you."

The words were narcotic. Natalie's shoulders relaxed, and the lamp dropped to the carpet and bounced once, then rolled a couple of inches to a stop.

"Then why are you here?" said Natalie.

"Because I have come to care very deeply about him," said Loreli. "And I don't want him to suffer any more than he already has."

"Will is suffering? Why? How?"

Loreli now managed a sad, friendly smile. "His heart is breaking. Because he sees into the future, and he cannot imagine a future with you."

"But . . . but you just said—"

"He loves you, Natalie, but he's convinced, as I am, that your love is doomed. He's the son of—" Loreli paused, faking disgust. "—the Dark Lord."

"I know that," Natalie said. "And I love him anyway." Though still drugged, Natalie was starting to feel better, emboldened by Loreli's words. Will still loved her. She knew it. She *knew* it!

"He loves you with all of his heart, but . . ."

"But what?" said Natalie, suddenly dreadfully nervous.

"But . . . he knows you two can never be together. Not the way you want. Not forever."

Jab! Jab! A knife stabbed into Natalie's heart. At least it felt that way—just as real, just as painful, just as deadly. What was Loreli saying?

Loreli felt the power of her words and savored their effect on Natalie. She was putty in Loreli's hands.

"Hearing him pour his heart out made me cry," Loreli continued. "Because . . . when two people love each other like you do, and the universe conspires against them, well, it's just so . . . terribly sad."

"We *can* be together," said Natalie. But her words lacked conviction because she too feared that a future together—the whole life-long, get-married-and-have-children kind of future—was nothing more than a dream.

"That's right. You *could* . . . but don't you see? He's half demon and he'll always be half demon. He can't change that about himself. If he could, he would. Believe me. But he can't. So he's trapped. You, on the other hand, have a choice."

Natalie cocked her head to one side, puzzled. An idea began to form in her mind: a seed planted, watered, now sprouting through the loamy earth, growing, enlarging, expanding, flowering. The upside-down, inside-out logic of it, to her addled mind, was at once repellant and appealing. It was unthinkable. Wasn't it? Of course it was. But . . .

She also knew how much she loved Will—how she could not survive, could not breathe, could not live without him. What Loreli was proposing had not just taken hold; it had seized Natalie entirely. It had grabbed her heart and would not let go.

"You want me to become . . . infected," said Natalie, her soft words dropping into the stillness.

"It's not what *I* want," said Loreli.

Though Loreli didn't say the words, Natalie still heard them clearly. *It's what Will wants. It's what Will needs.* Natalie looked deeply into Loreli's eyes, searching for some kind of truth. But all she saw was pain, and took it for the pain of a girl scorned. Will had chosen not to love Loreli, even though she was fiercely, maddeningly beautiful. He had eschewed the great Loreli's sultry perfection, choosing instead Natalie's own girl-next-door appeal. He *did* love her. But his love for her was tormenting him. Was that why he'd been acting so strange and distant?

"You must have noticed that Will has been getting . . . darker . . . himself," said Loreli. "As demons age, they become more consumed by their wicked side. Will is young, but it's only a matter of time before he becomes more like his father, as all boys do."

Will had been growing more remote, doing everything he could to stay away from her—as though he had a beast growing inside him and he didn't want to expose her to it. It all made sense now. He was *protecting* her. From himself. But . . . for her to cross over to the dark side meant she would lose so much of herself, of her life as she knew it. Then again, in some ways, maybe that was what growing up was about.

"Demons, humans," said Loreli. "There's a great divide between them, and never the twain shall meet." She was laying it on thick now. "It's just like the Capulets and the Montagues: arch enemies. Poor Romeo and Juliet! If only they'd been able to change their blood. Of course, they couldn't." Loreli paused again, letting the idea come to Natalie on its own, letting Natalie think the words before Loreli said them. "But *you* can."

She'd played her last card. Either Natalie would take the bait or she wouldn't.

"Close your eyes," said Loreli. "Do you hear something?"

Natalie . . . Natalie . . . Natalie.

He was there. He was always there, if you were willing to listen. And Natalie was hearing him loud and clear. The next move was up to her. She thought of Loreli and glanced at the blood-splattered lamp on the floor. It was an evil thought, an immoral thought, a sinful one, but she opened the door and invited it, *welcomed* it, into her brain. She imagined finishing the job, picking up the lamp and bringing it down upon Loreli's head, once, twice . . . a hundred times. And *enjoying it.* Natalie's body seized up, her muscles constricting as she felt a new kind of consciousness trying to surge through her body. Could she do it? She imagined herself with Will. She looked in the mirror and saw a sad, plain, lonely girl with dull eyes staring back her. But then the lonely girl blossomed into a deadly dark rose, a dangerously beautiful girl with crimson lips. And her eyes were fierce, the kind of eyes that said, *For his love, I will do anything.*

The light bulb from the lamp had broken, and a single shard lay at Natalie's feet. One . . . two. And now came three. She reached down and picked up the shard. She thought of Will. Perhaps he would be angry at first, no doubt clinging to some noble ideal, but he would quickly realize that she'd done it for love. He would accept, even admire, her sacrifice, and he would love her all the more for it. Their lips would come together and they would never have to part. As she was lost in thought Natalie noticed Loreli slipping out of the bedroom door. It didn't matter. It wasn't important. The only thing that mattered was the possibility that she and Will could be together forever. She continued to stare at the shard of glass. It was so very sharp.

Wake up. Open your eyes. Where am I? Try to remember. Think. Think. Wake up. Wake up. Wake up! Will was fighting, caught between worlds, semi-conscious but unable to force himself awake. Try as he might, he couldn't gain purchase in the material world, and he had a vague, unarticulated fear that he would be suspended in this limbo for eternity. Thoughts raced through his mind with blistering speed and he couldn't lock on to any one long enough to use it as a true reference point. It was like chasing snowflakes in a blizzard. Then he clutched at a single notion: to pinch himself. *Pinch me, I'm dreaming,* his mother used to say when she was giddy with joy.

Focusing as hard as he could on moving his right hand, Will used his right thumb and index finger to pinch the flesh on his thigh. The pain made the connection he was looking for and he was suddenly rushing toward a blazing white light. He opened his eyes. He was back. He felt light-headed. And as he turned his head to one side, he found himself gazing into the face of a small mammal. Sebastian. Will started to smile, but Sebastian bared his teeth and emitted a low growl. Uh-oh.

"Sebastian . . . good boy . . . good boy . . ."

Will rose to a sitting position. The room was spinning. He stood and felt pinpricks racing up and down the backs of his legs, like when he slept on his arm wrong and it fell asleep, only the sensation covered his whole body. Sebastian skittered across the room and up onto an overhead water pipe.

"Loreli?" Will called.

She didn't answer. He looked around. She wasn't here. Maybe she was upstairs, packing? He moved to the sink, turned on the cold water, and drank deeply. He was feeling better now. He flexed his muscles, feeling his strength coming back. He sensed movement and turned just in time to see Sebastian leap down from the pipe and sink his tiny, knife-like teeth into Will's neck. Yelping in pain, Will grabbed Sebastian's jaw tightly and squeezed hard. The little animal released his grip and Will flung him across the room, where he slammed into a shelf, knocking over a jar and bringing both it and Sebastian crashing to the floor.

"Holy crap, Sebastian! What did I ever do to you?"

Unfortunately, the jar that had broken open held the same yellow concoction that had doused the ants during Will's first visit. Just like the ants, Sebastian rapidly began to grow, morphing larger, looking more like a rabid dog than a ferret.

"Oh, great," said Will.

Sebastian was now two feet tall, a killer who looked like he fully intended to rip Will to shreds. He went into a crouch and Will knew the little beast was going to spring up at him. So he anticipated the move and dove right as Sebastian, emitting a terrifying screech, flew through the air, barely missing Will and slamming into the wall above the sink. Will jumped up, felt woozy for a second, but had enough presence of mind to grab a pipe wrench, which he swung upward with all his might. *Wham!* He caught the beast with a brutal uppercut that knocked him senseless. The mutated ferret dropped to the floor, unconscious, and began to shrink back down to his normal size. Will shook his head, picked the little creature up, and gently placed him back in his cage.

He felt the blood on his neck and found a mirror to examine it. The wound wasn't bad. He pulled a healing patch from his pocket and applied it. Then he took a few seconds to look at his new self in the mirror. His eyes looked the same. So did everything else. But he somehow felt . . . different. *Of course you feel different,* he thought to himself. *You've been cleansed.*

He went upstairs and moved through the hush of the house.

"Loreli?"

She didn't answer. Her mother was asleep on the couch. He walked out to his BMW, feeling woozy. But maybe woozy was good, maybe it was all part of the process. He wished Loreli was around so he could ask her. He didn't like the fact that she'd disappeared. Something had gone awry, he just didn't know what. He took a few deep breaths and then smiled. For the first time in his life, he was pure. And for a moment he thought he could feel all his strength surging back into him. He would be stronger, smarter, and better than before. Best of all, he would not be distracted by rage. Now he was ready to fight the Dark Lord to the death.

But first there was someone he had to see, someone he couldn't wait a moment longer to kiss.

Chapter Twenty-One:
The Rising

Dread cloaked the Under City as demons, demonteens, and shedemons impatiently awaited the rising of their leader. His head had been found, retrieved, and reattached. Why wasn't he rising? They were restless, agitated, disturbed. More fights than usual broke out. Rumors proliferated. Their Leader was dying. The demon race was doomed. All manners of disinformation and misinformation spread through the cursed population, and many felt that their time in the underworld was coming to an end. Demons were not, as a group, optimistic. So they ate and drank and smoked to obscene excesses, and spit curses, tossing blame and recrimination back and forth. Someone would have to pay. The question was: who? The obvious choice was the Black Prince's prodigal son, Will Hunter. But could any of them brave an attack on him without orders from the supreme leader?

Another rumor began to circulate, and it spread like a virus, infecting quickly and striking fear into the demons' hearts: their Leader was already dead and a coup was being planned. Sects met and spoke of the future in hushed tones. Clans pledged support to one another, and alliances were negotiated and then reneged upon. More fights broke out. It was clear that something had to be done to restore order. A new leader, if only an interim one, had to be anointed or chaos would reign.

Several Alpha demonteens jockeyed for the inside track in the race to see who might act as the interim leader or supplant the great leader should he indeed expire. Among them, Rocco Manelli battled his way to the fore. A young Russian, Milanokov, also stepped forward and had much support, as did a mature Nigerian demon, Abdul-Aziz, who stood seven-feet-two-inches in human form. Since none of the three enjoyed unanimous support, it was only fair that the matter should be decided in the typical demon fashion: they would have a cage fight, each demon using the weapon of his choosing.

Abdul-Aziz felt confident as he entered the iron cage—a huge ball forty feet in diameter—carrying a massive spiked war club. Milanokov, too, felt emboldened as he made his entrance to cheers wielding a tri-blade sword and shield. Then the cavern erupted with a sound like tearing metal as Rocco stepped into the ring holding two roaring, thirty-two-inch Craftsman chainsaws.

A throng of demons crowded around and crawled onto the cage as the match began. Milanokov faked a hit toward Rocco and, whirling, swung his tri-blade at Abdul-Aziz, cutting a gash in the giant's left leg. Abdul-Aziz responded by charging Milanokov, cursing and swinging his juggernaut club. He was twice as fast as Milanokov had expected and succeeded in blasting his club into the Russian's shield, knocking him backward, spewing a string of Slavic demon curses. Rocco stood waiting, patient, as Abdul-Aziz and Milanokov sparred, with the giant Nigerian landing another blow that broke the Russian's shield in half. But Milanokov wasn't done—he leapt up, flipping over Abdul-Aziz and landing behind him, then lancing the towering man through the shoulder. Bellowing like a sacrificial cow, Abdul-Aziz turned and swung his club with all his might. The Russian ducked and was preparing a counterstrike when he felt the hot blade of Rocco's chainsaw pass through his left arm, lopping it off. Blood spurted from the stump, and Milanokov had only a moment to reflect on his plight before Rocco's other chainsaw blade raked through his legs, severing them both.

As Milanokov toppled into the dirt screaming, Abdul-Aziz attacked Rocco, who ducked and whirled and counter-attacked with his big churning saws. The first cut into Abdul-Aziz's battle club and then seized up, surprising both demons. But Rocco was quick and used his opponent's surprise as an opportunity to drive an uppercut into Abdul-Aziz's torso, carving out his beating heart. As Abdul-Aziz fell sideways, Rocco lopped off his head for good measure. The cage floor flooded with blood. Rocco held the chainsaws aloft and the demons went wild, screeching like baboons on fire.

The cavern echoed with a sustained chant: "Rocco! Rocco! Rocco!"

Rocco's chest puffed up as he gassed the chainsaws, keeping them throttled to the max until finally their engines overheated and they exploded. The cheers grew louder. *This* guy was a showman.

Then a mighty roar shook the cavern. Debris rained down.

The Dark Lord was standing in the vault doorway.

He had morphed larger, into his baddest, most monstrous demonic self, and he was seething with fiery rage. He spit a stream of fire that arced toward Rocco, who, thinking quickly, dropped and grabbed Malinokov's battered shield in a defensive move. The crowd was ecstatic. Their leader was back!

"Kill! Kill! Kill!" they chanted, lusting for the immediate and gory death of Rocco at the hands of the grand evildoer.

Rocco, his hands, arms, and feet badly burned, bravely rose up, ready to accept his fate. But the Dark Prince, now greatly weakened, instead of finishing him off, fell sideways. A group of loyal shede-mons lifted him up and carried him hastily back into the vault as the crowd began to rumble their shock and dismay. Now the backbiting began in earnest.

"He's old!"

"He's ill!"

"He's not fit to lead!"

"He's finished!"

A mass mutiny was only seconds away. The wounded Prince of Darkness had emerged from his vault intending to quell all such notions, but instead—by showing his weakened state—had only succeeded in adding fuel to the fires of dissent.

Rocco and his cohorts took up swords and lances and stared at the shedemons guarding the vault entrance. The shedemons pulled their daggers and stood, ready to fight to the death.

But then a deafening noise rang throughout the massive cave: a high-pitched whistling that grew more and more intense until all assembled were covering their ears. The awful noise ceased as quickly as it had begun, and a blessed silence took its place. As the demons and demonteens and shedemons caught their collective breaths, they heard a voice.

"The Dark Lord is not finished!"

All heads turned to find Loreli, clad in a striking blue hooded duster, holding the blood valise.

"I have what is needed!" she shouted, lifting the valise up for all to see. "With this . . . the blood of his first-born son . . . *I will cure him!*"

The shedemons wasted no time rushing out and surrounding Loreli and whisking her toward the vault. The assembled throngs were confused and uncertain.

Fueled by a sudden swift rage, Rocco jumped on a boulder and yelled, "You're not curing anyone, you little bitch!" He was poised to attack.

And then he was lanced—run completely through—by a hooded shedemon who had been lurking behind him in the crowd. Rocco looked down at the blade sticking out through his torso, realized that it had pierced his heart, grabbed at it, and then fell over dead, his body convulsing and then disintegrating into sparks.

Another dissenter made a move to intercept Loreli, but the she-demons quickly dispatched him in a flurry of nail and dagger slices, and by the time they were done the offender was in a pool of his own blood and Loreli was well down the tunnel to the vault.

She approached the Dark Lord as he lay on the marble slab, his chest heaving. He was clearly in bad shape. His body parts seemed to be, rather than working in concert, engaged in some kind of repulsive internecine battle as his skin morphed from scales to flesh covered with pustules and back again. His patchwork body was bulging at the seams where the healing worms had done their work.

He was sweating, and his head tossed back and forth as he fought the pain that was engulfing him. In his brain, he saw goodness and light, acts of kindness projected on an inner wall. He saw a small child kissing the snout of an adorable puppy. He saw a man and woman at an altar exchanging vows of eternal love before God. He saw an elderly couple walking on a beach, smiling, gnarled old hands clasped together. The images of goodness and radiant love tormented him. *If this is death*, he thought, *then bring it swiftly!*

Loreli placed a hand on his forehead. "Don't worry, Father, it's going to be okay. I'm here now."

He opened his evil yellow eyes and stared up. It took him a moment to recognize her. When he did, he was not pleased.

"I do not wish to die with your face as the last thing I see."

"But because of me, Father, you're not going to die." She extracted the necessary equipment from her duster and went to work. "You are going to rise up and be stronger than ever!"

The Dark Lord's eyes narrowed as she jammed the needle into his arm. He grabbed her wrist with a mighty claw. He could crush it easily. But he did not, because she began pumping the blood of Will Hunter into his veins. He briefly lost consciousness as the blood spread throughout his body. The effect was completely euphoric. The Dark Lord experienced a rush greater than he'd ever felt before.

Minutes later, when the transfusion was complete, he stood up and let loose a powerful roar that echoed throughout the entire Under City. Then he cast his gaze upon his daughter.

"Come to me."

She did. He held her shoulders and then pulled her close to him in a fatherly embrace. Her nostrils flared. He smelled of death and decay, like the carcass of a beast of burden. She was repulsed, and yet . . . this was her father, the being whom she'd spent so much time fantasizing about, yearning deep in her heart for his acceptance. Even as waves of disgust washed over her, she forced herself to remain still.

He lifted her chin with a finger. His eyes were like pools of boiling saffron. She felt dizzy. His voice was a low, husky whisper.

"You have done well, my daughter."

"All in service of you, my Lord."

The Dark Lord felt a surge of pride and smiled at his offspring. "Now," he thundered, "we will celebrate!"

The Dark Lord was in the huge cavern standing upright on a rise, a roiling sea of his minions spread out before him. He was tall, strong, and powerful; no sign of illness remained. As for his worshippers, they were an adoring group, flush with the joy that their great leader had returned. Many of them reveled in the rumor—which had now become a belief—that he had in fact died and then risen again like a truly invincible being, cementing their faith that he was, indeed, a deity worthy of eternal, unquestioning worship. And to show their spirit, their great joy, they drummed a thousand drums. They beat congos and madals and dholaks, and hammered on ashikos and bodhrans, leaping up and down, working themselves into a frenzy.

A behemoth wielding a massive hammer struck a gong, and from out of the vault came Loreli adorned in a black and red velvet cape. She was flanked by shedemons and they all marched slowly, a royal procession. The shedemons had done the impossible—they'd helped make her appear even more beautiful than she naturally was. She was radiant. She was beaming. She exuded tremendous pride. She was led out to the ledge where her father was waiting, and the assembled crowd whispered amongst themselves. This mysterious girl, this savior, who was she and why was she being presented in this manner to them? Some said she was the Dark Prince's daughter. Others said no, she was his lover. Would she be the princess? Or the queen? The excitement was building.

The shedemons presented Loreli to the Dark Lord, removing her cape, revealing a stunning outfit underneath. She still wore her blue duster, but underneath was mesh and leather and lace combined in a mind-blowingly sensuous manner to create the perfect ensemble, beautiful and bad woven together like night and day.

The Dark Lord approved. Taking her hand, he twirled her around once, twice, three times, and raised his other hand to the crowd, exhorting them to empty their lungs. And they did. They cheered as though their team had just won the Super Bowl, their army the battle, their kind the war. Whoever this girl was, she was to be granted the utmost respect.

"I give you my one and only daughter," said the Dark Lord. "*Loreli!*" He stretched the word—her beautiful name—out into three distinct and lengthy syllables. *LORE! ELL! EYE!*

And the demons screamed even louder. "*Lor-el-i! Lor-el-i! Lor-el-i!*"

Blood rushed into Loreli's face as she bathed in the adoration. She could feel her entire body tingling. Her blood was hot and fast as it raced up and down her legs and arms, through her torso, swirling around her spine, driving her wild with delight and desire. She could hardly stand it; the intensity lifted her into a state of drugged euphoria. The Black Prince gazed at her once more.

"Tell me, dear daughter, how do you feel?"

"I feel . . . ecstatic . . . wonderful!"

"Pride for others is not an emotion that comes easily to me. Yet here you are. And I am so very proud of you."

"Thank you, Father."

He pulled her close again. He smelled even worse, sweat rolling off him like rain from a roof. He was rancid, toxic, and repulsive. But she didn't care. She had dreamed of this moment for years. They were reunited. They were powerful. They would stand together as immortals! Her cheeks were flushed. Every cell in her body buzzed with delight as her father spoke to her.

"You will be a great asset in the coming Armageddon. Together we are doubly strong. Invincible. Thanks to you, your brother, the traitor, has no chance now. No chance whatsoever."

Loreli smiled because she knew this was true. Will Hunter was soon to be dead and gone, forgotten, his pitiful soul wiped from the face of the earth.

Will pulled his BMW into the garage and got out. He could hardly contain himself, was nearly mad with joy. He had done it. He no longer had the blood of the Dark Lord running through his veins. He had lifted the curse, and could now live his life on his own terms, as a normal human being. Of course, he still had much to accomplish, but with the curse gone he would be stronger, no longer allowing anger to pollute his thoughts. He was pure. He would kick ass like he'd never kicked ass before. He looked forward to meeting his adversary on the field of battle.

But first, *Natalie*. He'd subjected her to far too much pain in the last few weeks, but now he would make it all up to her. Once he held her in his arms, all would be forgiven. He realized now that he would have to tell her everything about Loreli. No more secrets. He would tell all and deal with Loreli when the time came.

He entered the old stone mansion and climbed the stairs, his heart pounding with anticipation.

"Rudy? Emily?" he called.

He got no response, so he moved up the stairs and headed right for her room. He could picture her rushing into his arms.

The door was closed. He knocked.

"Natalie?"

When she didn't answer, he opened the door.

As he crossed the room he heard a roaring in his ears. And all at once, he started to feel weak. His skin felt flushed and yet, when he caught his reflection in the mirror, he thought he looked *pale*. What was going on? He was sweating. He didn't feel good. In fact, he felt wretched. But then he saw her—Natalie. She was lying on her bed, splayed out, looking so beautiful. She was, in her own way, perfection. He moved toward her, the world now in slow motion. All the hours, the days, the weeks, the months that he'd loved her—it all added up to now, this moment, this time.

"Natalie . . . it's me, Will."

She stirred, moaned (*oh, how delicious a simple sound!*), but did not open her eyes. Words began to spill from Will's mouth, straight from his heart.

"I know you've thought about these words before. At least, I'm hoping you have, because I have, I've thought of them a thousand times a day, every single day since I first met you. I've wanted to say them to you forever but . . . the way things have been, all that's happened, I was afraid. Not for me, but for you. I was always worried about you getting hurt, or worse. As much as I've wanted you, I've also known that, until now, we could never truly be together. Not the way we wanted to, *needed* to, forever. Because I was . . . who I was . . . because I carried his blood, I couldn't risk letting go, letting you know how I really felt."

Again she stirred, shifting slightly on the bed. Her fingers reached out for his hand and Will knew she could hear every single word he'd said.

"Every time I see you," he said, "every time I'm near you, my heart sings. It sings your song. And it sings only for you." He took a deep breath, and then uttered the words that would free his soul. "Natalie . . . I love you. And I will love you forever."

There. He'd done it. In no uncertain terms, he'd proclaimed his love for her. Will was so happy, so free, he felt like he could fly.

And then, suddenly, he was paralyzed with fear. Natalie had opened her eyes.

They were liquid black.

ABOUT THE AUTHOR

Author/screenwriter/filmmaker Temple Mathews, a graduate of the University of Washington and a producer at the American Film Institute, has written dozens of half-hour animation TV episodes and several animated and live action features and direct-to-DVD and video films. Mr. Mathews has sold scripts and/or worked for hire at every major studio in Hollywood. His credits include the Walt Disney animated feature films *Return to Neverland* and *The Little Mermaid II*, and the MGM feature film *Picture This!* Mr. Mathews lives in Santa Monica, California, with his daughter, Manon.